A Raven Series

Spellbound

Book 1

SITTA JAYNE & EVERLY ROSE

Acknowledgements

We would like to take this moment to say thank you to all of you for your support as we create this series. For reading along as we've weaved together Elena & Killian's world. A special thank you to our community for their daily interactions and support.

Dedications

To our families and husbands for understanding our need to go hide away and write for hours on end. We love you.

To our team at Native Publishers, thank you for your guidance and insight and making this dream of ours come true.

We dedicate this book to everyone that has been on this journey with us; through social media, our short stories leading to Amazon Vella. Thank you so much.

To all the writers out there; keep writing. No matter if it's a few hours a month. It all adds up. It's attainable. Just keep writing.

Contents

Spellbound, /ˈspelbaʊnd/, adjective; hold the complete attention of as though by magick

Prologue

Killian, a warlock and a seer with a gift that both blessed and burdened him, stepped out of his bedroom one fateful evening, unaware of the vision that awaited him. As he crossed the threshold, a sudden wave of disorientation washed over him, and he sank to his knees, overcome by a vision so vivid and intense that it felt as though reality itself had been torn asunder.

His eyes, usually sharp and perceptive, clouded over with a haze that obscured the world around him. In that moment, his senses were assaulted by a cacophony of emotions - a surge of anger so potent that it felt like a raging inferno in his chest, fueled by the magical powers that lay dormant within him, waiting to be unleashed.

The vision unfolded before him like a twisted tapestry of nightmares. His coven, those he had come to call family, lay strewn across the ground in a scene of unspeakable horror. Their bodies were contorted in unnatural poses, their hearts ripped from their chests, and their eyes gouged out, leaving empty, accusing sockets that seemed to follow Killian's every move.

A primal scream of anguish threatened to escape his lips, but Killian choked it back, his jaw clenched with a mixture of grief and fury. With trembling hands, he forced himself to approach the fallen members of his coven, each step heavy with the weight of impending doom that hung in the air like a shroud.

As he drew closer, a chilling laughter echoed through the chamber, drawing his attention to a figure cloaked in darkness. The man, clad head to toe in black, his features obscured by a sinister mask, exuded an aura of malevolence that sent shivers down Killian's spine. Despite the fear that gnawed at his insides, Killian's voice rang out, a mixture of defiance and desperation in his tone.

"Who are you?" he demanded, his voice quivering with a mixture of fear and anger.

The man in black regarded Killian with a cold, calculating gaze, the corners of his lips curling into a cruel smile. "You hold a title that was never rightfully yours, boy," he sneered, his voice dripping with malice. "I have come to claim what is mine by right."

Killian's eyes blazed with a fierce intensity as he met the stranger's gaze, his fists clenched at his sides. "No one gave me anything," he retorted, his voice laced with determination. "I have earned my place through blood, sweat, and tears. Your presence in my visions signifies a connection, and I will not rest until I uncover the truth."

The man in black chuckled darkly, a sound that sent a chill down Killian's spine. "You may think yourself a hunter, boy, but in truth, you are the prey," he taunted, his form beginning to fade back into the shadows from whence he came.

But Killian would not be cowed. With a voice that rang out like a clarion call in the darkness, he issued a solemn vow that reverberated through the chamber. "I will hunt you down," he declared, his eyes ablaze with a fierce determination. "No mask can conceal you from my sight. No shadow can shelter you from my wrath. I will seek you out, and when I find you, no mercy shall be granted. Not even the devil himself will protect you from my justice."

The man in black offered a final enigmatic response before vanishing into the darkness, leaving Killian alone with his thoughts and a burning desire for vengeance that consumed his every waking moment. As the vision began to dissipate, the remnants of his coven fading into the ether, Killian rose to his feet with a renewed sense of purpose.

The path ahead was fraught with danger and uncertainty, but Killian was undeterred. Armed with his powers of foresight and a heart that burned with righteous fury, he set forth on a journey that would lead him into the heart of darkness itself. The mystery of the malevolent figure who had infiltrated his visions beckoned to him, a puzzle waiting to be solved, a confrontation waiting to be had.

With each step he took, Killian drew closer to the truth, to the answers that lay shrouded in the shadows of the unknown. The legacy of his coven, the memory of their untimely demise, and the specter of the man in black haunted his every thought, propelling him forward on a collision course with destiny.

And as the echoes of his vow to hunt down his elusive adversary reverberated through the chamber, Killian knew that his journey had only just begun. The stage was set, the players assembled, and the stakes were higher than ever before. The battle between light and darkness raged within him, and he was determined to emerge victorious, no matter the cost.

1

Elena gazed skyward at the unimpeded view of the night sky. In the clearing behind Gran's house, no one would see her; the woods thick and peaceful here. With the absence of light from the city, the sky was crystal clear, with just a few constellations peeking down at her.

This was her favorite place in the world. Maybe that wasn't quite right. She hadn't seen too much of the world. But it definitely was one of the places she felt most grounded and safe.

Some might think her life was pretty simple and boring, but she liked it that way. She didn't live in a cage, but there were times she definitely felt like she put herself there. But not in a bad way. More in the way of, she liked her life just as it was, with no surprises. She'd had enough of those and some had not been of the good variety.

Her emerging power was immense, or it would be. She could feel that. It frightened her and excited her at the same time. When it came time to call it forth, her heart would race, her skin would pebble in anticipation, throw in a pinch of angst, and whatever else you could find.

Fire-witch.

She was fire and still had days where she couldn't process it. Elena had often asked her Gran what her elemental power would be when she fully transitioned.

The little lines at the corners of her eyes and mouth would crease and deepen, and she'd smile, but it would never reach her eyes; just concern would stare back at her.

"My red flame, your power will be perfect for you. Just remember to always protect yourself and listen to your voice within."

Their coven had not had a fire witch in attendance in at least two generations. It was the ultimate prize of the four elements. It could create and destroy in the blink of an eye and was highly unstable until mastered. So that it lay dormant inside her, just waiting until she called upon it, still freaked her out at times.

That moment, her gaze catching as a star shot across the heavens and fell toward earth, glowing against the backdrop of night. Nature was truly spectacular, and she made a wish.

She was supposed to attend a coven meeting tonight, which wasn't mandatory, but the invite had been extended her way. Elena had weaved a small fabrication of a white lie so she wouldn't have to attend. Not that the invitation had been fully genuine, but she knew how her coven saw her. She wasn't really liked; she was tolerated. Elena didn't care. Right now, at this point in her life she was being a bit selfish. Self-care was a thing and she needed it. Her uncertainty between coven vs solitary would have to wait for another day.

Tonight, she wanted to be alone in her own space and practice her magic undisturbed. Learn to manipulate it and stay in control; be its master and not the other way around.

She had brought some old ledgers from the store home with her, tearing pages out and stacking them in piles out here in the clearing. This space had been her testing ground for every stage of her witchcraft. She felt truly connected to the sky and earth here.

Taking a calming breath and slowly calling a tiny ember to life in the palm of her hand. Letting it burn brighter before guiding it toward the piles she'd constructed. One slight touch and a pile was engulfed, and in moments, nothing but ash was left.

Drawing her fire back in, she smiled. She was getting slightly better as the weeks went by. Could she do that with a moving object? Her heartbeat magnified as the enormity of her gift started to dawn on her.

Words softly whispered, the incantation repeated, over and over, her mouth getting dry – *goddess of air, goddess of night, grant my wish, my wish of flight, objects to rise, objects to lift, hear my wish* – until each leaf of paper rose and drifted upward within the clearing where she stood. Calling her flame to life, it instantly rose, her magic tingling between her breasts. Concentrating, sending tendrils towards the dancing sheets of paper, each strand latching on, little fireflies of power brightening the meadow within the towering trees for a few moments before what was left fell to the ground.

Gran had always said that her power was hers to command, but she also needed to believe. It was as simple and as complicated as that. The impossible was possible if you listened and accepted the whispers that often begged to be heard.

Plopping herself down, her back finding the soft ground, the silence of the evening around her, she missed Gran so much. It had been twelve months and fourteen days without her. She missed her voice, how she used to call her a girl on fire because of her red hair. Her touch, when she used to give her long tresses a gentle yank in affection or to get her attention, which wandered adrift at the most inappropriate times. A marvel of nature for a copper to be born to their lineage, she repeated often and for all to hear.

Elena knew a few things without a doubt. She burned quickly, her freckles were sprinkled everywhere, and she was not a fan of being called Carrot. And Gran would smile that quirky smile and say red was for luck and romance. Elena would agree to disagree. She'd never been properly kissed, so Gran's logic was definitely off the mark.

Elena should have known better than to throw thoughts like that into the universe because someone was always listening.

2

Killian gazed out his bedroom window, sipping his morning coffee as he watched the sunrise. He always cherished the quietness that greeted him at the start of each day, a brief moment of tranquility before the bustle of life began.

After taking the last sip and setting down his mug, Killian turned away from the beautiful view, stepping into his walk-in closet and picking out his clothes for the day; black shirt, black dress pants, and his favorite pair of boots.

As the high Warlock of his Coven, each day was filled from start to end and today was no different. Killian had a pressing matter to attend, a meeting with the sister witches. There had been a disturbance among them, an uneasiness, and he needed to address it quickly. He didn't allow situations to fester; nothing good ever came from that.

Killian valued order within his coven and would not tolerate chaos, especially among the sisters. Each sister had been handpicked for a specific reason, possessing a unique ability and hailing from a different coven to maintain the peace.

Killian's mother was the leader of the sister witches because she was the oldest among them. He knew that his mother could sometimes be harsh and bossy, always insisting on order and discipline her way. She was strict and wouldn't tolerate any kind of disobedience.

A sudden knock on his door interrupted his thoughts, making him realize his daydreaming might have put him behind schedule. Wondering who could be at the door so early in the day, opening it to be greeted by his brother's smiling face – "Keegan, what have I done to be graced with your presence this morning?"

He playfully slapped Killian on the shoulder and walked past him. "Hey, why don't you skip today's meeting and hang out with me instead? I want to share my plans with you about my girl."

Keegan had always been in love with Iris, Killian's best friend, ever since they were kids. Iris had the same feelings for him and it was clear to everyone around them that they were meant to be together.

However, their parents had other ideas and there had always been a constant push for Killian and Iris to get married, oblivious to the fact that Keegan is the one who truly deserves to be with Iris.

Keegan and Iris decided not to tempt fate because she could throw wrenches in where she decided. So eloping had become an urgent need, a private wedding in a beautiful and serene location. However, planning a wedding can be quite stressful, especially when you need to keep it a secret, which at any time could be difficult but within a coven of witches almost impossible. That's when Keegan turned to his brother Killian for help.

Killian was delighted to assist. He believed that the two lovebirds were perfect for each other, and he hoped that their parents would realize it too. As a supportive big brother, Killian took care of all the planning. Iris had expressed her desire to have a tropical wedding, so Killian paid for all the expenses and even surprised her with tickets to Bora Bora.

On their arrival, Keegan and Iris were greeted with a breathtaking view of the island and a carefully planned-out wedding ceremony. They exchanged their vows in front of the ocean, with Killian as their only witness. It was hard to believe that was two years ago. Their parents finally accepted the fact that Iris and Keegan were truly soulmates.

Kil, himself, had not been lucky in love and was in no hurry to find his significant other. He trusted that the powers at be would guide him towards his destiny. For now, he was quite content with being single and would leave the romance to his younger brother.

He would love nothing more than to spend time with Keegan, but he had to first address the issue. His mother's attitude was threatening to ruin the alliance he worked hard to establish with the other covens.

"Keegan, you know this needs my attention. I want to reassure the other sister witches that I have everything under control. As for our mother, I will not allow her to destroy the one thing I worked so hard for. Let's hope it doesn't come down to replacing our mother with another witch."

Killian knew that convincing his mother would not be an easy task. She was an elder witch, pure dark magic running in her veins and she would put up a fierce fight if things weren't done her way. If anyone dared to deny her orders, she would go to great lengths to make their lives miserable. However, Killian believed in being a compassionate leader and showing his coven understanding. He wanted his coven to trust him to do what was right and fair rather than resorting to cruelty.

"I am coming with you, Killian. It would be best if you didn't put up with our mother's fits when she doesn't get her way. It's ridiculous how she acts, and how our father tolerates her is beyond me."

His brother was right, and even he wondered how their father could handle her. Killian didn't understand this new behavior of hers. She was so loving and nurturing when he and his brother were younger. It was like a switch had been flipped. Killian hardly recognized her anymore. "I need to address this issue as soon as possible before it worsens. I only request that you do not intervene. Let me speak with her first. I can't have rumors spreading among the other covens about this matter; it will lead to division, and I can't permit that."

A few moments later...

Killian, followed by Keegan, walked into his mother's office without knocking. She was organizing books on a shelf and didn't bother to turn her head towards him. "I know you're here to discuss what happened, but

I'm not in the mood to discuss it right now. I have somewhere I need to be. So, if you don't mind, please go."

Keegan stared at Killian, then turned to look at his mother. He couldn't believe she had just dismissed the high Warlock so easily. Killian did his best to stay calm, but he could feel his anger building up inside him. How could she do this? This wasn't the first time Killian's mother had made another witch leave. Even when his father was the high Warlock, she had forced her best friend to leave the coven. Killian didn't know all the details, but he was determined to discover what was happening.

"I understand that you might be my mother, but that doesn't mean you can talk to me like that. I have worked very hard to become the head of our coven and fix everything that you have destroyed. Thanks to my efforts, we have established alliances with other covens, and I will not tolerate your behavior. If you do not tell me what happened, I will permanently remove you from the sister witches."

She turned towards Killian and glared at him like he had grown two heads. "The audacity of you speaking to your mother that way," she said. "Do you want to know why Marisol left your Coven, Killian? It's because she was the weak link among the strong. And you know what that does, my son? The enemy will see it as a way to get in. Marisol isn't cut out to be a sister witch. She would cave in a second when faced with a challenge. As I said before, I have somewhere I need to be."

Killian slammed his fist against the desk in anger as his body glowed around the edges with the rise of his inner flame. "I cannot believe you made Marisol leave my coven!" he exclaimed. "I trusted you to guide her and help her with her powers. She is a young witch and Iris's sister. Do you know what that girl can do? She possesses a power I have never seen before. It would take patience and building her confidence, but instead of doing that, you prefer to tear someone down. Her father's coven is our most valuable ally and also one of your husband's close friends. She chose to come to us, to learn from us. However, I recall you discarded your previous best friend due to a disagreement. Regrettably, she has passed away, and you won't have the opportunity to make things right with her."

Killian felt his jaw clenching as he struggled to control his anger. He didn't want to speak to his mother that way, but she left him no choice.

Rissa stepped closer to him, unleashing her magick, making it hard for him to breathe. The icy chill creeping up his spine smothering his flames. His mother was known as the Ice Queen for a reason, she could manipulate water molecules and turn them into ice.

Keegan's voice thundered through the room, "Stop this right now, Mother. What you did was wrong, and we all know it. Killian is the head of our coven, and your actions are putting everyone at risk. He has worked tirelessly to bring the covens together. Marisol is only nineteen years old, and she needs guidance. Why would you be so cruel to her?"

Killian chanted a spell breaking free from his mother's grasp. He pinned her to the wall with a wave of his hand, towering over her. "Mother, I want to make myself clear; this is the only time I will say this. You need to fix your mistake and apologize to Marisol and her father. You also need to help Marisol with her powers. Please put your pride aside and ask for their forgiveness. I'm giving you some time, and not a lot to make things right. If you fail to follow my order, I will be forced to remove you from your position. Do you understand me?"

Killian's mother was furious, but he remained indifferent. Her actions were unforgivable, and he warned her that she needed to listen to him. She glared at Killian with her lifeless black eyes, and through gritted teeth, she declared, "I'll do it."

3

Every morning, she woke up and looked out the window: same window, same room. Yet, every day, she saw something new. That was the power of magick, she thought. To keep yourself open to the possibilities of anything and everything. Sometimes, it felt like nothing was changing, but it constantly was.

Elena felt Essie jump up onto the bed, her expressive amber eyes finding her where she'd pushed herself up against the headboard, her pillow bunched up behind her, giving herself a few minutes before the hustle of her day started.

Even though her feline feet were small, they sure could give a poke, especially when hunger was a motivation.

Her coven sister and assistant Sophie was coming in late today, so Elena needed to be up and have the store open by nine this morning.

Beliefs had been in her family for centuries. Started by her great great Gran, she had supplied medicinal healing items, and then it had slowly evolved to where it is today, catering to the needs of the witch community and beyond.

Curiosity brought many through their door, and she was always willing to educate those who seemed genuinely interested in the lifestyle.

Being centered right in the middle of the French Quarter of New Orleans, the epicenter of all things supernatural, they were kept pretty busy. Add in the weekly meetings of her coven, never mind the special events during the month; each day sped by in a few blinks.

The nudge of Essie's head along her jawline brought her back to the moment she was in. Her familiar always knew when she was in a melancholy place. Elena's hands lifting, fingertips threading through the softness of her ebony fur; she knew all the late nights, including last night in the woods, and the time spent going over Gran's journals would eventually catch up with her. She had felt it slowly building over the last couple of weeks.

She hadn't really cried since the day she had laid Gran to rest. Being the only Payne descendant left, the weight of everything now fell to her.

When her Mama had passed, Gran was there, and she'd been there every day since, raising her, guiding her. She had been teaching her to be a good witch, a benevolent soul, to follow the guidance of the light.

Now, it felt like so much of the colors of her world had disappeared, and Elena didn't want to disappoint anyone. But last night, sitting with Gran's grimoire on her lap, her writing just beneath her fingertips, she knew the months of tears were caught up inside her.

With the lights low except for the reading lamp next to her on the bed, it struck Elena that the book that sat nestled on her lap had been held and cherished by the one person in the world who had meant the most to her.

She should let it out. It would relieve the awful pressure in her chest. Sometimes, you had to let that cleansing happen, bare the wound in order to heal. She knew if she let it all go, it would be a full-out ugly cry, soul-bearing, heart-wrenching, a full storm.

Gran had always said to show emotion was to show your courage. It eliminated all the clutter and gave your soul a place to thrive and flourish. And Gran was usually right about things, most things anyway.

So she had. She'd let her guard down and faced what she'd been trying to hide from. In her honesty, she just hadn't wanted to revisit all the pain. The pain of Gran's eyes closing for the last time and how she'd sat there praying and wishing for a miracle. How Essie had sat next to her, making the most heartbreaking wail she'd ever heard. How everything in this house and the store reminded her of her.

And Elena had let it all out to the point she'd felt physically sick, and her head had pounded like a bass drum. Essie had curled up on top of her chest, and their link was never more apparent as she tried to take some of her pain from her. And they'd fallen asleep like that, together. It was a proper purging, and she hadn't realized how badly she needed it.

So even though it was early on a Wednesday, the morning felt lighter, and she felt lighter. Her vision back to seeing full colors, the muted shades disappearing, the deep purring of a contented Essie bringing her own chestnut hues to that of her cat.

"It's going to be a good day today, Essie. How about I feed both of us, and we'll head in and see what mischief we can find today? How does that sound?"

She spoke to Essie a lot, and she sometimes wished that she could talk back to her. It was just the two of them now, but it would be OK. She was a Payne. Her magical inheritance was so rooted in the extraordinary, so what happened to her she wasn't quite sure, but historically, she came from fiercely powerful witches.

From mothers to daughters, again and again, gifted down the line. It was her time to shine, but first, she needed to master her new Nespresso machine. But after that, watch out.

4

The rain pounded against the rooftop, waking him from his slumber. Killian rolled over, looking at the clock; one o'clock in the damn morning. He knew he would need more sleep, but his raven pecked at his thoughts.

Killian had been restless after the argument he had with his mother. It had been close to a week since they had said something to each other. He knew she was up to something and it was probably in the no-good variety.

Why she had to be so damn defiant lately was maddening. His raven was restless, rousing him from his sleep wanting to investigate and discover what she was up to.

Kil's mother had changed so much over the years. She was rough around the edges and demanded everything to be her way, but she wasn't always like that. Something had shifted to make her so cold and uncaring. Meddling in his business was a bad move on her part. She needed to realize that he was a grown man and could make his own damn decisions. Why was she so persistent to know everything he was doing was beyond him but he was going to find a way to stop her nonsense.

Killian did not earn his position because of who his mother and father were. No, he worked his ass off to get where he was. There was no handout to be given. Just hard work and lots of dedication.

He rose, the silent call within him and his raven took form, stretching out his wings as he let him have his freedom. His heightened senses could feel something was off within the darkness of the night, hence waking from his sleep, his heart racing and pounding steadily against his chest. He lifted and flew out the window, following the threads of unease, searching for what had woken him.

The raven unites the light and dark. A channel beyond the realm of time. A seer and a bringer of messages. A bridge beyond the magical veil and the unknown. The omen of change to come.

Bram was his raven side. Killian could sense his agitation, the thumping of his heart starting to double time. Something was definitely out there in the cover of night. Giving full rein to his raven, their sight one in the same – "It's fine, Bram. Slow and easy."

Bram bristled up his feathers and poked out his chest telling Kil to be quiet and let him handle things. Bram thought he was the alpha when it came to Kil and him. He rolled his eyes at Bram, not saying a word, letting him think he ruled the roost, their spiritual bond inseparable.

The sound of footsteps caught his acute hearing, Bram's eyes locking on the two people that finally came into focus. A woman and a man stood below them, and as soon as she spoke, Killian knew precisely who it was. It was his mother, and he could feel his magick rise, his flames begging to be released. Bram tried to soothe him, but even he realized it wouldn't be easy, especially with who Killian's mother was talking to.

You never make plans with the devil unless you are ready to sell your soul to him. His mother did like to walk that fine line, but he never would have thought she would cross it. Killian was fucking outraged that she was making some kind of deal with Damaris. He was from the coven of Night Grove, and he had never been known to play nice with others.

Damaris was cunning and egotistical. He would do whatever it took to get what he wanted, even if that meant killing members of his coven. Kil's mother spoke of getting information on someone, but he couldn't make out the name she had said. Damaris held his hand out, and his mother shook it, sealing whatever deal they were both a part of. As soon as they both disappeared, Bram flew lower, doing a few sweeps of the area then he headed back home, back through the window, and Killian shifted to his human form. He was utterly outraged by his mother's betrayal.

Just as Killian believed his mother had grasped the lesson; she had approached Marisol with a heartfelt apology, embracing her once again as a sister witch within the coven. Additionally, she offered to mentor Marisol in mastering her magick skills. Then she turns around and does this and snatches away a glimmer of hope of her being the mother she used to be.

Damaris was his grandfather's right-hand man. Second in charge of their coven. Did his grandfather know what was going on? For fuck's sake, his mother was once Damaris's betrothed. Did she not care how this would affect her husband, the one that she claimed she loved with all of her heart.

Kil slammed his fist against the wall. He would get to the bottom of this and save his Coven from her bizarre behavior. No one would suffer from her cruel intentions. This had to end, even if it meant exiling her and treating her like she had treated others, like an abomination against her own kind.

5

Essie ran out the back door like her furry derrière was on fire. The squirrels taunted her familiar all hours of the day and night as she watched them from one window or the other, jumping from trees to the ground and teasing her black ball of attitude. The caterwauling made Elena's ears threaten to bleed, and she was sure one day it would be the death of her.

She was already late for her day, and now the black fluff-ball that was her Essie was gone down the cobble-walk, disappearing into the miniature woodland that was her backyard.

Hoisting the strap of her bag over one shoulder, balancing Essie's carrier in the other while juggling her keys and phone, she gave into the moment and let her frustration ebb away. Her gaze touched on the sanctuary she and Gran had nurtured and loved, every perennial and tree planted by one or the other. It made Elena's heart a little fuller, knowing pieces of her Gran were still here with her. The gardens offered a serenity to those who listened with more than their ears. The ones who existed by root and wand, nature cradling all life that dwelled within. Gran's words were a part of her daily journey, and she cherished every reminder to rejoice in the majesty of the elements, all the wild and tame parts.

The calmness of the moment was broken by the silken shadow of blackness that walked through the bluebells on silent paws, the look of utter annoyance in those amber eyes. Elena almost felt terrible until the chorus of Witchy Woman drew her gaze to her screen, and crap, she was really running late now.

"Essie, enough is enough. That squirrel has your number. Now get in here and stay put." – watching as Miss Grumpy-pants grumbled her way into her carrier and settled. Elena strapped the seat belt around the cage to be on the safe side because Essie might drive her crazy at times, but she loved her with everything she was.

Sliding into the driver's seat, her bag thrown onto the passenger, she drove the half hour to Beliefs, parking in her usual stall, unlocking the back door, giving Essie her freedom within the warded walls and a moment of deflation looking at all the orders to be filled waiting on the counter. The sooner she started, the sooner she finished, she supposed, trying to give herself a pep talk.

Flipping the sign to open, the first order of business was cleansing. Elena felt like after her emotional purge, she was ready to start fresh. She felt lighter today, her heart felt happier. Gran would want that for her. So she was going to try her best.

Selecting some burn bundles of rosemary and lavender, her choices for today, setting them in holders, their smoky scent filling the air in minutes, purifying the store where she spent most of her days.

Negative energy was everywhere and it was important to neutralize it, and create a more positive, harmonious living space. Plus, she loved the scent and so did the customers that visited the store.

Next she went about selecting ingredients for the orders. Reminding herself to concentrate on one order at a time. Sometimes, she got ahead of herself and that's when oopsies happened. Some herbs looked very much alike but mixed with certain other ones, and catastrophe could follow.

The bell above the front door heralding Sophie's arrival; Elena realizing close to an hour had gone by already.

"Morning Elena. I brought us some of Mabel's special lattes from the bakeshop. Thanks for coming in early today. I really appreciate it. "

Sophie had worked with her for just over a year. When Gran's illness had got to the point that she spent most of her days at home, Elena had needed help. Between the store and wanting to spend more time with Gran, she couldn't do it on her own.

Sophie was one of the very few witches that had been friendly to her over the years. She wasn't stuck up like many of the others in her coven. So one day when she'd been in the store, Elena asked her if she'd be interested in a job and the – "Yes I would" came out so fast they both had laughed.

"Awe thank you. That sounds perfect right about now. Set it down anywhere, I'm just getting the orders organized."

After a few more minutes of chit-chat, Elena turned to finish off where she was interrupted while her coven sister handled all the walk-in traffic.

A few hours later, the ache in her shoulders couldn't be denied any longer. She needed a break and food.

"Sophie, I'm going to grab a late lunch; you want something?" – Essie weaving in and out of her ankles at the mention of food.

"Remember, I'm leaving early today too. The coven is in a meeting. I'd ask if you were going, but I already know the answer." - Sophie's brows lifting slightly.

That was one discussion she didn't want to have, especially now that all she could think about was eating.

The Coven of the Divine Spirit was becoming an issue. She knew that. She knew it would as soon as her fire presented and the whispers of fire-witch started. She was going to be pulled in whether she wanted to or not. And she didn't. The problem was she was a Payne, the only one left, the last of her line.

She was expected to honor her place in the coven; Elena wasn't sure she wanted that for herself. She simply wanted to enjoy her life within the walls of Beliefs, practice her magick and live simply.

That was the bubble she wanted, but as her element grew, the whispers of the strength of her flame reached beyond her walls and the forest behind her; others felt the rise, and there was no hiding. They needed her element to complete their coven, to be strong, and to have the full cycle of nature represented.

Sunlight filtered through the windows of the store, catching her gaze. This was her second home, possibly her first. The walls of Beliefs had seen her first baby steps, her first failed incantation, her first heartbreak, and her deep sorrow at the loss of her Mama and now Gran. It really was her heart and soul; everything she was was because of her life here in Nola and the love she found within the small community of friends that kept Beliefs afloat.

Essie purred at her feet, her head tipping, those amber eyes all-knowing. You couldn't appreciate the good without experiencing the not-so-good. Her past and heritage would make her choose a road to follow, and she just wished Gran was here to talk too.

Her gaze took in the wallpaper they had hung so many years ago. Outdated and fading like so many things around her, but she would never replace any of it. Elena was a bit off-center; material things, wealth, none of that stuff interested her. The building that housed Beliefs was paid off; she had Gran's old house to live in, and she just wanted to live her life in peace.

Realizing she'd drifted off and Sophie was staring at her like she'd sprouted horns- "How about you feed Essie for me and lock the doors? I'll come back and finish tomorrow's orders after I get something."

Bag in hand, the screen door slamming its weathered frame behind her, the midday heat instantly adding to her array of freckles. The sun and her had a love/hate relationship, but it was a quick few steps to the busy side street, then a right turn and a push of a door to one of her favorite little retreats.

Twenty minutes later, sweet tea in one hand, sandwich in the other, Elena turned to head back to the semi-coolness of the store, her eyes lifting to the gentleman standing behind her waiting his turn, her smile always a play on her lips, his slight nod not reaching his darkened gaze.

She walked back out into the heat, stopping a few times to say hello to regulars that visited the store. A slight trickle of sweat dripped down the curve of her spine along with a prickle of awareness that had her glancing behind her to see the man from the bistro not too far behind her, his gaze not directly on her, but her imagination was always overactive. Her eyes back forward, Beliefs sign straight ahead, and now talking to herself - "C'mon Elena, it's a public street; just get inside and eat, you're hallucinating."

Half a dozen more steps, the closed sign turned at the front window telling her Sophie had left, her shifting both items to one hand while fishing out her keys and unlocking the front door, quickly closing it behind her, and flipping the lock. She shrieked as Essie jumped off the counter in greeting - "Damn cat, you scared the bejesus out of me. Stop it." Turning and peering out the window to the street, not seeing him anywhere, she grumbled at herself for being so paranoid.

"Essie, you're on guard duty while I eat. Make me proud." - Heading to the nook off to the side, she'd fill her tummy and then the orders and hopefully shake off the willies she was trying to ignore.

6

Killian's discontent was palpable. His growing exasperation with his mother's unwarranted intrusions was reaching a tipping point. She had a habit of appearing uninvited to matters that didn't pertain to her, offering unsolicited advice.

He slammed the door behind him as he walked into his house, his anger rising, and he could feel the element of his flames wanting to react. The one thing that seemed to calm him lately was his secret escape. One he rushed to get to every night for the last few months.

Quickly heading to the shower, the warm pulse of the spray removed some of the tension and washed the day away. He reminded himself that cool heads prevailed, especially when dealing with his mother. He couldn't let her get to him as she did and he foresaw another discussion with his father coming. But that was for another day.Opening the shower door, grabbing the nearest towel, there was just one place he wanted to be right now. Hanging the towel over the warming rack, he headed into his bedroom, slipping into his bed so he could drift off to sleep, to dream of the woman that had invaded his thoughts every night over the last while.

It didn't take long before she appeared, and a smile crept along his lips. There was something very familiar about her, but he couldn't quite place why. She sat in the middle of a field, picking what looked like herbs.

The sun shimmered on her beautiful red tassels of hair, and a black cat sat by her side. Her fair skin was peppered with freckles that made his hands itch to touch her, to see if she was as soft as she appeared to be.

He walked closer with careful steps. He didn't want to frighten her away; Kil just wanted a glimpse of her face. He knew this was a sign from the goddess of fate, leading him down a road that could be his future.

A breeze blew, making the vibrant red locks swirl around her. Killian could smell the softest hint of cinnamon mixed with a hint of vanilla. He wasn't sure what he did right to dream of a woman he would meet one day and that he was certain of. It could be a week, month, or even years, but he knew when this happened, it would change his life in the most unexpected of ways.

Kil didn't want to push the goddess too far; it had to be at her pace, because he knew if pushed she would send him down another path that would be heartache.

The beautiful red-haired woman stood, making him stop dead in his tracks. He hoped he would get a glimpse of her face, but she didn't even turn in his direction. She walked towards what looked like a little white cottage surrounded by flowers. The black cat ran alongside her, but for a brief moment, she stopped and cast what sounded like a protection spell. His heart started to beat rapidly in his chest. Not only was this woman beautiful, but it seemed she was also a witch.

Not only was fate a part of this, but destiny seemed to be coming along for the ride. He wouldn't argue with whatever they had planned because he could escape here in his dreams with the beautiful witch that made his heart race and warmed his soul.

For now, this would be enough for him to be content. It was a secret that was his own, and no one could take it from him. To keep her safe from the darkness that resides in his mother, he whispered a spell that he hoped would reach the beautiful redhead.

𝕬 𝖘𝖕𝖊𝖑𝖑 𝖔𝖋 𝖘𝖆𝖋𝖊𝖙𝖞 𝕴 𝖈𝖆𝖘𝖙. 𝕬 𝖜𝖔𝖗𝖉 𝖔𝖋 𝖒𝖎𝖌𝖍𝖙 𝖙𝖍𝖆𝖙 𝖍𝖔𝖑𝖉𝖘 𝖍𝖊𝖗 𝖋𝖆𝖘𝖙. 𝕬 𝖘𝖍𝖎𝖊𝖑𝖉 𝖇𝖊𝖋𝖔𝖗𝖊 𝖍𝖊𝖗 𝖆𝖓𝖉 𝖇𝖊𝖍𝖎𝖓𝖉, 𝖙𝖔 𝖗𝖎𝖌𝖍𝖙 𝖆𝖓𝖉 𝖑𝖊𝖋𝖙 𝖕𝖗𝖔𝖙𝖊𝖈𝖙𝖎𝖔𝖓 𝖇𝖎𝖓𝖉.

Watching her walk away, knowing he'd given her an unknowing gift, Killian let her go, excitement and contentment following him into a restful sleep.

7

Her Gran had a word for it. She called it the dithers, and when those happened, you should pick up your wand and be at the ready unless it was more of the collywobbles. If those set up home in your tummy, shit would usually hit the proverbial fan.

Since earlier, that feeling of being watched hadn't left her. Elena had looked over her shoulder a few times since locking herself inside the store on her return with her late lunch. Her half-eaten sandwich was not sitting well between those dithers and wobbles that had taken up residence.

Her gaze shifted to where Essie had stopped midstep and stared off into the distance, her amber gaze fixated on nothing, which was not helping her current situation at all. Moments turning to minutes, her familiar just sitting there; still. Elena wondered where she had gone too. Possibly through the veil or into another realm, her head turning back to her, the shade of her element evident in Essie's gaze, wondering what had just happened.

"Essie, you really need to learn how to talk because you just notched my heebie-jeebies up to the next level."

But nothing, no meows or purrs, just the stare that made her arm hairs rise and wished she were holding a baseball bat in defense of things that she didn't see but knew were there.

That was that. She would leave what wasn't done and could wait until tomorrow. She couldn't concentrate anyway. She probably had already possibly mixed up one or two potions. It was pointless doing any more today. Elena was throwing in the towel on this day.

"Essie, we're going home, so stop your googly eyes and find your carrier."

A short time later, she was fed, Essie was fed, and her second glass of wine was half empty, and all things were right with her world.

The couch she sat on was worn but comfy. The patchwork quilt that lay across her legs was the same vintage, but it was home and always had been. When life or the day was too much, this was her retreat. Every day and year of her life had been lived inside these four walls.

The veranda out front had seen all the comings and goings. The flagstone path that led from the house to the front street had felt the footsteps of the generations.

Her favorite room by far, though, was the library. It wasn't big by any means, nothing larger than two bedrooms strung together, but Gran had seen to it that the books she housed and cared for were a fount of history and knowledge in one way or another.

So many of those books holding a deep emotional attachment to Elena, fond memories of being read to in the corner chair by her Gran. Peter Cottontail, still one of her favorites, and she wasn't ashamed to say she still read it on occasion.

But what had brought her here tonight was Gran's grimoire. Elena had promised Gran that she'd read as much as possible and practice and improve her craft. She was still far from being a fully transitioned witch, the divine force out of reach for now, but she'd get there.

She knew she wasn't the brightest, even with her red hair, but Gran had always said - "Drive your own broom, don't worry about anyone else."

So, keeping her word, she sat cross-legged in the living room with Essie contentedly purring at her feet. It was more snoring, and she'd told her that often to be whined at in return.

She lifted the grimoire onto her lap to have a shock jump from its cover through her palms, a hiss escaping her lips at the static discharge almost in the protection of the invasion. Essie's screech and arched back, adding to the moment. The scent of smoke hung in the air around her, and it seemed familiar, but yet she couldn't place it.

Pulling her hands back towards her, the book opened, pages rifling as if turned by unseen fingers, then stopped. Words from the page lifting as if written in fire, her own voice speaking them softly, control of her body taken away from her, the language foreign to her own ears, but power rose around her at each chant she recited.

Elena knew it was a spell but had no idea what for. The longer she sat there, held trapped, the sensation built around her. Her own panic rose, not knowing if this was good or bad.

She wanted it to stop. Needed it to stop. Then, slowly, the shifting of the letters before her, some dropping and disappearing, others rearranging, her eyes riveted as words hung suspended.

The raven will light your way.

Her gaze drifted over the suspension before her, the words repeating in her mind. Then, as if reading her angst, the book slammed shut, the letters falling like ash from a flame, leaving nothing behind.

Pushing the book off her lap onto the couch, she stood staring at it. What in all the heck had just happened? Grabbing the blanket and throwing it over Gran's legacy, she picked it up and moved it over to the floor in the corner of the room.

Quickly grabbing her salt from the kitchen, she placed a circle around where she'd left it because it couldn't hurt, her voice the only sound in the room.

"Gran, what's going on ?" - spoken into the quiet.

Holding the salt to her chest, her mind was a cobweb of thoughts. A raven? Elena didn't like ravens or crows. They always gave her an unsettled feeling. Like when they looked at you with those black coal eyes, they could see into your soul, maybe take it and never return. To her, they represented the dark side of the world and magick, like gatekeepers for the afterlife. Even now, just thoughts of one, never mind a collection of them, gave her the willies.

Keeping an eye on where the book lay, setting down the salt but keeping it close, she refilled her wine glass because what just happened required more liquid courage.

Elena couldn't let the grimoire lay there indefinitely, and there were more pages to look through. She just hoped it was done with the dancing letters and the light shows.

Today was a complete shit day. Killian's coven was feeling the ripple effect of his mother's defiance. As lead of the sister witches, she was failing at her duties. How could she leave such a quake behind her? Did she not fucking realize she was not only hurting the sisters, but she was also hurting her eldest son?

Rissa had a way of demanding things from Killian and Keegan. When she didn't get her way she would rant and rave. Their mother was turning into someone they hardly recognized. Memories of their mother from when they were boys now unrecognizable as he looked at her.

She was also wearing on Killian's last nerve with her fixation on his single status. Always wanting to marry him off, not caring at all that she was aggravating him in the process. Until one day he blurted out the secret he was trying to keep to himself. He told her he was indeed in love.

Killian told her about his beautiful redhead that he met in his dreams every single night. That she was his future. That it was only a matter of time. In typical Rissa style, his mother rolled her eyes, telling him how foolish he was to believe in such nonsense, then turning and walking away. His secret was truly out, a slight pang that it wasn't just his anymore but a slight chuckle knowing that sharing that with his mother would eat at her. Something she fucking deserved after the hell she has put him and his brother through.

Even his father had enough of her outrageous behavior. He felt terrible for his father because he knew how much he loved his mother. They fell in love when they were seventeen, built a life, and had children. And yet she was so distant and cold towards him.

After a long and tiring day, Kil transformed into his raven making his way toward home. The weight of some days could be too much to bear, and he longed for the solace of the night skies to soothe him.

He needed to forget about all that had happened today and find some peace in the quiet of the night. As he soared through the skies, he felt a sense of calm wash over him. The stars twinkled above him, and the cool breeze brushed against his face, bringing a sense of tranquility that he had been craving. Shifting, showering and jumping between his sheets, he needed his girl. And that's what she was, she was his.

Tomorrow was another day to worry about his mother and the decision he had to make. He only hoped to make her see how important her family was to her. Somehow, he would find a way to drive out the darkness that was taking hold. He didn't want to banish her to a life of exile because it would break his father in more ways than one.

Killian never asked for too much from anyone. He was a man who did what he had to do to keep his coven safe. He believed honesty and loyalty were most important when it came to any type of relationship.

Cowards lie and hide in the shadows, and those are the most dangerous people of all. Killian's mother was indeed one of those who would conceal her secrets, but Kil would find out soon precisely what she was up to.

Tonight, he would follow the path his dreams would lead him to of his redhead. One that warmed his heart and touched his soul.

It didn't take long for him to let go of his day and drift off. And there she was, and this time her face came into full view. Fuck she was stunning. The sun seemed to dance around her and make her freckles pop on her cheeks.

Fate was showing him a glimpse of the woman he was meant to be with. No he didn't know how long it would take for them to meet, he'd be content for now. Every dream showed him what was waiting for him, he just needed to be patient. Every night was a day closer to having her in his arms. He had to believe that. He had to believe there was a higher purpose at work. For now he was happy knowing his destiny was out there, making her way towards him.

9

Elena held her stare in the mirror as she spoke the words out loud, her hand still stung and itched from last night. Gran's grimoire would take years off her life at this rate. Whenever she thought she was making inroads, that darn thing attacked her. She couldn't think of an explanation for it. She was a Payne, Gran's blood descendant. So what was she doing wrong?

She knew she wasn't the master of the book; that was Gran. Elena felt like she was at its mercy, and she didn't like that feeling.

Gazing into the tawny brown reflection of her eyes, the color so much like her mother's had been - "C'mon girl, think" - so much aggravation at herself.

Then…Blood magic. A chill going through her at memories best forgotten or maybe just suppressed. That could go wrong in so many ways. You never knew how dormant magic could react to a blood offering.

Righting herself, her fingers lifting and slowly removing the curlers she had placed earlier, now thinking it hadn't been such a good idea. She didn't need to make her hair more noticeable, especially today.

What had she been thinking, and that was the problem. She hadn't been. She hasn't been lately. But that was her way. When an important decision needed to be made, she veered in another direction.

She ran her fingertips through the mess of liquid fire on her head, gazing at herself. She needed help, and she couldn't go to the Coven; she didn't trust her sisters, and how awful was that to say? They needed her, yet they hated her power of fire. She needed to get through today without the roof falling in or that damn book reaching out to her.

She was scheduled to have some of the council members in the store later today. Elena often offered her small nook area in the corner of Beliefs up for gatherings or meetings. When Mira, director of the Divine Spirit, had called her and asked if they could use her location for a get-together, her first reaction was to say No.

Just the thought of some high-ranking members only a few feet from her as she went about her day sent her tummy into the turns.

Plus, she found it odd that they would use her space; it was much smaller than their usual. They generally chose someplace on the grander scale in hopes that the whispers and the gossip made the rounds in Nola. They loved to be the wag on other's tongues; they lived for it.

Elena was so different from most members of her coven. She was sure all this was so that they could do some snooping and get a closer look at the witch presenting the rare and powerful element. For the most part, Elena was relatively quiet and preferred to spend time alone. So, keeping a low profile was now proving a thorn in her side because they were curious.

Ugh. She did this to herself, and after the evening she'd had, and then her night of dreams, she was only half herself. Why lately her sleep was more restless she didn't know either. She'd always been a good sleeper, never having a problem getting 6-8 hours in a row. But the last few months she just kept flipping and flopping. Sleeping but not a deep sleep which explained why she caught herself drifting during the day. If she could, she'd call in sick and keep the closed sign up, but that wasn't an option.

But she was going to help herself, and that's why she told Sophie she would be only slightly late and to start on the day's orders without her.

The idea came to her as she left the house with her coffee mug of dark roasted, extra sugar, extra cream. A grounding ritual was great for when you were feeling anxious or overwhelmed, when life became just a bit too much. Gran had always been about your whole health, and Elena knew she'd tell her to step away for a bit, attune to nature, and heal any imbalance that was unsettling her.

So, stowing her coffee and bag in the car, she took a detour behind the house down the familiar path and into the backwoods. She didn't need to go far before her eyes found an oak tree, which was perfect for the ritual.

Elena sat down, leaning her back against the trunk, taking a few deep breaths, and visualizing everything that made her feel weighted. She tipped her head back and gazed skyward at the branches above, knowing the tree's roots were just as widespread beneath her. Imagining herself becoming part of the tree, allowing all her negative energy to flow from her into the tree and the surrounding earth, chanting - *Powers of the earth in which I believe, bring stable energy unto me, take the energy that serves me not, let it serve the ground within this plot.*

The woods had always been her place since she was a baby. This spot, as much a place of comfort as her home was. Such a tangible bond between her and nature, a togetherness in its purest form when everything was right with her world.

She'd been correct in coming here before heading on with her day. That's what Gran had always said, and again, she was right. We had to listen to ourselves, really listen, and take off the filter. The answers were there if we opened our minds and hearts.

Pushing herself up, stretching her arms high, a smile lighting her lips, Elena turned, hugging the tree - "Thank you for being here through all my steps. I'm sure I'll be back."

Following the path back up to the house, she was ready to face whatever the day and her coven sisters tossed her way.

Spellbound

10

*T*he first time Rissa met her husband, Kaden, she could feel his power and the uniqueness within him. Their love for one another was undeniable but never would she have thought it would be tested in a way that could ultimately destroy them.

Their sons, Killian and Keegan, took after their father. Rissa was thrilled to see her boys inherit the ability to shift into a raven and hold a second unique power just like her husband; one having the gift of sight and the other bending time to his will.

Her name echoed as she walked through the halls of His Manor, her uncertainty a chill on her skin. She knew nothing truly ever escaped Him, but she always hoped. From as far back as she could remember He'd made her life so difficult and thought himself so much wiser than others.

She smiled proudly as she entered the room where she'd been summoned. His disappointment etched across His wrinkled face, her spine straightened as she held her head high. Her magic wrapped around her like a shield.

He had heard rumors floating within His clan, causing disruption. How could she be with a man that possessed more power than He did? Kaden became a threat out of mere jealousy and the sons by inheritance.

Both Rissa and Him held their own unique powers, both strong individually. His ability to crawl into others' minds, to unravel the deepest secrets and lay them bare. That should be a blessing, used for a greater good, but not when controlled by a nefarious soul.

He'd make her witness things that would shatter any soul. But she had a strength within her that even He could not comprehend, a strength born of love, motherhood, and the unbreakable bond between a woman and her children.

The words He spewed of her betrayal burned like acid on her skin. She had been faithful, loved Him, and stood by His side through life's trials. Yet He chose to believe the lies, to turn a blind eye to the truth.

Damaris sat beside Him like a vulture, his gaze fixed on Rissa with a predatory hunger. She was of His blood, yet His loyalty lay not with her but with the scumbag Damaris.

Rissa's love for her husband and sons was a flame that could not be extinguished, a jewel that shone in the darkest depths of her soul. But His jealousy licked through Him like a wildfire. His insecurity had twisted His mind and warped His perception of reality. He had become a monster, a shadow of the man she had once loved.

Killian had earned his place as the next elder of their coven through hard work and dedication. Yet He despised her son for it, and she could only hope that He didn't know of the other powers Keegan and Killian held. It would drive Him to the point of no return.

Rissa's heart ached with an almost unbearable love. Her sons were her world, her everything. And she knew that at any moment, that world could be shattered. But she would fight, she would claw, scream and die before she let Him take them from her.

As she stood there before him, that instant happened, her world crumbled. The threat hung in the air, tendrils wrapping around her heart. She screamed, a wordless wail that tore through the silence. The visions burst forth, a torrent of blood and pain and loss. Her husband, her precious boys...their bodies laid out before her, lifeless and mutilated. Raven feathers drifted down like ashes, a haunting reminder of what was to come.

A sob tore from her chest, wracking her body. She was helpless, powerless against the onslaught. Her magic had failed her; her strength was gone. All she could do was watch as her world burned until there were only ashes left.

... her sacrifice beginning

Rissa had been thinking alot lately about her past, her emotions running on high. The loss of her best friend and their rocky past had her heart in so much turmoil. She wasn't allowed to act upon it. She had to swallow her feelings and push them down in the pit of her stomach.

She needed to get her hands on the spellbook before the man pulling her strings got to it. Rissa knew that since Matilda had it, it was safe but with her passing it no longer was. It was of utmost importance to get it back in her hands again.

***

The sound of the alarm clock rang loudly in his ears. Was it seven in the morning already? Damn, it felt like he just went to sleep. Flinging the blanket off of himself and getting up, he headed to the shower. His dreams fully consumed by a beautiful redhead with piercing chestnut eyes, he knew she was the other half of his soul. The one that was his equal in every way.

Turning the warm water on, stepping under the spray, letting the water wash over his body, thoughts of her came flooding in, he imagined kissing her as he stroked his cock from base to tip. Her soft flesh pinned beneath him, moaning his name while he drove deeper inside the warmth of her pussy.

Pearls of precum dripped from the bulbous tip. Grunts erupted from his throat, his balls tightening as he stroked faster, fisting her crimson locks, snapping her head back so he could look into her chestnut eyes as he thrusted deep inside her womb. He felt her clench, erupting like a waterfall drenching his cock with her sweet nectar. Kil moaned; his seed shot out like a cannon. He leaned against the shower wall, catching his breath.

Finishing his shower, Killian smiled broadly. This woman had bewitched him like no other before. Drying himself off, he secured a towel around his waist and then selected a pair of black slacks and a gray polo shirt, laying them out on the bed.

He had a meeting to attend with his father, some protocols needed to be discussed over the representation of their coven at an upcoming grand meeting. The problem lately, he didn't want to hear him rambling on about when Killian was going to settle down and have children. It seemed that was all he wanted to talk about lately. Why couldn't he just concentrate on his brother and the love he has for Iris? But nope, he had to be his main focus as of late. His argument being that he wasn't getting any younger and he was his oldest son. He had obligations to continue the raven lineage.

The smell of coffee invaded his senses, his pre-set time always having it ready for him. Killian loved his coffee in the morning. He truly didn't know a better way to start the day.

His hair still damp as he made his way to the kitchen; grabbing the nearest cup from the cabinet, he poured almost to the rim. Just as he was about to touch his lips and take the first sip, the sound of his name was spoken out loud in the room.

Peering over the rim, his mother's eyes met his. Privacy obviously not high on her list either. What on earth could she want? He wasn't running late for their meeting so he hadn't a clue why she was here.

"Killian, save the look. I'm canceling the meeting today. I have other plans for you. Well, actually, I need you to do something for me. Something of importance and it can't wait. "

This wasn't good, not at all. His mother rarely asked him for any favors. So this had to be big or this was something he probably wanted no part of.

Setting his cup on the counter and crossing his arms across his chest, her tapping her fingers on the table waiting for him to respond.

"Mother, what favor do you need me to do?"

She gave him a pointed look and took a step closer. "Son, this is important. I need you to go and retrieve an old spell book of mine. It was gifted to me by our ancestors. I let a friend, Matilda, use it, but unfortunately, she passed away a number of months ago. Her granddaughter is now running her shop, so all you have to do is tell her that I sent you to get my spell book."

Scrubbing a hand down his face in disbelief. So she wanted him to miss out on a coven meeting because she needed him to play errand boy. Kil knew he wouldn't hear the end of it if he didn't do as she asked him to do.

As the High Warlock, he simply couldn't miss a meeting. He walked past her into his bedroom to get dressed, grabbing his shirt and pants, slipping them on, adding his socks and watch, then back into the kitchen.

"Mother, I am not rescheduling this meeting over a damn spell book. Send Keegan to get it, I have important things to do. Now, if you excuse me, I must be getting onto those."

Before he could get to the door, her magic swirled around him, pulling him towards her. He didn't fight it. He didn't want to fight with her again. **"KILLIAN SEAMUS RAVEN...** You will do as I ask of you or your father will know about this. Do you understand me?"

Well, his ass was grass that was for sure. She'd just used his full name and he was already dealing with her erratic behavior. A deep sigh fell from his chest and she released her magic and he straightened his shirt reminding himself to pick his battles.

"Mother, I will go but know this, I am not happy about it. And you can be the one to tell father we are pushing back the meeting by a couple hours. And don't forget to mention it's because of you." - a slight curiosity as to why she would give another her book – "What's the name of the store and where is it located?"

"It's in the French Quarter and the name of the shop is Beliefs."

A short while later...

Huffing down the street, he couldn't believe how his mother was acting. She could have gotten Keegan to get the book for her. It was that simple but her dramatics were seriously out of hand. He turned the corner and saw Beliefs tucked behind one of his favorite cafes. Why he had never noticed it before was beyond him.

Opening the door, he was hit in the face with a familiar scent that made the hairs on his nape stand up.

Approaching the counter but no one was around. He waited a few minutes then he yelled out, "Hello, is anyone here?"

A female voice answered. "I will be there in a second."

Looking around the shop, everything was perfectly placed. It definitely was run by a woman because a male wouldn't be this neat.

"How can I help you, Sir?"

His head snapped in her direction and he froze. His eyes took in the beautiful woman with hair the color of wildfire and eyes like warm cinnamon. It was her, the one he'd been dreaming about for months. He tried to speak but his words failed him. All he could manage to get out was..."**It's you.**"

***

"Sophie, would you mind going to the post office for me? I've had a parcel sitting there for a few days and as an incentive you can grab some money from the jar and stop at Lou's and get us a treat." - knowing that would do it because Lou's was one of her favorite local stores, anything New Orleans flavored you could find in there.

The blonde head of her friend poking out of their storeroom, "You don't have to ask me twice," her hands already lifting the apron over her head.

They needed to organize their storage space better before the next shipment of jars and stuff arrived. So, between customers and orders and the meeting being held here today, that needed to be done.

A smile lighting Elena's face, she had gotten so lucky with Sophie. They just clicked and were about the same age. She enjoyed the store as much as Elena did and she was great with their patrons, which included the coven members, who Elena tried more than not to avoid.

"I'll see you in a bit. Don't burn the place down while I'm gone." - a wink and laugh from Sophie as the back screen door banged as she left.

Her coven. Ugh. She really wanted to avoid what she shouldn't be avoiding. They wanted to tie her to them whether she wanted to be tied or not. And it's not that she disliked her coven; she had just always felt like an outsider. When Gran was alive, she was tolerated but now that she had no one, the feeling of alienation had grown. Maybe it was her fault; maybe it wasn't.

What Elena did know was she liked her tiny world, she felt in control for the most part. It was her, Essie and the friends that she allowed close. She wasn't ready yet to fling open the door and let just anybody in.

The whistle of the kettle breaking the spell she had momentarily been under. She should flip the Closed sign for a short while until she felt more like herself. The store was still quiet, it was early but then Essie started chattering and walking to her bowl and Elena followed behind.

Once she saw to Essie, Elena closed her eyes and let fate decide on her flavor of tea. Touching one first, then the other, her gaze taking a peek, mint was the winner.

The voice. His voice halted her stirring of sugar in her cup. She hadn't even heard anyone come in thanks to Essie and her complaining because she had run out of her food and had to go to the cellar for more. "I'll be there in a second," yelled out to the front, cleaning off the front of her dress and giving Essie her "behave" stare.

The blue of his eyes had an indrawn breath halting as she rounded the corner to the front counter. The look he gave her faltered her steps and then he spoke, the voice that had oftentimes disrupted her sleep had just walked into her store.

"It's you."

11

His breath hitched in his chest, and his heart slammed against his ribcage. He couldn't believe who he was seeing. The beautiful redhead with the captivating eyes from his dreams stood before him. Could this be real? Indeed, he must be dreaming again.

He stepped towards her without thinking and pulled her into his arms, stealing a kiss from her luscious lips. Fuck, she tasted like wildfire, which sent an inferno to his groin.

This was the closest he would ever get to heaven, and he didn't want this moment to end. Her hands snaked up the back of his neck, and her fingers tangled in his hair. She was as lost in the moment as he was. Did she dream of him as he had of her? Was it selfish of him to take what didn't belong

56

to him? Maybe so, but her lips begged to be kissed, and he couldn't control his desire.

She released him from their kiss, and he felt an aching deep within. This woman was his mate; he could feel it in his soul. Her beautiful eyes bore into him and he was at a loss for words. Indeed, she must feel the same, or at least he hoped so. Being rejected would kill him in more ways than one.

"I can't apologize for my behavior. I've been dreaming of you for a very long time, and I never thought I would come face to face with the woman who has taken my heart as hers. It may seem silly, but I only speak the truth. I may not know the real you, but I know everything about the woman in my dreams. I call her Red, and she calls me hers."

She took a step back, and he wanted to reach out and pull her against him. Fuck, he was an idiot to have acted so and to spill his guts to her. She must be thinking that he was an absolute weirdo.

He didn't wait for her to speak, he turned slightly, upset with himself for acting the way he had, so out of sorts forgetting the reason for why he'd come, he took a few steps, her voice lifting his head and holding her gaze. "Wait" were the words she had spoken.

***

His eyes captivated her, holding her in a spell of her own making. A face now to go with the voice that she'd heard for months. It had started off very randomly, on the evening breeze that came in through her opened window, and then another time waking her from a restful night's sleep. Then nothing for days, sometimes even a week or more.

But then it happened at Beliefs, her spinning so quickly she'd dropped a crystal goblet that had shattered in a thousand pieces, yet no one was there. She started to think someone was trying to contact her from the afterlife. And every instance, the deep timbre became a bit more clear.

His movement was as if he floated toward her; she was entranced. The thought swamped her to the point she just stood there mouth open, gawking at him like some schoolgirl.

Even when he stepped forward and kept coming, his arms wrapping around her, his lips on hers, her traitor body responding to his touch, her hands a slow glide around him, then up his back to thread fingers through the softness of his hair. She heard herself moan, moan into his mouth that coaxed her fire to rise and blister.

A blast of reality at that. Why hadn't she burned him? Her power had protected her on more than one occasion when she'd been threatened or touched unexpectedly.

She tore her lips from him, her arms slipping away from around the width of his back, her flames still dancing beneath her skin in awareness. Her eyes touched every aspect of him, confused at what was happening.

She felt like time had just been suspended. All the sounds around them had just fallen away. What if someone from the coven had walked in and seen? She didn't even know who he was. Her hand lifted, fingertips running across her lips, puffy from his kiss.

His voice filled the room, and she listened, not entirely understanding what he was saying. It was like she had drunk too much of Gran's wine, and everything was hazy around the edges, and her recognition was lazy and slow.

Then he turned. Was he just going to leave? And her mouth spoke before her brain, "Wait. I don't know who you are, but you can't just walk in here and start kissing someone, especially me," her sensibilities finally getting back on track. "I don't know you," *that was primarily true,* she thought, "and even if I did, this is my place of work, and anyone could have just walked through the door and seen us," that even sounded stupid to herself but once she started her redhead traits burst out. "Who are you anyway, and why are you in my store?"

***

What the hell was wrong with him? Never had he been so thoughtless, but she had been haunting his dreams in the most beautiful of ways. Her lips alone would bring a man to his knees willingly, and those eyes of hers spoke to his soul. Never in all his years had he felt this way instantly when he had met someone. He couldn't control himself; she had him under her spell.

The moment she whispered for him to stop was like an answer to a prayer. Maybe, just maybe, she felt the same way for him. Then, in a split second, she turned his world upside down. Like a knife had been plunged into his chest, piercing his heart. Her words came out so harshly that he felt like he was being scolded for taking the last cookie from the cookie jar. Killian didn't give two shits if anyone saw them; why did she even care?

He took a step towards her, and she took one back. She had to feel what he felt; there was no way to deny it. His fire sought out hers, and that fucking meant something to him. She is the one that he is meant to be with. His other half. Warlocks and Witches know when they have met their mate, and she was his!

"Red, I don't care who would see us. I know this seems so irrational, but every night when I close my eyes, your beautiful face appears. Fuck, I know this sounds so fucking crazy, but it's the truth."

Running his hands through his hair in frustration, he wanted to punch the wall. Red had to think he was fucking nuts the way he was acting, but she was the reason for his behavior.

He never craved something or someone as badly as he did her. Watching her reactions, Red's stare was locked on his every movement. He needed her to say something after his confession. Anything would be fucking nice right now. Her silence was deafening!!

"Say something, Red."

***

She watched him, listened to him, and watched him some more. The way his fingers kept threading through his hair, and then it fell across his brow, and he'd do it again. His voice was so compelling and captivating, and she knew it; she'd heard it before in her dreams. Or were they premonitions? But never a face to go with. And this was too real, too surreal, and right here standing in front of her in her store.

He wanted her to talk. She had difficulty putting the last few minutes into any order as to why he had grabbed her and hung on so desperately because it had been like that. Like a fever, she had gone up in flames. She could feel her tiny ember that always glowed, leap. It was like a torch lit to gasoline, instant and bright.

But she wasn't that girl, at least she didn't think so. She led a pretty quiet life and hadn't dated much. Gran had kept her pretty busy for the most part, and sometimes she wondered about that. She'd heard the odd whisper behind her back. She knew the fire element was powerful, whereas she was not, not really. But Gran said it was meant for her. Elena just didn't know quite what to do with it.

He wanted her to say something?

He looked distraught, and for some reason, that bothered her, yet, she took another step backward, then another, until the counter separated them, and she had something to hang on to.

"We haven't met before, and you walked into my shop, so why did you? Why Beliefs over another store on the block?"

***

Did he believe in the whole myth about love at first sight? Absolutely not! He had always thought you have to be with someone and get to know them before you could say you love someone and mean it. He stood in her shop, eating his words and wrestling with his demons.

It was love at first sight. His heart belonged to her if she wanted it. Night after night, he'd dreamed of her and all the wicked things they had done to each other.

Here, she stood before him in the flesh. How could he not touch her or not taste her lips against his? Yes, it was complete madness, but he didn't give a fuck. He knew she was the one he was meant to spend his life with, and he could feel her fire caressing his. She is his mate, and he would fight like hell to prove it to her.

His heart did a deep sink as her facial expression gave away what was warring within her. He knew she was fighting her emotions and didn't understand why this was happening. She took a step away from him, and all he wanted to do was pull her back in his arms where she belonged. Letting out a sigh, he didn't want to scare her, so he gave her the space she needed.

"My name is Killian, and I am the high Warlock of the Raven Coven. My mother and your grandmother were close friends, and she sent me to retrieve the spell book she let your grandmother borrow. It's been passed down from our ancestors and is extremely important to my family."

She chewed on her bottom lip as she listened to his every word. It made it hard to concentrate when he only wanted to be the one nibbling on her lips. Fuck, he sounded like a lovesick puppy. This woman had him by the balls and didn't even know it. He closed the distance between them, needing to feel her close.

"Do you feel that, Red? You are the flame to my fire?"

12

ℌe was tall and good-looking, and even though she put distance between them, Elena could feel his magick calling to hers. Why was that? She didn't understand the sensation she felt when their powers touched, like they were melding. It unsettled her.

Then he stepped forward again and again, every word he spoke raising her anxiety level because he was like royalty and he'd kissed her, Elena Payne.

"Stop," her hand coming up so she could get a few words in. "Killian, you shouldn't be here," her fingertips touching her lower lip, "and you shouldn't have kissed me. You're like the highest of the high, and I'm like … you shouldn't have," she started to pace, gathering her hair and pulling it over one shoulder, playing with the ends. "And yes, I feel my magick calling, but you need to stop it," was she scolding him? Oh geez, she needed the floor to open up and swallow her. "I think I know the book you

63

mean, but I don't have it here. It's at my home in our library. Gran kept all the special editions there. And my name is not Red. It's Elena. Elena Payne."

Her fire was stretching and reaching, and it was freaking her out. Turning back to him, her head tipping because of his height, "You need to turn down whatever you're doing. I feel like I'm going to combust."

***

Her words hit him square in the chest hard. He even flinched a little. Couldn't she see that there was no way to stop this? She had to know when two of the same elements met that, there was a chance at being fated mates. The calling of one to the other, the question unknown if there would be an answer. If there was? It's a connection that could not be severed.

Killian grabbed her gently by the arm and got her to stop pacing. "Listen, Red, this between us is out of our control, and there is no way to stop it. I never thought I would walk into your store and come face to face with the woman that has been filling up my dreams, night after night. This, as you call it, is our elements connecting, and that's why you feel the way you do and why I can't keep my damn hands off of you. We are fated mates, Red. There is no denying it. And your name is beautiful Elena but I've known you as Red for quite a while."

She stared up at him with her mouth wide open. He waited for her to say something but nothing came out. Red blinked rapidly, and he pulled her close to try to comfort her, but nothing seemed to ease her. Fuck, why did he just drop all this on her? Kil wanted to be gentle, but he needed her to understand what was happening between them. Did she think he gave a fuck about what coven she was from? That shit doesn't mean anything to him. All he wanted or needed was her.

***

She understood all the basics of what Killian was saying, but she couldn't fathom why it would happen to her. Gran often talked of our true fate being out of our hands. Even when a spell was cast, there was a counter for the spell. So, what happened in one place would affect another. So Elena never did them to improve her life or position. She sold spells and incantations in the store, but she always advised the buyer of the downsides.

But she could tell by his voice and stature he believed every word he said. Reaching out and stopping her mid-stride, he pulled her closer, and that simple touch burned in her soul. Thinking about the reaction sent her anxiety on a leap. Something was happening, but here and now wasn't the time, and she needed him gone so she could breathe.

Taking a step back again, which she'd been doing a lot of since he walked into the store, a chime from the front door telling her the day had officially started, she looked from her first customer back to Killian.

"I need to start my day. The book is at my home. If you want to pick it up, you could stop by later. I can give you the number. But no more kissing or whatever else it is that you're doing." Moving off to the side, she grabbed a card for the store and flipped it over, writing down her cell number. "Call me after four and we can work out the details." She handed him the card and went to pass him, almost tripping over Essie, who had decided to come be a bother, weaving in and out of her legs, then Killian's.

"Essie, stop being so nosy and go do your job. Whatever that is."

***

Watching her step away made his heart sink. He knew she could feel this thing between them, but why was she trying her best to bring logic into this situation? Was she scared? Kil knew everything was moving fast, and it wasn't very comforting, but this was real, and how he felt about her was undeniable.

Killian didn't give a fuck who saw them together, and he most certainly didn't provide another fuck if anyone didn't approve. She was the one, and he would stop at nothing to show her they belonged together.

Killian never was the type of man that didn't say precisely what he felt and he wasn't going to start now. There was no way in hell he would let his soulmate slip through his hands. Never in all his years had he felt a connection so strong in his entire life. It was like two magnets coming together and no one would pull them apart. It was near impossible to do so.

He could feel her powers and he knew how strong she truly was but Kil could also feel something else within her. Maybe she had a secret that he didn't know.

His fire was burning, calling out to hers, practically begging her to meld with his. Her grandmother must have told her what happened when twin flames met. If they didn't claim one another, their fire would burn out, pure powers would just cease to exist.

He could teach her how to control her powers and be one of the most powerful witches in her coven, but if that were to happen, she would need to open up and trust him.

For now, Killian would try to control himself around her, but he hoped she was prepared for what was going to happen.

Picking up the card and putting it in his back pocket, he wanted to kiss some sense into her, but that had to wait. A smile playing along his lips as a large black cat, apparently named Essie, came to give him the once over; *her familiar,* he thought. Kil watched the customer turn towards the back of the store as he whispered, "Red, expect my phone call at four. It seems we have a lot to discuss."

Drawing his powers in, Kil didn't wait for her to say anything else. He was gone like rain on a summer morning, materializing back at home, met by his mother's disapproving eyes.

13

How many times had she looked at the clock on the wall? How many times had she forgotten what she was doing to have to stop and give herself a shake? And how many times had she almost tripped over Essie, who was making herself a complete nuisance rubbing against her legs because she could tell she was in her "druthers" like Gran used to say.

It was no use; she was failing miserably. Elena took herself to the nook, slid in, and gave herself the what for. She let the morning events pour out instead of trying to hide them away like they didn't happen.

It had happened. Killian had walked into her store, gathered her against him, and kissed her. He kissed her, speechless and dumbfounded. Made her into someone she usually wasn't. Not that she'd been kissed by many, but the point was she wasn't a fall-over-some-guy kind of girl.

Her thoughts softened as his face appeared to her. He was something, though. Killian. The name alone was incredibly sexy like he was. She had caught herself twice wanting to reach up and push the fall of his hair off his forehead but had managed to stop herself.

Tall, sandy-colored hair, the bluest of eyes fringed by long dark lashes, a positively indecent mouth and a hard chiseled body, which she'd felt when he'd drawn her in tightly. Top that all off with ink she could see peeking out from the collar of his shirt and on his forearms, and now she wondered where else he had picture stories tattooed. A low groan escaping that she couldn't suppress.

He was a warlock, an important one in a powerful coven. That life wasn't for her. She knew she'd have to seal herself to one, but since Gran's passing and the rising of her element, she had become more stubborn.

But right now, she needed to pull herself together. Sophie had already given her the looks, asking if she was alright. It was simple, he was going to call. They'd meet at her place, she'd give him the book, hopefully finding it quickly, and then he'd go. Five minutes tops.

Even as she tried to convince herself, she already knew that wouldn't be the case after this morning and what he had said to her. But she could be very convincing when she wanted to be, so it meant letting him see reason. She'd have to convince him otherwise and he'd have to find another redhead.

Her phone ringing had her almost falling off the bench she was sitting on. A swipe of her screen, the 3:59 staring up at her, Kil was a minute early.

"Hello. Hi Killian. No, meet me at my place. I have my car."

Talking briefly and giving him the address, she put her phone down, reaching behind her for Gran's special wine. Two hours. She'd see him in two hours, not sure if it was a good or bad thing, but obviously, someone up above thought her life was too plain.

Filling one glass first, then another for Sophie, yelling, "Break time, Soph." Elena would see how she felt after one drink, but if her jitters hadn't disappeared, then a second was in order. And for now, she was keeping this to herself. No one needed to know how a kiss by a handsome stranger had thrown her off kilter.

***

Killian had been thinking about her all day and their last conversation. He knew she was scared about what was happening between them, but he wanted to reassure her that there was nothing to fear. This was fate bringing two souls together as one.

Red wanted him to meet her at her house, and he was eager to do so. This was his chance to prove to her they had something special that they couldn't deny. She made him feel things that he didn't think were possible. Kil honestly believed love wasn't in the cards for him, but when he met Red for the first time, he knew she was the one.

Opening the door to his Aston Martin, he slid in the seat, typed her address in Google Maps, started up the engine, and was on his way. So many thoughts of her flooded his mind. Her beautiful eyes had looked into the depths of his soul. Her soft lips begged to be kissed. Fuck, she gave him a hard-on just thinking about her.

Get it together, Kil, he muttered to himself.

The drive didn't take him long, pulling up at the address she had given him, and he immediately adored the two-story New Orleans home that came into view. It even had a white picket fence, gardens, and flowerbeds like his dream. It was a perfect fit for his Red.

Sliding himself out of the car, his gaze running over the entire landscape, getting a feel for her place, he walked up to the door, a firm press on the bell, his head turning this way and that, scanning the area.

A moment later, she opened the door, and his eyes raked over her. She was dressed in a yellow sweater that hung off her right shoulder with a pair of black leggings. Tendrils of red hair swept in her face before he could think what he was doing, his fingers reached up and tucked her hair behind her ear.

"You look beautiful, Red."

***

So she was a little on this side of tipsy. Not a lot. Just after two glasses of Gran's wine, you lost those inhibitions you sometimes had. She was nervous; that's why the afternoon had been a blur. Killian was coming. To her home. What had she been thinking? What was she thinking? She knew what she was thinking and shouldn't be thinking it.

Sophie had dropped her off on the way home after closing Beliefs early. She had made it home with enough time to change and tidy before the doorbell rang. Knowing he'd be in her space, just standing in the kitchen, set the butterflies to flutter in her center. Him in the store was one thing. Here was entirely another.

She should have told him to come back tomorrow to the store where there were other people and a place to hide if needed. And rushing in as she had, she'd just grabbed his mother's book from its resting place in the library, setting it on the counter with no time to take another quick look because her plans were slowly falling apart, looking down to see Essie whaling at the door. Just great; even the cat had a thing for the warlock.

Taking a calming breath, the handle turned in her hand, pulling the door open, and there he stood, their eyes colliding. That voice that dripped sweetened honey calling her Red again, then his fingers tucking a strand of hair behind her ear, and she might have stood and stared like a schoolgirl blushing at her first crush.

Common sense finally kicked in, "C'mon in," - turning and putting some space between them, the sound of the door closing making her heart kick up a notch. Elena swore she tried to steal herself against how he would look in her kitchen, but then she turned, and five feet away from where she stood earlier today in her knickers sipping her tea, she lost the ability to speak again.

So when the words finally spilled out, she sounded ridiculous. "I might have drank too much wine this afternoon and I was late getting home. Not that I drove myself but..." her words trailing off because he just stood there staring.

illian entered what appeared to be a living room decorated in a feminine and cozy style. As he followed her to the kitchen, he couldn't help but notice how gorgeous she looked. Even with her messy hair, he could imagine himself running his hands through all that red fire. She gazed at him with those darkened hues that had the power to make him weak in the knees.

Red struggled to get her words out, and Kil thought he heard her giggle. This was a side of her he found adorable. Did she really believe that he was there just for a book? No, he was there because he didn't want to miss the opportunity to be with her. She was extraordinary, and he wanted to prove how much she meant to him.

"That sounds like you had an interesting day, and if I'm being honest, you look totally adorable and sweet. How about we order a pizza or I could cook something for us? I'm pretty handy in the kitchen, and we could make something delicious together."

As he spoke, he noticed she was staring at him like he had two heads. He wondered if he had said something wrong or if it was because nobody had ever offered to cook for her. Perhaps she thought he didn't know how to cook. Chuckling to himself, he remembered that he had to learn to do everything since he lived on his own.

"Red, you ok?"

***

Elena was taken aback when he mentioned that he would cook for her. She had expected him to simply come in, get the book, and then leave. At least that's what she had expected, even though her mind had been imagining different scenarios all day long. Had she made herself so nervous that she used homemade hooch to calm her nerves?

She had been drinking wine, but it was wearing off, so she decided to stop lying to herself. She was intrigued by Killian, and her curiosity was piqued by his background and why he had said everything about them. And then there was the book that his grandmother wanted. She had looked through it a few times, not thoroughly, just a quick glance, and wondered why now? Why come for it when it had been out of her hands for quite some time?

She was always doing that, jumping from one thing to another. Barely finishing one thought, and she'd start on something else. Gran had constantly shook her head, telling her to complete what she was doing before going to the next, especially if she was preparing spells or incantations.

Elena realized that she had zoned out for a few minutes, and he was waiting for a reply; he'd been unsettling her all day without knowing it. If she were wise, she would have suggested getting the book and letting him leave, returning to where he came from.

However, she said something different, "I have some stew in the fridge I made yesterday. It just needs to be warmed up, and I also have a fresh baguette. So, if that's alright with you, we can eat, and then I'll give you the book." She couldn't help but stare at him as he stood there, so comfortable in her kitchen. He was trouble.

***

Her beautiful brown eyes widened in surprise. Why wouldn't he want to cook for her? After all, he was a man of many talents. Also, a home-cooked meal was much better than dining out. With a dazzling grin, he picked up the apron that hung from a nearby hook and chuckled.

"Kiss the chef?"

Her cheeks were flushed with fever, causing her freckles to stand out. Kil couldn't help but think how beautiful she looked, and he could stand here and stare at her all day, completely content.

He opened the refrigerator and took out the container of stew, placing it on the counter. Kil searched for a pot, and Red pointed at the lower cabinet beside the stove. He reached in, retrieved a pot, and poured the stew inside. Reheating it in the microwave was a hard no for him.

He turned the knob to medium heat and placed the pot on the burner. As he focused on the cooking, Essie appeared and pranced into the kitchen, meowing. Kil picked her up and hugged her to his chest. He stroked her soft fur, and Essie purred contentedly.

"I missed you too Essie."

Red rolled her eyes as Essie purred loudly and contentedly in his arms, then shook her head slightly while Essie seemed to stick her tongue out at her. Kil chuckled and gently placed Essie down. He stirred the stew, ensuring it wasn't burning, and then searched and found where the bowls were, setting two on the counter. Meanwhile, Essie kept walking in and out of his feet, much to Red's growing annoyance.

"Essie, be a good girl and behave."

The cat let out a loud meow like felines did when they weren't the center of attention. Elena bent and picked her up, taking her into the living room whispering to Essie, "You're a traitor."

He pretended not to hear what she said, grabbing a spoon, scooping the stew into bowls, and placing them on the kitchen table. He pulled out a chair for her and signaled for her to come and join him.

15

It was clear that Essie had chosen to side with Killian. Elena knew that animals had a keen sense of trust and would only befriend certain people. This spoke volumes about Killian, but Elena was a cautious person who took time to build trust. Essie's quick allegiance had set off her alarms.

Picking her up and taking her further away, she turned back and did a little stuttering step at the sight of him cooking.

As Elena stared at him, she couldn't help but notice how beautiful and rugged he looked simultaneously. When he caught her staring, she felt her face turn red, but he quickly found some bowls, prepared them, and set them on the table. He even pulled a chair out, making a warm, gushing feeling rise within her that she might have purred.

She gave him a smile and a thank you, and she'd never felt so self-conscious in her own kitchen. Pushing her hair behind her ears, then gazing across where he had settled himself, she wasn't sure if she could eat. He was just so intense, or that's how she felt.

"I'll get some drinks," - sliding out, her head in the fridge in a second, she returned with chilled water with lemon and quickly grabbed two glasses, setting them down. "I can get you something else if you want. Beer? Wine? A Cola?"- it's like she couldn't shut up or sit down.

***

As Essie left the room, he had a grin on his face when he saw Red glare daggers at her. The power play between the two was adorable and very entertaining. He loved how her freckles would show through her flushed face when she got flustered.

The image of him living here with her sprang vividly in his mind. The mere thought of her wearing nothing but his T-shirt and roaming around the house filled him with joy. Though he never admitted it, he was soft-hearted when it came to love. This woman was worthy of the world, and he was determined to make sure she got it. He knew he sounded love-struck but didn't care. He was a man who knew what he wanted, and her name was Red.

As he sat across from her, he was completely mesmerized. He couldn't understand why this woman didn't already have a partner; she was gorgeous and extraordinary. He watched as she fidgeted in her seat and twirled a lock of hair around her finger. Just in the motion of reaching out to touch her hand, but for some reason, it startled her, and she jumped up and headed to the fridge, asking him what he would like to drink.

Grinning wide. "I'll take a Cola with a side order of you."

***

Elena blushed bright red at his words. Cola with a side of her? Her eyes lifted to his, and she was prepared to stammer something, but her insides had decided to boil over and then erupt. She turned around, got his drink, set it back in front of him, and sat down.

Even then, she couldn't bring her gaze up to meet him, so she busied herself by filling her glass with ice water and then starting on her stew. Which was hot, and she nearly burned her tongue with the first mouthful, grabbing her drink and downing half of it in two gulps.

And then her eyes lifted to see him watching her. "Killian, you have to stop staring at me. Eat your stew and tell me if you like it. It's Gran's recipe. I just added a few extra things to it."

Was it wrong that she wanted to reach across the table and softly push his hair off his forehead? Run the pad of her thumb across his full lower lip? Having him here was a bad idea. He fit. It's like the space of her home welcomed him in and wrapped its essence around him.

Elena knew at that moment that her quiet life would change. She even felt a door behind her close and a new one open. Her gaze still holding his, she needed to say something because it was getting heavy in here, and he hadn't moved or answered her first question, "Why does your mother want the book back now?"

***

Killian had never felt so captivated in his entire life as he did with her. She buzzed around like a bee in its hive, and he knew she had cast a spell on him that had him utterly hooked. Her piercing gaze penetrated his soul, and he was willing to do anything to see her smile every day.

Kil chuckled when he caught her staring at him. He wondered if she realized how distracting she was to him. Her pouty lips seemed to beg to be kissed, and her alabaster skin, peppered with those cinnamon dots, begged to be touched. She was lovely, but Kil wasn't sure if she knew that fact. He did as she asked and took a spoonful of her stew.

He closed his eyes and savored the explosion of flavors in his mouth. Rosemary, thyme, pepper, and a hint of brown sugar blended perfectly. Killian was impressed by her culinary skills. He could visualize her dancing in the kitchen, wearing only an apron, while preparing dinner for him. He looked up and grinned.

"Red, this stew is amazing. I love how the spices just explode along my tongue. Not to mention the hint of sweetness of the brown sugar, giving it the perfect flavor. And if you like, you can call me Kil."

Her cheeks were flushed with fever, but she still smiled beautifully. Red thanked him bashfully, and he felt an overwhelming desire to embrace her and kiss her passionately. She was going to be his weakness, his undoing. The next question was difficult, but he was determined to answer truthfully.

"My mother is a dark and ancient witch of my Coven. Her magic is rare, making her a target. That book holds spells others have never heard of before, making that book rare and valuable. There are things about your Gran you might not know, Red. She was a sister witch to my mother's Coven."

16

She dropped her spoon at Killian's admission. She stared at him across the table because that couldn't be possible. Her Gran was all things light and powerful. There was no way that she was affiliated with Killian's coven. And to suggest she practiced the dark side of witchcraft was preposterous.

Her Gran had raised her. They were as close as a family could be. There was no way she would have kept that hidden from her, especially when she always encouraged Elena to stay on the good side, the light side.

She stood. She couldn't sit there any longer. Her mind was racing backward in time over conversations they had. She started pacing across the kitchen floor, Essie coming to where she did her back and forth.

"Killian, that's impossible. Gran would never practice dark magic. I would know. That's a feeling you can't hide. We spent so much time together, and I would have known. It's not possible," she stopped to look at him. "You're wrong. I don't believe it. I won't. Let's get your book, and you can go."

Elena turned to go, her stomach actually physically hurting because she hoped and wished and had started to dream of what could be. She wasn't malevolent or malicious. If that's what his coven was, if that's what he practiced and how he lived, then she couldn't continue with whatever this was. Her eyes closed where she stood, and she shook her head slightly because she wanted this, wanted him.

***

He didn't expect her to react the way she did, but it made his heart sad, knowing that he was the one who spoke of something she wasn't aware of. Kil didn't know why Red's Gran would keep it from her. It wasn't anything to be ashamed of, and black magick might not be the chosen magick of Red's, but it wasn't as bad as she made it out to be.

Didn't she know when black and light magick combined it was extremely powerful, and there is such beauty in the darkness.

Surely, the stars would not shine without the blessing of the night. He gently brushed his fingertips against her arm, trying to comfort her. Kil didn't like that she was upset. He wanted to pull her in his arms and reassure her that everything would be okay.

"Red, I had no idea that you didn't know; maybe your Gran was trying to protect you from something or someone, but that being said, there is nothing to fear. Black magick can be a beautiful thing if you let me show you."

She backed away from him as though he burned her; her scarlet-colored locks shook from side to side. Taking a step back, he picked up the spell book where he'd seen it sitting, flipped to the back of it, and stopped at the page that listed, sister witches. There was a name from each of the ancient Covens, and Red's grandmother was the next one down below his mother's.

Picking up the book and carrying it closer to Red, pointing to the name under his mother's. "Is that your grandmother's name?"

***

She didn't want to look because of that unease in her stomach, her sixth sense already told her what he said was true. But seeing it would make it real, which meant Gran had kept things from her.

The Gran she knew and loved couldn't have done that. Why would she have? It made no sense. None at all.

His touch brought her eyes to his. This wasn't his fault; he was just the messenger. Yet he was the one here for her anger and hurt to find an outlet. How could he say black magick could be beautiful? She knew what some of her sister witches did out in the woods of the coven's property. Whispers always had truth attached to them. Blood was spilled, and sometimes lives were taken, maybe not directly in that moment but as a result.

His eyes pinned to her, Elena already felt the shifting of the axis. Things would change at this time moving forward. Moving closer to Killian, she started at the top of the page scanning down until she got to the name that shouldn't be on the page or in the book. And she just stared at it, the letters becoming blurry because nothing made sense.

***

One thing that was extremely hard for sure was hearing the truth about something that you never knew, especially when it was about someone that you loved deeply.

Kil wanted to wrap her in his arms and hold her for eternity. Her sad eyes made his heart sink. He would have thought that she knew everything about her Gran and yet she had kept this from his Red.

Elena's finger gently ran down the page of the book, her eyes scanned every name written, and when she finally came across Gran's name, a gasp left her lips, making her shoulders slump. Kil could see the disappointment in her eyes. Why would her Gran keep this secret from her? There wasn't anything wrong with being a sister witch. The whole purpose is to unify the covens and protect one another at all costs. It was an honor to be chosen as one because they are the most powerful witch of their coven.

"I am sorry that I even said anything, Red. I honestly thought you knew. I promise I will get to the bottom of this and why your Gran left the sister witches. There has to be a reasonable explanation why she kept that hidden from you. There is something else I need to know. Is Essie your Gran's familiar before she became yours?"

Her eyebrows pinched together like she was confused about the question he asked her. If Essie was actually Gran's familiar before she became Red's, then she knows exactly what happened.

Familiars are for protection, and it is their job to know where and who their person is at all times. It would be so much easier retrieving the truth from Essie. His mother, on the other hand, had made a vow and was sworn to secrecy to the sister witches.

"My beautiful little witch, I need you to answer my question?"

***

Elena stood and stared between Killian and the book, so many thoughts ricocheting around inside her head that she wanted to grab her hair with both hands and give a hard yank so they'd stop swirling.

She thought she knew everything about her Gran and her Mama whether by the stories she was told or the reading she had done. Gran and her were close. Closer than close. Everything she had become was because of her and her patience. Even when she'd screwed up a spell or anything, Gran always said it was a learning experience. Elena would have sworn on her life that they held no secrets.

Yet Killian had proof that there were things about Gran she didn't know. Things she never told her, felt like she could never tell her. Thoughts that she didn't trust her cut deeply and tears actually did start to fall.

At Killian's question about Essie, her mood changed. Elena wasn't even sure how old Essie was, but she'd been around since as long as she could remember. It was almost at times like they shared her insight. Elena had never had a kinship with another animal, just Essie.

Her fingertips cleaned up the mess she had made under her eyes, looking up at Killian, "Essie was ours, together, but she's been around since I was born. So I guess the answer is yes she was Gran's." She turned to grab a tissue from the box that sat on the counter, giving her face a blot, weariness settling over her.

Between the wine and food, and now this unexpected hurt and confusion, never mind how Killian made her feel, Elena was exhausted and done for the night.

"Killian, if you don't mind, I'm done. I just want to have a hot shower and go to sleep. I have an early start tomorrow, and all of this has been a lot. You can take the book back to your mother. Thank you for…" The shrug of her shoulders even seemed heavy to her. She didn't know what else to say to him.

***

Killian understood Red's need for solitude to absorb the revelations he had shared with her. The disparity between what she believed and the actual truth was causing her immense pain and disappointment, emotions that Killian empathized with deeply. He yearned to offer her reassurance, to convey that everything would eventually fall into place and that her grandmother's intentions were to protect her.

As he gently kissed her cheek and took a step back, Killian spoke softly, "Red, I deeply regret the distress this has caused you. I never intended to cause you any harm, and I wish I could undo the pain you're feeling. I will honor your space and decisions."

With a heavy heart, Killian left with the spellbook, the door quietly closing behind him.

17

ooking up at her very insistent feline, Elena said, "Essie, that paw touches me one more time. You're not getting fed. I mean it."

Her familiar totally ignored her and touched her cheek again. A meow that sounded like 'get up, it's late' grating into her face.

Elena knew it was late, she'd slept like crap after Killian or Kil had left her, her heart heavy for more than one reason. She'd even watched him, hiding from behind her kitchen curtains as he got into his fancy car and left.

How could you want something so much that hadn't really even started? He just...a deep sigh leaving her. He just touched her in a way she never had been before. And she wasn't talking just about the kissing, which was like how her fire felt, hot and all-consuming, but it was other things about him too.

But she needed to let it go because she didn't think she could take anymore hurt in her life. Not right now. Her grief over Gran was still fresh.

She had already decided that she'd brew herself a potion today because she needed her rest. Between the coven demanding her presence at an upcoming event and the information Killian had dropped on her about Gran, she was going to need help getting her zzz's.

Another swipe across her face and more caterwauling.

"Okay, okay, I'm up," she gave Essie her best steely-eyed gaze, muttering she might turn her into a squirrel, loud enough for her to hear. That got her a nice look from her cat.

A short while later, she stopped as she walked into the kitchen. Less than ten hours ago, he'd been right here in her kitchen, her gaze falling to the bowls and such in her sink. She'd just rinsed them off last night and left them there, too exhausted to do more.

Well, crap. She'd let herself start a walk into a fairytale, her foot already in the imaginary world of love and promises. And was it possible that his scent still hung in her home because she swore she could still catch a whiff of him? Essie took that moment to start again, the princess needing to be fed.

"You and I need to have a talk about your attitude." Elena and Essie both knowing how much love she had for her familiar. A dawning just then that she'd left her car at the store because she'd been drinking, and Sophie had driven her home.

Double crap. Looking out the window at the sunshine and blue skies-
"Well Essie, it looks like you're getting a ride in the bicycle carrier today, or you stay home. Which is it?" She was fully expecting some kind of answer, which she got when her black feline rubbed herself against the back door. "Ok then. A bike adventure it is."

***

Looking up as the coven members ended their once-a-month meeting, Mira gave her a nod, "We'll see you again, Elena," Her gaze followed them as they made their way to the front of the store, the tinkle of the bell marking their exit.

She still didn't know why, out of all the places they could meet, why they chose here. Elena knew they did hit up other spots, but with her being more an outsider than a real member, she didn't get it. But she caught their gazes on her as she went about her day. Nosy. That's what they were.

With their departure, she was left alone; Sophie had gone to deliver a few orders to their older clientele, then looked to see Essie asleep, curled up in her bed. The life of a cat, she thought. Then, her eyes settled on the stack of boxes that the Amazon driver had delivered earlier. He must practice magick, she thought, because how could all these boxes fit inside that small van he drove.

The sooner you start, the sooner you'll be done, that mantra hoping to give her incentive. Slicing open the closest box, bubble wrap was the first thing she saw; sifting through to find the new collection of candles she'd ordered and placing them on the counter to the side. She could already tell that some of this order was going to have to go into their storage area.

She'd over-ordered again. It's not like it wouldn't sell, but they had limited space.

Then the next few boxes were opened, various sizes of jars, then crystals and stones and it went on and on, the final box filled with books.

Books sold really well in the store. It was a shame she didn't have more time to read them before they left out the front door. Sorting them in genre, then placing them into what spaces she could find along the side wall where she had all her reading items, the bell turning her head.

"Hello Elena."

"Hi Jared," her smile was genuine. "I have your order ready for you. Just give me one moment to pop these on a shelf." She placed the last few books where they could be easily seen, then made her way to where he waited by the front counter.

His eyes lifted and met hers, something in them for a moment, something dark and painful. It was gone as quickly as she'd glimpsed it. Like storm clouds rolling in and just as swiftly gone. His gaze intent on hers, an awkward silence between them where they stood amongst the stores this and that.

"Elena, thank you for helping me through this, not judging, not asking. I'll let you know if the spell works." After paying for his order, he then turned to leave, his purchases held in the brown bag clutched in his hand. "You look like her. Your mother was a beautiful woman too," his words left trailing behind him.

The little bell above the door going off again. She truly hoped this helped him, his wife's death was hitting him hard. Sleep deprivation was exhausting on all levels, and in Jared's case, he had been staying awake, hoping Amy visited him from the other side. But by the look of the dark circles beneath his eyes and his haggard appearance, it was taking a toll.

He couldn't go on this way that was for sure. The ingredients in the potion she'd selected for him, held not the magick within the elements but in the spell spoken. And it would hit quickly and hard once the words left his lips. Elena had emphasized that point.

What she hadn't mentioned was she was making a stop on her way home. Once he slept, Elena was going to ward his home against negative energy. She would make regular visits over the next few weeks just to keep an eye out. Jared and Amy had both been long-time friends to her Gran, Mama, and herself. She'd try to do whatever she could. She understood the loss and pain he was going through. They had never had children, so the quietness of the house, where before there used to be the hustle and bustle could make an ordinary day seem even longer.

Shaking off where her thoughts were heading, it was time for tea, and then when Sophie got back, they could decide what to tackle next.

And that's when he entered her mind. She'd managed to keep him at bay while she'd been busy. But now the store was quiet, and she was idle, and there he was, Killian of the Raven Coven.

She wondered what he was doing now.

<h1 style="text-align:center">18</h1>

Killian had so many emotions running through him that it was a bit overwhelming. He had no idea that Elena didn't know things that a witch should have known. Why did her grandmother, her Gran, remembering that's her name for her, keep her in the dark about these things? The hurt in her eyes made him want to pull her in his arms and never let go.

He had this strong urge to protect her and keep her safe. Maybe that was her Gran's intentions by not telling her, but that also made her vulnerable. Killian wrestled with the thoughts of Elena that consumed him. He tried to sleep, but it didn't come easy.

The next day...

Killian was an early bird, and he made sure to get up every morning to go for a run. He found that this daily routine helped him keep his mind clear and allowed him to view things with fresh eyes. The sound of his feet pounding against the pavement, the cool morning breeze, and the chirping of the birds were all part of the experience.

As he ran, he would let his thoughts wander and reflect on the responsibilities of the day. It was his way of preparing for whatever challenges lay ahead.

He had a meeting within the next couple of hours with his coven, but first, he wanted to look through his mother's spell book to see what she was hiding; maybe he would find out exactly why Elena's Gran left the sister witches.

Finishing up his last mile, Killian took a quick shower and got dressed, leaving himself thirty minutes before his meeting.

Kil opened the spellbook and flipped through the pages, looking for any clues, but what caught his attention was a specific spell that he had never seen before. It was written in his grandfather's handwriting. It was a binding spell that practically held the victim hostage. Killian was outraged; there was dark magic, and then there was evil magic, which was prohibited in his coven.

I call to earth to bind your magic and make it mine. Air to speed its travel. Bright as fire shall it glow. Deep as tide of water flow. Count the elements four-fold. In the fifth spell shall hold.

Why would his grandfather want to steal another witch or warlock's powers? This spell would render them powerless. Killian knew his grandfather was strict and stern but never was he hateful or evil. Whatever this might be, Killian would get to the bottom of it.

He called to his raven. 'Bram, I think we need to make an entrance to my mother's house. Let's find out the real reason why my mother wanted this book back and why my grandfather wrote such a spell. Maybe this is the real reason Elena's Gran left the sister witches and never came back.'

His wings unfurled gradually, his body contorting and bending to assume the form of his raven. Bram catapulted out the window, maneuvering through the trees like a seasoned performer.

Flying through his mother's office window, he transformed back into his human form. With a casual wave of his hand, he was fully clothed. Kil reached into his pocket, retrieved the page he had torn from his mother's spellbook, and slammed it onto her desk.

"Would you like to explain this, mother?"

Rissa picked up the piece of paper to examine it. "Kil, I've never seen this spell before. Where did you get it from?"

Killian crossed his arms across his chest. "From the spellbook, you told me to retrieve. Did you pay attention to the handwriting?"

Rissa's hands began to tremble; she knew exactly whose handwriting it was. She dropped her arms to her lap, trying her best to hide her nervousness. "It's your grandfather's handwriting, but this is the first time I have ever seen it. I read every page in that spellbook, and not once was that spell in it."

Killian saw her shaking like something had rocked her to the core but his mother recovered quickly. He didn't understand why she would be upset over the spell her father had written. Maybe she realized the severity of the spell. Either way, he wanted to make sure that his grandfather did not perform such a spell, or Killian would see him reprimanded severely.

"Mother, you don't think he would ever use this spell on anyone, would he?"

Rissa wanted to say yes, but she knew better. "Of course not, Killian. Maybe he put the spell in the book in case an enemy should attack."

Killian hoped his mother was telling the truth. He was giving her the benefit of the doubt. "Maybe that was grandfather's intentions." Yet that unsettled feeling stayed with him, "I have a meeting to attend. We'll continue this later."

An hour later...

Killian's meeting with the sister witches filled his heart with joy and hope. Witnessing Marisol's growth and newfound confidence in her magic brought a sense of peace to his soul. However, amidst the success, his thoughts inevitably gravitated towards his little witch, Red.

She lingered in his mind like a precious gem, her well-being a constant concern that tugged at his heartstrings. The thought of her experiencing any form of pain or distress pained him deeply. Killian was acutely aware of Elena's feelings of betrayal by her Gran; his heart ached with a fierce desire to shield her from further hurt.

He retrieved his phone and composed a heartfelt message to her. [My thoughts have lingered on you all day, and my heart aches for how our evening parted ways. Would you honor me with your presence for dinner, so we can talk things over?]

***

How was it possible to get so dusty and sweaty reorganizing shelves? Between her and Sophie, they dusted the store every couple of weeks. Plus, stuff didn't sit around the store long enough to gather dust. Yet, looking down at the apron she wore over her clothes, it looked like she'd gone five rounds with the trash bin. Her gaze swinging over at Sophie, who looked slightly better but not by much, "I'd say we earned a cold glass of cider. I'll grab the pitcher, and you flip the Close sign. That's enough for today."

"That sounds good to me." A smile lit her face, and Elena took the moment to send up a thank you to the universe for sending Sophie her way.

Grabbing two glasses from the shelf and the pitcher from their small fridge, she set that out in the cozy nook where the tabletop held her life's work of artistic design. Elena had sat here coloring or painting while her Mama and Gran had put in their hours at the store. There was even a small burn mark where she'd tipped over a candle and hadn't shouted out to either because she hadn't wanted to get in trouble. Which she had anyway from both her Mama and Gran. It had been a double whammy. But now looking at the markings, they brought comfort and warmth to her, like a hug.

"Penny for your thoughts. Or maybe it's a quarter now. Inflation is crazy." Sophie slid in, her blonde hair tied with a ribbon and her blue eyes sparkling with mischief.

"Nothing, really. Just memories, the good kind though." She poured them each a fill of cider. "I haven't said how much I appreciate you lately, Sophie Savoy. You make every day so much fun. I can't imagine you not being here with me. So, a toast. To sisters from different misters." She held up her glass to clink with hers.

"I love it here, too. It feels like home. And I'm learning so much. I really love talking to everyone that comes in. Some of them feel like family now. You're really lucky to have all these people who care about you. Some of them have great stories about your Gran. She must have been something in her day. Even the members in the coven regard her highly."

"She was something. I miss her so much," lifting her glass, she took a mouthful of her drink. "You know this cider is her recipe, yet it doesn't taste the same as when she made it. I guess that's the way of things."

"You're really lucky to have your memories, Elena. I know how hard it's been on you, but you also know without a doubt how much they loved you." The blue of Sophie's gaze was saddening a bit.

"I know they loved me. And you're like a sister to me, Soph. I'm here if you ever need anything. You know that, right?"

Sophie had told Elena shortly after she'd started that she had no real family except the members of the coven. She never gave her explicit details, and Elena didn't pry because it seemed like a really sad subject.

"I know Elena. And the same goes for me. And I'm sure if you gave the coven a chance, you would see that they really do care about you."

Elena let a slow breath out, not wanting to tarnish the nice few moments her and Sophie were having. The Coven of the Divine Spirit and her were on rocky grounds. And she didn't want to think about them right now.

"We'll see Sophie," her phone decided at that minute to go off.

Sliding her butt off her side of the bench, her screen lighting on the work table, Elena leaned down, her hair forming a curtain around her face, where she looked down at her phone, tapping in her code, and her heart did a lurch. It was Killian.

Elena's thoughts instantly drift towards his lips, his body, his everything.

"Elena, you ok?" Sophie's voice broke into the moment, and her blush was instant like she'd got caught doing something wrong.

"It's all good. Just a friend."

Did she want to meet him? Her heart said yes, but what did it know? Remembering she had to stop by Jared's house tonight.

Sending a text back - [I have one thing I have to do later in the evening. But we could have dinner first. No kissing though.] and she sent that before she could talk herself out of it.

Turning back to Sophie to see a look on her face as she gazed down at her empty glass, "Sophie, you ok?"

Her friend's gaze lifting and finding hers - "Yeah. I'm fine."

***

Sophie took those few minutes while Elena went and checked her phone. She had to tell Mira and the others that she wasn't going to spy on Elena for them anymore.

She didn't want to do it from the beginning. Elena was her true friend, but they threatened to remove Sophie from the coven if she didn't. And then where would she go? She liked it here. Especially here at Beliefs with Elena.

It was getting harder and harder to lie to both them and her friend. She'd have to tell Elena what was going on. That was the only way out. If they threw her out, so be it. She should have had the backbone to say No from the start.

Elena was a total sweetheart and didn't deserve this from herself or them. She'd have to tell her and hope she understood or at least gave her a chance to make things right.

***

"Sophie, I'm gonna head home. I have something to do. Plus, I need a bath. Are you ready to head out, too?"

"I am." She slid out and grabbed her bag. Sophie's arms came around Elena so quickly that she let out a soft "Oof" at the squish.

"What was that for?" Elena's smile was instant.

"Just because you're the world's best boss," Sophie pulled open the back door and headed down the steps - "Drive safe. See you tomorrow." Knowing she'd have to talk to Elena soon. Her gut couldn't take more of this.

Killian couldn't tear his eyes away from his phone, anxiously waiting for Red to respond. He was filled with uncertainty after what had transpired; unsure if she would ever want to see him again. It pained him to realize that so many aspects of witchcraft had been kept from his beloved Red, and he despised the thought that he was the one responsible for shattering her perception of reality.

The song, "I Put a Spell on You," began to play, and a smile spread across his face as he glanced at his phone. It was a ringtone he had chosen specifically for her. Killian thought it was rather fitting, considering that's exactly what she had him under. Red had enchanted him in every possible way. Kil chuckled as he read her text, sending one back.

[I can't make any promises that there will be no kissing, but I will try my best to refrain myself. I will pick you up around seven.]

Kil hit send and headed to the bathroom, stripped down, and took a cold shower. Every time he thought about her, he couldn't help but get hard. It wasn't a bad thing, and he wasn't complaining.

Chuckling as he grabbed a towel, wrapping around his waist. Giving himself a little pep talk- "Get it together, Warlock. You can't walk around with a stiffy every time you are near her. She is going to think you're a perv." Killian pushed back those thoughts of how her flesh would feel against his, a smile on his face.

Killian whispered a spell, snapping his fingers together, and grinned as he looked himself over in the mirror. He loved the convenience of glam magic, and he wondered if Elena would recognize it as well. It was important for a witch to recognize these things. His Red had been sheltered, and he realized it was for her protection, but he would show her what she truly was made of.

Thirty minutes later...

Kil pulled into the driveway and admired the quaintness again of Elena's little cottage. The exterior was adorned with an array of beautiful flowers, creating a picturesque scene that exuded tranquility and peace. As he took in the serene surroundings, he could understand why she loved it so much; it truly felt like a little slice of heaven.

Killian got out of his car, a Bugatti La Voiture Noire. It was one of his favorite new purchases, done in matte black. He was usually a fan of older cars, but this one just screamed 'warlock.'

Killian walked up the pathway to her porch and knocked on the front door again. And then there she was, a radiant smile illuminating her face. Dressed in a stunning floral sundress that perfectly accentuated her crimson locks and charming freckles, enhancing her already enchanting beauty. With an air of elegance, she stepped forward as he extended his arm towards her, a silent invitation for her to join him. A soft blush tinted her cheeks as a soft "Hi" left her lips, her arm gently entwining with his.

"Hi Red. Just so you know, I was thinking about you all day." And he just left that there for her to think about.

As he opened the car door, he couldn't help but notice Elena's keen interest in his Bugatti, her eyes tracing its every curve and detail with an appreciative gaze. It was evident that she shared his admiration for the car. With a subtle smile playing on her lips, she lowered her head gracefully, slipping into the plush leather seat with a sense of quiet delight. Closing the door behind her, he made his way to the driver's side and settled in, the subtle click of the door sealing them within the comforting confines of the car. Killian reached out to turn on the radio, opting for a low volume as he pondered what type of music would resonate with Elena's preferences.

After a moment of silence, Elena finally broke the quiet, "Killian, this car smells brand new and expensive," she observed, her voice tinged with curiosity and admiration.

Chuckling warmly, Killian nodded in agreement, his eyes reflecting a hint of pride. "It is," he admitted with a smile, "I'm typically more of an old-model type of man, but when I laid eyes on this beauty, I knew I had to have her." His words carried a sense of fondness and appreciation for the sleek vehicle that now surrounded them, an unexpected but welcomed addition to his collection of cars. "And she handles like a dream."

As they drove towards the restaurant, Killian's hand found its place on Elena's thigh, a gesture of comfort and closeness rather than anything intimate. Elena, feeling the warmth of his touch, didn't pull away but instead found herself drawn to his presence. A sense of connection and trust enveloped them as they shared this moment together. Their unspoken chemistry seemed to ignite a gentle flame between them, a silent understanding blossoming as they journeyed towards their destination.

They arrived at Salam's Charms, one of his favorite restaurants. He loved that he personally knew the owner and the fact that everything he cooks is fresh and homegrown. Kil got out of the car and opened the door for his witch. He held out his hand to help her and just so he could touch her.

Her fingers laced his as they walked through the ornate double doors of the elegant restaurant, immediately drawn into an atmosphere of sophistication and refinement. The soft glow of crystal chandeliers cast a warm light over the richly decorated space, illuminating the intricate details of the luxurious décor.

The walls were adorned with tasteful artwork and mirrors, reflecting the flickering candlelight on each elegantly set table. Plush velvet curtains draped the windows, adding a touch of opulence to the room. The soft strains of classical music float through the air, creating a sense of timeless elegance.

The tables meticulously arranged with crisp white linens, sparkling silverware, and delicate china. Each place setting accented with a fresh flower, adding a pop of color. The chairs upholstered in sumptuous velvet, inviting guests to relax and enjoy their dining experience.

In the center of the room, a grand floral arrangement set as a stunning focal point, its vibrant blooms perfuming the air with their sweet fragrance. A polished mahogany bar stretching along one wall, stocked with gleaming bottles of fine wines and spirits, ready to be expertly mixed into signature cocktails.

Killian smiled as Elena's eyes twinkled with amazement. Her head turned in every direction as the hostess walked them to their table. Elena took her seat, and Killian whispered to the hostess. "Let him know we are here."

The hostess nodded her head his way, Killian sitting down, grinning. "I am assuming you like the restaurant I chose."

Elena's voice was full of excitement. "Killian, it's so beautiful and elegant. I almost feel out of place here."

His brows furrowed. "You are the most beautiful woman in here, and I never want you to feel anything less. Plus, I know the chef very well and the lady behind the elegant decor design."

Elena smiled wide. "You do?"

Killian reached across the table, holding her hand. He nodded slowly. He was about to say something when his brother, Keegan, and his beautiful wife interrupted. Keegan playfully punched his brother's shoulder playfully.

"So, are you going to introduce us to your lovely lady?"

Kil chuckled, "Elena, I'd like you to meet my brother, Keegan, and his beautiful wife, Iris. They are the owners of this fine establishment. Keegan is the chef, and Iris is the designer."

Iris held out her hand to Elena. "So you are the beautiful redhead that's been showing up in my best friend's dreams?" She giggled. "Kil was right; you are stunning."

Killian watched Elena fiddle with her napkin, shyness looking so adorable on her.

"Red, Iris has a big mouth, and she can't keep any secrets to herself. She has been my best friend since we were kids. So she thinks she can say anything when it comes to me."

Keegan's laughter rumbled out across the restaurant. "Is my wife embarrassing you, brother, or should I say elder."

Iris pinched Keegan. "Okay, okay. Let's leave these two alone so they can get to know each other better. Kil, order the chef's special for yourself; it's one of his signature meals today."

Keegan grasped his brother's shoulder, laughing. "Killian taught me everything I know when it comes to cooking. So his favorite dish is the chef's special today. It was nice meeting you, Elena. We hopefully will see you soon."

Killian scrubbed his hand down his face, holding back a laugh. "They live for embarrassing me."

Elena smiled, "Awe, I think it's rather sweet."

Kil rubbed his thumb across her hand. "There is something I need to say. I am sorry about the other day. I had no idea that you weren't aware about your Gran."

***

This time, Elena made sure to leave herself plenty of time to get ready and she stayed clear of the wine cabinet. There were two days a week she stayed open till 7 PM. So, leaving early today was no biggie. Plus, they had got a lot done.

She wasn't going to lie to herself either. Her and Killian may have parted in a real odd way when he'd been over at her place, but she hadn't stopped thinking about him. And it was obvious how smitten she might be as she sat behind the wheel of her car behind the store, minutes passing by as she daydreamed and hadn't even moved yet.

"Get a grip, girl," she spoke as she started Gran's car.

Pulling out of her stall and turning onto the lane, a double honk at her because she hadn't really looked right and left. Killian was going to get her a ticket for distracted driving, a shake of her head at her thoughts and a friendly wave to the other driver.

"Pay attention," she muttered to herself.

Less than half an hour later, she was inside her door, Essie, the first thing she almost tripped over, the second being her food dish, "I'll feed you right now, and then I'm going out." She did not mention Killian's name because she'd probably start meowing and never stop.

Minutes later, her clothes from the day were lying in a pile on her bathroom floor. Shower or bath? She had time and much-preferred baths.

Her plan earlier was to have a night to herself; at least, that's what she thought when she had woken. She'd cleansed the tub before bed, her candles arranged, and the current book she was reading sat on the ledge.

But that was before Killian's call.

If she didn't wash her hair, just pinned it up and out of the way, she could soak.

Decision made, she ran the water, adding rosemary and sage first, then lavender and rose for relaxation, followed by eucalyptus and peppermint for invigoration. And at the end, dandelion and chamomile for their healing properties, mindful as each ingredient was added, a spell chanted as she settled herself into its warmth. Her hand lifting, passing over the wicks of each candle, the call to fire instant as she lit each one.

Leaning back submerged up to her shoulders, a peace found her as she cleared her thoughts and let the tub work its magick. But it didn't take long before she wasn't alone. Even here, Killian invaded her thoughts, remembering that she'd told him no kissing.

Her eyes drifted shut, and here in the quiet, just her by herself, her body and mind knew how false that was. She really wanted to be kissed again and pulled tightly in against him, to feel the hardness and heat of his body. Images taking flight, but she had no time for those; the water already cooling, but she'd come back to those later when she was alone in her bed.

***

"Killian, it's not your fault, and there's no need to apologize. I, kind of was shellshocked seeing Gran's name in the book. There's obviously things I don't know, and yeah, I'm confused and upset, but how about we leave that for another time," Her gaze drifted down to where he held her hand, "How about we just enjoy tonight."

Their server arrived at that moment, taking their orders of two of the chef specials with one bottle of wine. The whole while, Killian had not let go of her hand.

"Now tell me about what you have to do after we eat? Is it top-secret, or do you need a plus one?" His smile was mischievous, "Because I'm available for late-night shenanigans and sleepovers," his thumb was doing a sexy stroking along the inside of her palm.

He was deadly, thought Elena. He was like one of those hot, sexy, inked bad boys in her books. She wasn't sure how she was going to eat her dinner. The wine showed up, thank goodness, giving a minute reprieve, a tasting poured for each of them, and then they were alone again.

Using her freehand, she lifted her glass, ready to take a sip, when Killian gave a "Wait, we need a toast" the blue of his gaze capturing hers, "it's not really a toast, Red. It's more a wish to many more nights of you and me," the edge of his glass found hers, and her eyes held his as she took a sip, hoping it cooled her off and settled her a bit. The wetness of the wine leaving a sheen on his lips, her thoughts going to where they'd been in the tub. She knew a blush had fully infused her body at that point, and he knew where her thoughts had dipped too, if the slow smile that crept over his lips was a tell.

Deciding she couldn't sit here gawking at him, her mouth opened, and words just spilled out, "I actually am going to stop by very quietly, more like on the down low, to place a warding around a friend's home. He lost his wife not too long ago, and he's been having a hard time." Killian's stroking of her hand stopped.

"You were doing that alone?" A more serious side of him appearing.

"That was the plan, why?" She lifted her glass to take another sip.

"I'd like to come with you. I could help and then make sure you get home safely. Say yes."

Honestly, with him sitting there, looking the way he looked, the way the natural pull was between them, the answer was already spoken, even though she hadn't said it out loud.

"Come on, Red. I want to help your friend."

"OK," Was all that came out because anything more at that point and she might lean across the table and take her own kiss.

And as their meals were delivered by Keegan himself, Elena knew fate had just truly taken hold of her life.

20

as gobsmacked the right word? Maybe. Or was it mystified? Elena wasn't sure, but there must be some kind of word for what she was feeling.

All through dinner, her sight was fixated on Killian. Their choice of food for dinner was incredible and she truly wished for Keegan's sake she could have been more focused on it, but not with his brother sitting across from her.

And when she managed to draw her gaze away from him and take in the magnificence of the restaurant, she caught a few other eyes on him, jealousy rearing up to greet her. And Elena had to put a Whoa on that because she and Kil barely knew each other. But that didn't stop her from sending dagger-like looks to the women who were eyeing him too long.

He did look like sin, mouthwatering sin, but it was so much more. It was his mannerisms, the way he held himself so confidently, plus the way he talked about his family. He was one of those guys who could caveman a girl back to his place by her hair, and she'd smile the whole way.

Whoa again.

If she kept this up, her imagination was going to set the tablecloth on fire, and how embarrassing was that going to be to try to explain. And she wasn't joking. Her inner flame was close to igniting, her bones turning to warm honey. She was developing a fever; correction, she had a fever; all stages of feverish, running through her, because of him.

After they said their goodbyes to Iris and Keegan, and Killian had closed her safely in the passenger seat of his new ride, and she watched him walking around to get in on his side, she decided that yes, gobsmacked was the right word.

The night had closed in around them as the engine roared to life, the turning of his head finding her already staring at him. "So tell me where I'm going?"

She had this overwhelming urge to lean over and kiss him again. The closed-in space making her more aware of his musky scent, and she was going to be squirming in her seat any minute 'Talk girl, c'mon, put words together,' She kept reminding herself she had zero experience in the art of seduction, and she'd probably end up knocking their heads together.

"Jared lives on Dumaine Street. I'll know the house when I see it." His address was totally lost to her at the moment.

"Dumaine it is then." As he pulled away from the curb, his hands looked far too sexy on the wheel. And it was like he could read her mind because one of his hands found hers, giving it a squeeze and not letting go, "And why the warding?"

Her eyes drifted downward to where the warmth of his touch was playing havoc with her insides, "Jared's wife passed away a few months ago like I told you, and he's not sleeping well at all. He wants to stay awake in case she visits him." She moved her hand so they were now palm to palm. She wanted to entwine their fingers, but she was too shy. But he obviously wasn't. Killian fit their hands together, not taking his eyes off the road. "They did everything together. They even worked together. They never had children so the house is feeling very quiet. He picked up a spell from me to help him sleep because he can't go on like he has been. I told him Gwen wouldn't want him running himself down. But something feels slightly off. I can't explain it. He has a cleaning service that goes into his home twice a month. One of the girls did me a favor, she's been a friend of mine for a long time, and she was close to Gwen. She did a cleanse of his house so I thought it would be a perfect time just to add a ward against any negativity he or others are bringing into his home. It can't hurt, right?"

Stopping at a red light, Kil turned his head at the same time that he lifted their joined hands, bringing them towards him and placing a soft kiss against her skin, "I love your heart, Elena," he tightened his grip slightly and placed their hands on one of his thighs. And she was again gobsmacked, her mouth slightly open and her insides turning into a gooey mess.

The bright lights from the downtown District long behind them, now more guided by old lantern-style street lights, casting an ethereal glow within the car.

"Here we are. Dumaine Street," he said, turning the car right onto a quieter street than they'd come down. "Tell me when you see it, and I'll park just past it."

Dumaine was a really quaint street, and she knew the house by the wrought iron fence that circled it on all sides.

"There, that one on your left with the high fence."

It was close to 11 o'clock, and the house was dark, which was perfect, but Elena hadn't taken into account how close the other houses were to Jared's. And on top of that there were still a few people outside milling around or on their front porches.

"Killian, this isn't going to work. There's too many prying eyes still around. I was hoping to walk the perimeter, but I guess I didn't think this out properly." her sigh more for herself because she should have just asked Jared if she could do this for him instead of trying to be all sneaky.

"Maybe you should just drive me home, and I'll think of something else."

***

Killian found himself utterly enchanted by everything about Elena. Her deep caramel eyes seemed to pull him in closer; that hint of cinnamon that seemed to be a part of her enveloped his senses, and her freckles twinkled like stars when she smiled.

Being in close proximity to her was insufficient; he yearned to feel her touch, savoring the sensation of her skin as smooth as silk. The allure of her presence ignited his primal side, urging his passion to surge and envelop her entirely. Elena Payne, the enigmatic witch with cascading crimson locks, held him captive in the intricate web of her enchantment.

In a room filled with people, her beauty would radiate like a beacon, drawing his gaze; she was the epitome of allure, the one who held his unwavering devotion. He would move mountains and cross oceans for her; so profound was his affection.

Killian adored her considerate nature and the way it melted his heart. She cherished her friends and was fiercely protective of them. Killian couldn't help but smile. She was the whole package, and the most wonderful part was that she was oblivious to it.

Her pouty lips looked adorable when she realized she wouldn't be able to ward off her friend's house without drawing attention. His hand gently grasped her thigh, giving it a soft squeeze; he took that moment and leaned in, his lips meeting hers in a gentle kiss.

"My beautiful Red, no pouting and no giving up. Let me do this for you because your red hair is like a vibrant sunset in a world of shadows. It shines brighter than any warding spell we could cast. We would have to get creative to keep you incognito."

Elena's face glowed with laughter. Just when he thought she couldn't be more beautiful, she laughed, and it was infectious. He could listen to her laugh all day and be perfectly content.

"Red, I can ward the house in my raven form and go unnoticed. No one would suspect a thing. Your friend will be protected, and we won't alert the cops."

"You're what?" Her eyes were like round saucers.

His smile was instantaneous "My raven. Killian Raven at your service, beautiful. Here to assist damsels in need and shit on others as needed."

Her look of surprise was so adorable. Killian belonged to her completely; no other woman could compare. Though they hadn't known each other long, their connection felt timeless.

He mindlinked with his raven 'Time to shine, Bram. Let's show Elena how handsome you are.'

Killian's body began to bend and twist, black wings stretching along his back, soft feathers slowly covering his flesh. His eyes transformed to the color of midnight. A squawk from his beak, then his head nestled against Elena's cheek. Bram was such a flirt.

Killian talking through the link 'get your head in the game, Bram, and keep your beak off my witch.'

Bram, in his smug tone 'She is our witch.'

Killian chuckled 'agreed, so let's get this warding spell going.'

Bram lifted out the opened window, taking flight, and flew around the house and its perimeter numerous times as Killian chanted the spell.

Bless this house, may peace dwell within. Protect all that enter, Whether friend or kin. Bless every door, window, ceiling, and wall. Bless every room. Bless them all. Bless the roof and ground surrounding your protection, love, and light. Bless the days and nights as above and below. So it mote be.

The spell complete, Bram flew to the front of the house, shifting Kil into his human form 'smooth move, Bram' walking to the car as quickly as he could, sliding back into his seat. Elena gasped, her eyes leaving a heated trail over his form.

Killian grinned, "I might have left out the part about shifting back from my raven form would leave me naked." He knew Bram could have done that a bit more eloquently.

***

Invasion of the Body Snatchers. That's the movie that popped into Elena's head. She knew many things were possible, but seeing Killian shift into a bird right in front of her had not been on her list of things for the evening.

'And did it hurt,' was what ran through her mind as he altered from a six-foot-plus man to a black-as-night raven. Even then, he was bigger than any raven she'd seen before.

Did that mean his entire family could shapeshift? That would seem legitimate, considering they were the Raven Coven. Her mind was off on all different possibilities now until the softness of feathers touched her cheek, startling her.

"Killian, I don't know how you're ever going to top this on another date," Her hand lifted and softly touched his downy appendages.

Then he was gone, out the window so quickly, her head bending to try to see him against the darkness of the night sky, but it was virtually impossible. He blended in so well and she would have stuck out like a beacon of light.

And then he totally topped his top by transforming from his raven back into himself, in the middle of the street, fully naked. Like she could see everything. Everything! And holy moly, it was so much better than her books.

A blush infused by the hottest fire covered her body and she was sure her cheeks glowed in the night. And then, in all his nakedness, he was sitting back in the car next to her.

'Don't look down, Elena. Don't. You've never had sex, and you don't want to start in a bazillion-dollar car. And how could you even? Where would stuff go? Who sits on who?' her thoughts again going everywhere, his voice grabbing her and bringing her back to the moment.

"Please tell me you have clothes with you because if we get stopped, I can't even think up a story for this." A laugh decided at that moment to bust out, and she couldn't stop.

***

Killian grinned from ear to ear at Elena's blushing face. Her cheeks flushed a deep shade of crimson, a striking contrast against her fair complexion. Her amber eyes sparkled with a mixture of surprise and admiration as she took in the sight before her. He wasn't one to boast about his size, but the way her gaze lingered on him told him all he needed to know.

Bram's voice sounded through the link, a playful edge to his tone. 'Don't let that blushing of hers get to your head. Remember, I have one hell of a beak, old man.'

Chuckling at Bram's remark, Killian replied, his voice laced with amusement, 'You're the man, Bram, I mean the bird.' The banter between the two friends was a familiar comfort, a reminder of the bond they shared beyond their magical abilities.

With a wave of his hands over his head, a shimmering ripple of magic cascaded down his form, his clothes materializing seamlessly on him. The fabric clung to his muscular frame, accentuating his powerful presence. Leaning in toward his witch, he placed a tender peck on her cheek, the gesture filled with affection and warmth. "Did you like what you saw, Red?" he inquired, a mischievous twinkle in his eyes.

He was only teasing her, but her nervous giggle was the cutest thing he had ever heard. As his car came to life with a push of a button, Killian casually laid his hand on her inner thigh, squeezing gently. The night air was cool and crisp, a gentle breeze ruffling through their hair as he drove her home.

A short while later, after more laughter and a few shared secrets, Killian accompanied Elena to her front door. The soft glow of the porch light illuminated her features, casting a warm and inviting aura around her. Killian turned to her, a smile playing on his lips.

"I had an amazing time tonight, Red," Killian said, his voice soft and sincere. "I can't wait for our next date."

Pulling her close, he kissed her deeply, savoring the sweetness of the moment. Their connection felt electric, a spark igniting between them as they lingered in the embrace. Reluctantly, Killian let her go, his baby blues locked on hers with a promise of more to come.

Elena watched as Killian made his way to his car, his silhouette outlined against the night sky. The engine roared to life, a gentle purr that faded into the distance as he drove away. She stood there, her heart racing with excitement for what the future could hold. She was in deep, in a very short time.

21

𝕾ilken sheets whispered against her bare skin as she stirred, dawn peeking through her window. Silence for a moment until Essie decided to intrude and make her demands. Elena's thoughts go to the night before and Killian. She was in some serious heat for the warlock.

Dreams of them together had woken her during the night. Not fully, just enough that she drifted into a state of arousal. She was wet and needy, her fingers finding her bud inside her lacy undies. All it took was a few strokes, and she bit her lip, keeping her orgasm to herself, riding it out, and falling back into her dreams.

She was waking up differently today; she could feel it in every fiber of her body. How fast could you fall in love? She knew it was too soon to

122

feel the way she was feeling. She needed to slow down and not jump too far ahead. And with that stuck in her head, she got up, met the day, and hoped she could put off texting Killian until lunch.

***

The chamber resembled a crypt or mausoleum, the walls, and floor carved from the same gray stone, the ceiling crafted with a grim artistry of the morbid. The air acrid, holding the scent of death and the malice of ages passed. She heard her own pulse as she turned in circles, trying to see into the darkening corners. There was no door. She turned and turned but none to be seen.

Then it sounded like whispers drifting around her. Elena tried to call her flame, but nothing came. No surge of embers or enlightenment, no power, just her standing in the waning light that drifted through the one filthy windowpane.

Then, as if she called it to happen, low flames flickered alive from wicks that stood atop black candles, their stature all but crumbled.

Shadows reached tall and irregular around her, restlessness creeping along her skin. She couldn't breathe, thoughts a stranglehold on her throat as the walls closed in, a low scraping sound where mortar and brick fell away from the wall before her, a stench of rotting soil so potent, one hand lifting to cover her nose and mouth.

Her eyes held the niche in the wall. Was it? A few steps closer, her thoughts confirmed a hidden grimoire. At first glance, it was thick and old, her hands both reaching while her mind screamed-**No**.

The instant her fingertips made contact, pain shot up through her arms, the book making an audible moan. This was the blackest of magic, and she'd disturbed it. She needed out, out of here.

Trying to scream for Killian, but no sound came; fear and anger a turmoil inside her, then her breath halted. The whispers again, but now she heard her name, 'Elena'.

Frantic to leave, but the walls were closing in, and the window had disappeared- 'Elena soon.' She spun and spun.....

Wrenching her head up off the counter to fix on Sophie's panic-stricken eyes of blue in front of her, "Elena, are you all right? You scared the crap out of me. You were mumbling and definitely upset, but I couldn't understand what you were saying. Are you OK?"

Looking around, the sun beamed in through the store's windows. It was midday, and she was sitting at their workbench filling orders. She was at Beliefs; she was safe.

"I'm OK. I guess I'm more tired than I thought." Her own gaze took in the deep concern of Sophie's. "I swear I'm OK. I didn't even feel myself dozing off. Don't fire me for sleeping on the job." She was trying to make light out of something that had really scared her and worried Sophie.

That wasn't a dream, she thought; that was foresight. And why now? She was really happy. The first time she felt lighter and more herself since Gran's death. She'd had premonitions before, but nothing ever as horrifying as this. She needed air.

"Sophie, I'm going to step out for a few minutes. I'll drop the two orders we just finished along the way. Be back in like half an hour." sliding off her stool, she grabbed her bag, and gave Sophie a quick hug. "I'm just going to walk off my sleepiness, and then we can finish up the last of the orders. If you want to take lunch now, you can. Or wait for me, and we can do take-out?"

***

Sophie could tell that whatever happened to Elena had startled her. She'd offer to go with you, but sometimes you just needed your alone time. She understood that. "I'll wait for you. I can clean up the mess we made and set up the jars for after lunch. Go get your air."

Watching Elena leave, Sophie really needed to talk to her. Today was not the day, though. She didn't want to upset her again, which it would. She really hoped she wasn't going to lose her best friend.

***

Kil stood in the middle of the room, his magic swirled around him like a cape. Pure raw power running through his veins, chanting the words of the elders falling from his lips. A ritual that had been passed on for centuries to keep enemies away or causing harm.

I cast this spell into the night.

To bind my enemies and limit their fight.

By earth, by water, by wind, by fire,

I wish to stop their evil desire.

As Killian finished chanting the last of the spell, a vision brought him to his knees. His eyes clouded over, and suddenly, he found himself standing in the middle of a tranquil field surrounded by towering trees. As he looked around, everything appeared to be perfectly ordinary, yet there was an inexplicable sense of anticipation in the air, leaving him both puzzled and intrigued.

As Killian roamed the area, taking in the surroundings, his dual nature as a warlock and a seer gave him the ability to glimpse into the future. Unexpectedly, a vivid vision began to materialize, causing him to come to a sudden stop as the world around him faded and the vision came into focus.

Killian's mother lay sprawled on the ground, her shoulders shaking with sobs. Rissa, looked up at him, her lips moving, but the words were lost in the rush of the wind through the leaves. It seemed as if she was trying to warn him about something urgent, but her voice was muffled and distant. Killian had never seen his mother cry before, and the sight of her tears brought a pang of sorrow to his heart.

Despite his mother's recent coldness and distance, seeing her like this stirred a deep longing to comfort her. As she stood up, her fists clenched at her sides, a gut-wrenching scream escaped her lips and echoed through the forest, reaching up to the skies.

Killian's hand reached out to cup her shoulder, to comfort her, but everything went black. He lay in the middle of the floor, completely drained from his vision. He slowly rose, trying his best to shake off his vision, but he knew it would linger in the back of his mind, they always did.

An hour later...

Killian couldn't help but stare at the clock, its hands pointing straight up to twelve noon. He felt a surge of excitement as he gazed at the array of food packed in the basket before him. He was planning a surprise picnic for Red, and he couldn't wait to see her reaction. Unsure of her food preferences, he'd prepared homemade chicken salad sandwiches, tasty ham rolls, a refreshing strawberry salad, and a delicious lemon meringue pie for dessert.

He climbed into his customized Raptor pick-up truck. The sleek cherry red exterior with bold black pinstripes never failed to turn heads. He was a bit of a fanatic when it came to his rides. He had a separate building for his wheels and he could drive a different one for every day of the week.

As he pulled into the parking lot next to Elena's shop, he couldn't help but feel a surge of elation. With a basket full of surprises, he stepped into the store, eager to find his enchanting witch.

A blonde popped her head around the corner. "I will be right with you, Sir. Just putting up stock."

Killian carefully set the ornate basket on the polished counter, anticipation building as he awaited the appearance of his beautiful redhead witch. He hoped the blonde could help by telling him where Elena was. Taking in the quaint surroundings of the shop, Killian couldn't help but grin. Elena's store was a treasure trove of herbs, glistening crystals, flickering candles, and countless books meticulously arranged to create an enchanting ambiance. The air was filled with the soothing fragrance of scented candles, creating a warm and inviting atmosphere.

The blonde finally appeared smiling, holding a stack of books in her hand. "How can I help you?"

She sat the stack of books down and wiped the sweat from her brow. Killian extended his hand out, shaking her hand. "Hello, I am looking for the owner of the shop. My name is Killian and who do I have the pleasure of meeting?"

The blonde gave him a firm handshake. "My name is Sophie, and you must be the warlock that Elena can't stop talking about."

Grinning wide, showing off his pearly whites. "In the flesh. It's nice to meet you. Is Elena here?"

Sophie started to put the books on the shelf, one by one. Making sure they were in alphabetical order. "Elena should be back at any moment. You are more than welcome to wait. Would you like a glass of herbal tea while you wait?"

Killian nodded his head. "Yes, that would be great."

Sophie put the last book on the shelf and headed to the back of the shop. She was out like a flash, holding a glass of tea, setting it down on the counter beside him. He picked up the glass, taking a sip. "This is delicious."

A smile tugged at Sophie's lips. "It's one of our best sellers. We can't keep it on the shelf long enough. It's Elena's Gran's recipe."

Killian set the glass down, "I can see why. It's a perfect mixture of herbs. It's really refreshing."

Sophie took a step closer, her face taking on a different demeanor. "Elena was right about you. You are definitely some serious eye candy but that being said, if you hurt her in any way, you will be answering to me. Capisce!"

Killian nodded, Sophie was very protective of Elena, and he respected that. It was nice to know that Elena had a friend that she could count on. "I will not hurt her, Sophie. That is a promise."

Sophie grabbed the empty glass as the bell of the door caught his attention. Elena walked through the door, her face in shock. Killian walked over and kissed her cheek. Her face flushing with hints of pink.

"I wanted to surprise you with a picnic." He turned, giving her a glimpse of the basket, then his attention to Sophie. "I am stealing her for a couple hours."

Sophie winked at Elena. "You two go have fun. I will take care of the shop."

Killian grabbed the picnic basket, took Elena's hand, and headed to his truck. Elena looked up at him, her eyebrows pinched together. "This is your truck?"

He chuckled, placing the basket in the backseat. "Yes, isn't she a beaut? Red seems to be my favorite color."

Elena blushed even more. "She is pretty, but I need a step ladder to get in."

He scooped her up in his arms. "That's what you have me for."

Elena's laughter bubbled up joyfully as Killian gallantly assisted her into the passenger seat of his sturdy truck. With a gentle closing of her door, he swiftly made his way to the driver's side, placing the basket in the back seat and then sliding in effortlessly before starting the engine with a confident turn of the key. The powerful hum of the engine resonated through the vehicle as they set off down the winding road.

As they traversed the scenic route, the warm touch of Killian's hand on Elena's thigh provided a comforting sense of closeness between them, enhancing the serenity of the drive. The gentle sway of the truck as it navigated the twists and turns seemed to echo the rhythm of their budding connection.

Upon reaching their destination, Killian was once again the gentleman scooping Elena from the truck.

Bogue Chitto State Park stood before them, a hidden gem that held a special place in Kil's heart. Towering cypress trees adorned with delicate Spanish moss enveloped the park, casting a mystical aura over the lush landscape.

As they strolled leisurely through the vibrant park, the gentle swaying of the moss overhead creating a soothing backdrop, Killian and Elena walked hand in hand, their fingers intertwined like a promise of togetherness. The sun cast a warm glow around them, painting the world in a golden light. Killian, his voice barely above a whisper, leaned in close to Elena's ear, his breath soft against her skin as he confessed, "I am falling for you hard and fast."

Elena had been a constant presence in Killian's dreams for months, her image haunting him in the quiet hours of the night. It was as if she had always been a part of his life, her essence woven into the very fabric of his being. How could he not be in love with her? To Killian, she was more than just a woman; she was his soul flame, the one whose presence ignited a fire within him every time they were near each other.

Finding a perfect spot beneath the sprawling branches of a majestic Cypress tree, Killian spread out a checkered blanket on the soft grass, a cozy setting for their impromptu picnic. Elena knelt down gracefully beside him, her eyes alight with a mixture of curiosity and affection. With a smile lighting up his face, Killian reached into the picnic basket, revealing his homemade delights, unveiling his savory sandwiches, rolls, salad and the lemon meringue pie that promised a sweet ending to their meal.

"I hope you're hungry, Red," Killian quipped playfully, the endearing nickname rolling off his tongue, a testament to the bond they shared. His laughter mingled with the rustling of leaves overhead, creating a harmonious symphony of shared moments and whispered promises.

***

You could never judge how a day was going to turn out by how it had started. Never would she have thought after being frightened so badly earlier that she could be so incredibly happy a short while later. But Killian's surprise lunch had changed the pulse of her day.

"I can't believe you made all of this yourself." Her insides did a somersault upon realizing that he'd been thinking of her as much as she'd been thinking of him. "Killian, Kil," her gaze found his, and she did what she had been thinking about since leaving him the night before. She leaned forward, the palm of her hand softly resting against his cheek, and she took a kiss. Her lips barely stroked along his, her tongue tentatively giving a graze along the fullness of his mouth, his opening, and his own hand threading through her hair, and the kiss turned into liquid fire.

It was his groan that lit a fuse inside her, and Elena crawled herself closer without breaking the kiss until her front awkwardly met his, and they fell to the side, forgetting where they were.

She had no idea what she was doing, but her body guided her, Killian's hands everywhere, pulling her in tighter, and the kiss was now tongues and moans and everything she'd ever read about.

It was the sound of kids' laughter that brought her back to the moment and possibly Killian, too. The frantic clutching changed to a few last parting touches of their lips. Her eyes opened to see his right there, and her blush steamrolled over her cause she'd never thrown herself at anyone. But there was nothing that could have stopped her at that moment.

"So Red, I'm taking it that you really must like picnic lunches," His fingers tucked her hair behind her ear, and it's like he must have known. "You can kiss me like that anytime you want. And I mean anytime." His wink brought a smile to her face.

It was then she pushed herself back and looked around her to see a few families and others joining in the day.

"I haven't been in this park in a really long time. Years, in fact. It's strange how you can get so busy with your life you forget to take time out and enjoy what's around you."

Killian couldn't stop staring at her. Her hair was like someone had lit a torch against the backdrop of the blue sky. His dreams had somehow led him to her; to the here and now. He was living his dreams, and as he thought that, a desperate angst ran through him. He knew as a seer how his spiritual eye clarified the past, present, and future. He knew Elena was part of that eternal truth, his intuitive powers telling him so.

Grabbing her one more time, he brought his lips against hers in more of a **you're mine** kiss. Declaring that to anyone who might be watching. Then releasing her just as quickly. "I just needed one more before we eat. You're the sweetest treat here, Red." When did he become the guy with these cheesy lines?

The urgency of that next kiss and Elena was ready to haul him down onto the blanket he'd brought. He was so far out of her league, but she didn't care. If it wasn't for the other people nearby enjoying the nice day, she'd show him how far down her freckles went.

"Elena? Hey, you there?"

She'd obviously dipped into fantasyland as she cleared her head to see Kil holding a plate out to her and cutlery wrapped in a napkin, "There's lots, so have as much as you want. And you can take the leftovers back to the store if you'd like. Oh, and just so you know, that isn't all for the kissing. There's going to be more of that, too."

And she just stared at him as those words sunk in, watching him load his plate with bits of everything, wondering how she was going to eat with thoughts of him filling up her head.

But she did eat. And she ate a lot. "Killian, everything is so good. Keegan isn't the only chef in the family. You're going to spoil me with food like this. Sometimes, lunch is just a quick granola bar or salad. Well, sometimes we order in but we end up eating what was once hot, cold because the store gets busy."

"Be prepared to be spoiled from now on. If I can sneak away during the day, I'll be on your doorstep, beautiful."

And she just stared at him again, not knowing how this had happened to her. She owed that spellbook for bringing them together that was for sure. Her phone ringing, and she set aside her plate to see it was Sophie.

"Hi, Soph. What's up?" Her eyes were on Killian's "You sure you don't mind? I'll owe you. Thank you. See you tomorrow then."

"Anything wrong, Red?"

"Sophie has just informed me that I'm know longer needed at the store today. I'm supposed to hang out with you and have fun. So it looks like you have me if you want me."

His slow smile reminded her of a Cheshire Cat, and her body did that whole skip-a-beat thing it did around him.

"Sophie deserves a raise. I like her way of thinking, Red. Now, what to do with you." His blue gaze dipped over her from head to toe, and she was sure she squirmed. "Hmm, some things are more adult-rated, but I could cast a spell and cloak us from outsiders. I really like that idea, but how about we finish up here and take a walk around. There's a few trails nearby and I can hold your hand and whisper dirty things in your ear. How does that sound to you?"

She was becoming a gooey mess. Did she know a spell for that? Even if she did, she didn't know if she could cast it properly that's how much he affected her.

"I think that all sounds really nice." Elena knew her freckles were standing out amongst her blushing. He'd had her in that state ever since picking her up literally in his arms to put her in his truck.

"Good. So let's dump the basket back in my truck, and we can go explore a bit, and then I'll take you home."

Killian pulled her up by her hands, and his lips found hers again before she'd had a chance to get her balance. "I told you there'd be more of that. Get used to it. My lips love your lips, Red."

Speechless. She wanted to say something cute back but her mind was blank except for thoughts of him, them. Oh boy, she was in deep.

***

The trail they found after he stowed away the basket was just off the parking lot and would take about an hour.

"Gator Bait trail? Really Killian. We couldn't have taken one that didn't sound like we might be eaten at any moment."

And by the look on his face and the devilish smirk that was pinned to his mouth, it dawned on Elena what he'd thought of, and her shade of red deepened.

Stopping at the side, Killian pulled her against him, "It wouldn't matter what the name of the trail was; if you're with me, I'm always hungry. And fuck me, Red, but my mind has had us doing all sorts of nasty things together. The good nasty and the bad nasty. For months, it's only been you in my head and heart." His head dipped again, and her lips met his halfway. There was no softness this time from Elena. She grabbed a fistful of his shirt and hung on for dear life.

"Ewww gross," A Few boys rode by on bikes, breaking their lip lock, a laugh falling from her lips as she saw Killian smile.

"They think that now, but give them a few years. That ewww is going to turn into ahhhhs," The tone in his voice had her falling in deeper with him.

"Come on, Romeo, let's walk off all that lunch, and if you're good, I think I remember there being an ice cream spot somewhere in here. Maybe a trail map will show us the way. But only if you're good."

"I can't promise that. Not with you looking like you do, Red. I'm a bad boy. You should know that right now."

She knew it. She knew it that first day he'd walked into Beliefs.

"I think I might like bad boys."

Holy heck, had she just said that out loud. Looking sideways at him, at his face, at that sinister smile; she had. Maybe the ground would open up and swallow her.

"You meant bad boy. One. Singular. Me. You like me, Red? How much? You can tell me. And then I'm going to use it against you. Cause that's what bad boys do."

And he never missed a step. Just kept walking, his hand finding hers and holding tight. "I'm waiting. Tell me."

"You're serious?"

"100% serious Red. Tell me you like me. Tell me you think about me at night when you're lying all alone in your bed. Do your hands wander? Cause I'll tell you a little secret. Mine do. My eyes close, and there you are, and I'm hard as stone."

Her feet sorta tripped over each other, but he was there to right her and pulled her to the side again, his face hovering over hers-" Tell me. I dare you."

He was being cocky; he knew that. But there was a hot passion inside of her to go with that hair. How no one else had ever seen it, he couldn't believe it. But no one else ever would. She was his.

Dare. Did he dare her? Did he think she wouldn't tell him? She could say stuff. She wasn't that shy. She'd just never had a guy before.

His gaze was challenging her; she could see it. He was so ruggedly beautiful.

"I like you, Killian. I may be even more than like you. There, I said it."

His tug on her hand pulled her in closer to his side, "Was that so hard. We'll work on the loving me part." his wink giving her a warm feeling.

She didn't even know what to say to that, so she kept quiet and just enjoyed their time walking together and enjoying this new feeling.

"So I'm curious, and you can tell me not to be, but your fire element is new to you, isn't it? And before you say how can I know that it's because I'm a lot older than I look and I have a sense about these things. I'm not just a pretty face, Red."

Elena was always pretty private about her life; that was something Gran had sort of instilled in her. She never questioned it then but now she did wonder why. There were obviously reasons but she had no one really to ask. And asking the wrong person could maybe cause problems.

Giving Killian a quick glance then she refocused on the pathway they were on, "Gran knew it was fire. She always said when the time was right that, my element would be perfect for me. I think maybe I kinda came into it later because it frightened me. The first time I called it forth, and, it came was just a few months before Gran started to not feel well. She'd take me into the woods, and we'd practice, but there were a few times I lost control and set some trees on fire. It's so unpredictable and still is. I practice, and I'm getting better, but I can tell how volatile it is, and I really have to concentrate to keep it harnessed. I don't know if I'll ever master it."

Killian just walked and listened. He remembered that feeling of the overwhelming intensity of his powers when they were manifesting but he'd also had his family's help and a few other elders of the coven. Everyone had helped him understand his element and his gifts.

"If you'd let me, Elena, I could help you. Fire is my element, too. I've had years and years of training. I know how it feels when it pulses and tingles. How it stirs in the center of your chest, how it warms and unfurls like a blossoming rose. I can help you feel more in control." And he just kept walking them along the path, hoping she said yes.

She'd never really had anyone she'd trusted other than Gran. She'd been so young when her Mama had passed that she was more just hazy images now. Gran had taught her spells and potions and such, everything she'd need to keep Beliefs afloat. When Gran had finally said it was time, it was already too late. No witchcraft or magick could cure her body of the cancerous cells.

"Maybe Killian. I usually practice out behind the house where there's lots of room. Less chance of anything going up in flames. Plus, there's a long water hose just in case, which I've used a time or five." - shaking her head, remembering how she'd run like a bat out of hell to turn the water on.

"Well, the offer is open. I'm going to be spending a lot of time with you, so use me, woman. I'm yours to play with." His brows gave her a waggle.

"Is this your bad boy side coming out?"

"You haven't seen anything yet, Red."

***

Two hours and two double scoops later, they were on their way back to Elena's. Not only did Killian lift her back into his truck, he pushed the center console up and pulled her in right next to him, "I want you close. Don't even think of arguing. I can drive and touch you at the same time."

She'd lost track of how many times he'd kissed her or just run his fingers along her skin. This afternoon was like the rest of the world had just drifted away, and her and Kil had been in their own bubble.

The low growl of the truck and a few turns out of the park and they were back on the highway, "I meant to ask you, did your mother say anything after you returned the spellbook to her?"

Did Elena realize how his fingers had stopped playing across her thigh? Killian still hadn't figured out why, after all these years she'd needed the book back now. And that spell that he'd come across before handing it back to her, what was the motivation behind that.

"She was in the middle of something when I returned it but said Thank you. And I'm sorry that finding out about your Gran upset you so much. I'm sure we can find out more with a bit of digging. I can help with that, too, Elena. I want to help. I feel like I ripped open a secret, but now that it's done, you should know your history. It's important to know because it will help you evolve into what you're meant to be."

Turning his head to see her looking straight ahead out the windshield; she was so gorgeous. And he had to pry his eyes off of her to concentrate on the road.

"I guess I don't understand why she wouldn't tell me. It seems like it was a pretty big deal to be in the sister witches. And then the falling out which changed her life. I wonder if my mother knew any of this or if Gran didn't tell anyone? And now, who would really know or tell me."

As soon as she said that, an idea popped into his head. Whether it would work or not, he didn't know. But if it meant helping Elena find out answers he'd do anything. He wanted her happy and content in every way.

"Did you leave Essie at the store, or is she home?"

"She's at home, probably raising the roof because her dinner is late. What's new, though. That cat has a bottomless pit for a stomach."

Perfect, thought Killian.

22

" I'm just going to change if you want to find a spot on the couch. We could watch a movie if you have time?"

"I'll always have time for you, Red."

They had barely opened the door, and Essie was meowing. And not the nice type. The type that said she was starving and how could you make her wait type meowing.

"I know I'm late but I'm here now," Elena talking to the annoyed ball of black fur.

Killian watched Elena get Essie's food from the fridge and warm it up in the microwave for her.

"I won't be long, Killian."

His gaze followed her as she disappeared up the stairs to her room. Then he could hear her moving around upstairs, and a smile touched his lips. He loved the feel of her house and how it just felt like her. There was love and contentment here; he could feel that.

That he'd brought unhappiness to her world really bothered him, and he needed to make it right, his eyes dropping to where Essie sat and ate. No time like the present. The sooner he knew if this would work, the sooner Elena would get answers.

There had to be a reason why her Gran didn't tell Red about being a sister witch to their Coven; there was nothing to be ashamed of. He could only hope that Essie would tell them what happened cause he knew his mother wouldn't be so easy to get information from.

Familiars usually don't give up information easily because they are completely dedicated to their witch. But Red needed answers, so hopefully, Essie would play nice. Usually, cat familiars are family members. He wondered if Red knew that. Did they mindlink with one another to communicate? Or had Essie been staying silent for a reason.

Hopefully, Red wouldn't freak out when Essie started to talk, that is, if she spoke at all. Killian knew she had that ability, but that being said, the longer she'd been in her animal form, the more comfortable she could have become and she could refuse to talk.

The soft tread of footsteps on the stairs had Killian's gaze shift and then stop. The fall of red hair around her shoulders, those freckles that begged to be kissed; he wanted a life with her, he wanted everything with her. So this was a step toward that.

"You haven't moved from the kitchen. Aren't you staying for a little bit?" were her words, seeing him where she'd left him.

The purr at his feet and the rub along his pants got his attention. He bent down and scooped Essie up in his arms, stroking her fur. "Oh I'm staying alright. I just hadn't gotten that far. I was daydreaming about what you were doing up there in your room." He gave her a wink, watching how the blush rose and dusted her cheeks. "I thought I would try something first if that's ok with you."

Elena's brows came together, not sure what he was getting at. "Ok. But what is it?"

"You'll see or you may not. I'm going on history and magick here."

He kept his voice low and calm when he began to speak. He didn't want Essie to feel that she was being ambushed.

"Essie, I need your help with something, and I was hoping you'd understand why and why now." His hand gently stroked her, sending good intentions into her, opening up his side of Bram so she felt a link to his raven side. "Who are you really, and why would Gran leave the sister witches?"

Killian knew Essie had been listening to their conversation. That was part of her station in life, to gather information, be a protector and a conduit to the other side.

Essie pushed away from him, jumping out of his arms to the floor, and shook her head from side to side. Her back arching, the hair standing on edge, a chafe sound like nails on a blackboard or she was spitting up the largest hairball in existence. Then a female voice, slightly rough where before a gentle meow was only heard.

"Firstly, you know as well as I do, Killian that I am sworn to secrecy. Secondly, I am Red's great aunt, Gran's sister, Esmeralda."

Red gasped in surprise, her hands lifting to cover her mouth from Essie, revealing who she was. Killian moved close to her, wrapping an arm around her and gave a gentle squeeze. Kil kept his voice at a gentle tone when he asked the next question.

"You aren't betraying anyone, Essie. And the time has come to bring Elena out of the dark. I...we have hurt her by keeping this hidden. What was the reason that Gran left the group? I know when you are sworn in that it is nearly impossible to leave."

***

She wished she could read minds because the way Kil was staring at her, there was more going on than he had imparted on her. Butterflies were lifting off in her stomach and fluttering a mile a minute.

Essie did her strut around Killian's legs, begging for attention because she was a traitor. And he indulged her, lifting her with those defined arms of his, Elena a bit jealous even now within the situation the way it was, Essie getting the cuddles and stroking.

But then he spoke to her cat like he expected a response and when it actually happened, Elena's mouth fell open like she was in a time warp of some kind because she knew that voice, remembered it from somewhere long ago.

Her great aunt? Elena's gaze stayed locked on the talking Essie. She wanted to say something because it was obvious she could have spoken back to Elena anytime she wanted. How many times had Elena talked to her, her mind just emptying itself of problems or thoughts? Not once would she have imagined that Essie could have spoken back to her. Even then she would have thought she was losing her mind or some kind of spell had gone haywire.

The warmth of Kil's arm around her brought her sensibilities back on line and she had questions too.

"Why haven't you talked before this? When Gran passed, I could have used a friend. When her grimoire was hard to read, you could have helped. I know the questions Killian has asked you, but why would you let me hurt so badly on my own? That was just mean." She was leaning into his body, her arm going around his waist.

***

Kil knew this was a lot to process for his beautiful witch. He could tell that she didn't have a clue that familiars were not only passed relatives, but they could communicate with one another.

Why didn't her Gran tell Elena important things such as this? It was almost like she treated her like a child. Now, she's here on her own, has been alone for some time and Essie had not once spoken to her. He could feel a bit of anger stirring in his gut.

He looked over to Essie and ran a hand through his hair in frustration. It is an elder witch to instill in their young on how to survive and protect themselves. To understand their powers and learn how to control them.

He did his best to wrangle in his anger so he wouldn't frighten her, but he was teetering on the edge of losing control.

A sigh fell from his lips as his eyes diverted back to the talking cat and waited for her to respond to Red. Essie started to speak and Red eyes grew wide. "Elena, I promised my sister I would watch over you and that's exactly what I have done. She made me promise not to speak until you were ready. We were both grieving at the same time and I tried my best to not break a promise I had made. For that, I am truly sorry. Elena, I did try my best to give you hints and connect with you but you never did."

Killian watched as Elena's shoulders slumped and tears ran down her beautiful, freckled face. Essie moved to close the distance between her and Elena but she backed away from her familiar. "I needed you Essie and you weren't there to comfort me. Why would Gran not tell me things that were so important?"

Fire danced behind his eyes, he couldn't stand to see Red upset. "Enough of beating around the bush, Essie. We need to know what happened and why she left the sister witches? We both know when you are branded, you are in for life. It used to come with a death sentence if one of the sisters decided to leave. Tell me how she got away without being hunted down and killed?"

Red's head snapped in his direction as if he hit her in the gut with his words. There are so many things he would teach her but he needed the truth.

"Killian, she isn't ready to hear the truth and neither are you. Your mother was her best friend and they were practically glued at the hip. They did everything together, but Elena's Gran, my sister, fell in love with a human and we both know that's forbidden."

***

To say the room was starting to spin was an understatement. Elena was having a hard time processing everything falling from Essie and Kil's lips. She wasn't sure what hurt worse at this point. That Gran had kept so much hidden from her or that Essie was her great-aunt and let her suffer over the last year.

Elena had a soft heart; she always had. She never wished anyone harm. Even her spells and incantations were meant for benefit. Gran had always said she needed to embrace all aspects of witchcraft to be well-rounded. Many in the coven practiced on the darker side. It had always made her feel fearful. And now, knowing fire was her element, it even left her feeling more uneasy.

Fire was extremely volatile and powerful. She'd been practicing out back in the woods, but even the tiniest flame seemed to hold so much. It's like it wanted to reach out, lash out and feed on everything around her. She couldn't understand why it chose her. Elena Payne, redhead, an oddity.

She felt Killian's anger building and felt his temper rising. Looking up to see his own flames dancing in his eyes. His admission that Gran should have been killed for leaving the coven startled her to push back from him.

What the blessed hell? What kind of covens were these? And why would Gran agree to bind herself to something like that?

Then Essie dropped another secret she never knew. Her grandfather had been human. It's like the last 22 years of her life weren't hers.

She backed up further, the kitchen counter hitting her in the back. Her chest felt tight, a warmth rising within her. Her hands reached out to grasp the edge of the granite. She'd woken up this morning to a perfectly beautiful day, and now … she just couldn't understand how everything had changed.

Turning, she took a few steps to the back door, flinging it open, her feet taking her down the stairs, and she ran. Ran across the grass, passed the flowerbeds, and down the path into the woods. She heard her name being yelled behind her, but she didn't care. The one person she loved and trusted beyond anything had lied to her every day of her whole life.

23

Killian was struggling to hold back his anger, not towards Elena but for the fact his mother would hold back such a secret. Why didn't his mother tell him what happened with her best friend? He knew his mother could be extremely rough around the edges; she saw life differently than others did. When she wanted something, she would stop at nothing to get it, regardless of the path to get there.

He shut his eyes as his raven came forth to show him where Red ran too. She was lying in the middle of the woods weeping and mumbling out words that he wished he couldn't hear. He knew she had every right to be hurt and angry, but her words felt like knives piercing his heart. She didn't understand the truth about the rules of a coven. Why did her Gran shield her from everything she was?

Red was stronger than she realized; all she needed was to believe in herself. He just hoped she wouldn't end what had only begun. Kil couldn't even begin to imagine what his life would be without her in it. One thing he truly believed in was to always tell the truth, even if the truth hurt. He never sugar-coated anything; secrets could cause the most damage. They could turn someone's world upside down in an instant.

"Essie, please explain why your sister didn't want Red to know who she truly was? Why shelter her granddaughter from such truths?"

"Killian, we both know things aren't that easy. I begged my sister to help Elena to evolve and how to use her powers but she refused my request. She didn't want Elena to know about her past and the lies she kept. Elena was the only light left in my sister's life. You and I will help Elena grow into her power. She will see there is beauty in the darkness like there is in the light. Killian, you are proof of that beauty. I can feel how true you are, and I know how much you care for your Red. Now let's go get our witch back."

***

She ran passed the tiny bridge that ran over the creek, passed the grave markers of all the animals and birds she found dead on the property and buried, passed the swing Gran had hung years ago where Elena used to sit, swing, and watch her practice her spells.

She saw none of it. The socks she wore offered no protection from the stones or sharp pieces of debris on the ground, and she'd pay for it later.

Elena felt the warm streams of tears running down her cheeks and off her chin. It was all too much, her world shifting on its axis.

The clearing opened up in front of her, traces of ash littering the grass and the scent of fire clinging to the trees. This was her spot, and she fell to her knees and let the gates of her anguish run out.

She cried for herself, for Gran, her Mama. She cried for all the memories she thought she had that now weren't true. Was everything a lie? Why would she hide things from her? Nothing made sense; she felt completely alone.

Maybe Gran knew she didn't have the strength of character to carry fire. Of all the elements, of all the other traits she could carry, why the most powerful? What if she could never fully harness it? What if she was an absolute failure and she became ridiculed, the Payne name a black mark in the book of legacy.

Her anger rose, her head a jumble of thoughts. Elena's palms warm against the ground she sat on, no idea she was the conduit or what she was calling forth. Small embers lit, licking across the dryness of her surroundings. Flames slowly burst, eating their way to small bushes and then trees. She sat in the middle, unaware, until she looked up to see the wall of destruction she had created.

"Oh my god!" fell from her lips.

***

Essie knew where Red would run too. It was a place her sister would often go when she needed to clear her thoughts and be alone with nature. Kil felt awful that his witch had to find things out this way. It was never easy to hear that someone you loved would keep secrets. He knew precisely how Red felt; his mother often kept the truth from him.

Killian's fire danced behind his eyes, and he could feel Elena's fire reaching out to him. Something was very wrong. Essie must have felt the same and took off like a shot. She yelled back. "There is no time to waste. Elena doesn't realize that her emotions control her powers. She is going to burn everything around her."

He was fucking furious for the fact it seemed that Red's Gran kept her living under a rock. She didn't even mention that her emotions control her flames. Why on earth would she not tell her these important things? She was a witch, not a damn child that needed to be treated like a fragile doll. How was Red supposed to protect herself? Hell, how was she supposed to control that element if she wasn't told?

Elena was sitting on the ground, surrounded by burning trees. Killian ran to her and lifted her into his arms. Her fire was completely out of control and spreading rapidly, whispering to her, "It's going to be just fine, Red. I need you to try to wrangle your fire in. Calm yourself, and don't let it spread any further. You can do this. Just concentrate."

Sobs broke free from Elena as she tried to get herself together. Killian could feel her anger stirring, and he tried his best to calm her, but she was too hurt to see reason. He hated to see her this way, but he had to find a way to get her to stop.

Essie jumped in mid-air and shifted into her human form. "Don't worry, Elena, I told my sister I will always protect you, and that's exactly what I will do."

Red gasped and watched her aunt suck in each flame, then blow out nothing but smoke. Killian was impressed by Essie's unique powers, and Elena blurted out. "What kind of witch are you?"

He whispered against her ear. "Your aunt is a Siphon."

24

Kil's whispered breath in her ear that her aunt's gift was siphoning registered slowly. His warmth reached her first. He'd picked her up and wrapped himself around her, trying to settle and calm her. Told her to breathe and get control but she couldn't.

Her mind had all its doors and windows open, and gale-force thoughts were bantering about, and she was in a storm. She knew the destruction she was causing; she could see it. She just couldn't do anything about it.

Peering out from around her red strands, her sight must be wrong, wasn't it? Because Essie had just changed into a woman right before their eyes. Her aunt manifested where, up until this moment, a cat had always been. The hurt lacing deeper that she was, in fact always able to transform yet never had.

Elena's amber hues watched, mesmerized as her aunt siphoned the flames and, in its wake, left smoke and ash. Relief cascaded through her because this clearing, these woods that were part of their property, meant so much to her. Memories abounded here since Elena could walk. Remnants of her Mama and her Gran's power lay within the makeup of fabric in this place.

She'd never known a witch with the ability to take another's power and use it as their own. The duration might be short-lived, but any power was up for grabs if it could be harnessed. It was remarkable, but at the same time, she had heard that witches with this ability had been considered abominations and thrown out of covens to live a lonely life.

Shifting in Killian's arms, she kissed his cheek, holding his gaze when theirs met. "Can you put me down?" His hold tightened for a moment before her feet found the ground, and she turned to her aunt. "You need to tell me everything because from where I stand, both you and Gran have been cruel. Didn't it even matter that you both knew you were hurting me? 'Cause to me, it seems like my entire life has been one big lie."

***

Kil did what Red asked of him and gently put her back on her feet. He took a step back to give Essie some room to explain her reason for not telling Elena her secret. Killian could see the hurt in Essie's eyes; he knew this wasn't easy for her, so he hoped Red could understand her reason. She was the only family Elena had left, and he didn't want this to cause her to walk away from her aunt.

Essie took a few steps closer, gently touching Elena's arm. "I know you feel betrayed by me and your Gran, but please let me explain why I couldn't tell you who I was. When I was a fledgling, I wasn't like the others. My sister was five years older than me, and when she realized that I could siphon others' powers, she tried her best to protect me, but what I didn't realize was I became a threat to the others. The elders called me an abomination and demanded that Matilda, my sister, end my life. She couldn't do it, so she turned me into a cat and made me her familiar. No one knew, and she kept my secret to keep me safe. When you have been living as a cat for so long, you forget you were ever human."

Killian's heart went out to Essie. He knew what she was saying was the absolute truth. Siphones were either outcasts or burned at the stake. Maybe this was the secret his mother had discovered and why Red's Gran left the sister witches. It would make perfect sense.

He knew his mother was a woman who only saw things one way, which was her way only. She could be exceptionally selfish, but if this was why she left, he couldn't blame Matilda for wanting to protect her sister. He would have done the same thing for his brother.

"Elena, you are so very loved, and I don't want you ever to forget that. Please don't be mad with me or your Gran. We had to keep secrets to protect you. I have known Killian since the day he was born. My sister and his mother had been best friends since they were teenagers. They did everything together and even came up with the idea of the sister witches. It was a way to bring covens together and protect special witches with unique powers so they wouldn't be outcasts. As Killian's mother got older, her dark powers strengthened, turning her into someone we didn't even recognize. Matilda tried her best to help her, but she refused to see reason, which broke her heart, so she left the sister witches, and Rissa let her go. No other reprisals. This was the hardest thing for her to do because she loved Rissa and her sons like family."

***

Elena's bubble of anger burst as she listened to Essie's explanation. That elders, ones who are meant to lead by example and guide the young ones, that they told one sister to kill another sister, seems archaic. It wasn't the dark ages. Thoughts of witch hunts and burnings so long ago yet the pain and destruction still lingers. Non-believers and haters setting the torch because of fear and paranoia and 'If-one-witch-was-bad, they-were-all-bad' mentality.

But that it came from within their own family was atrocious. How could someone ask another to kill another, let alone a sister?

That was the power of fear. All it took was the planting of little seeds, adding in the right amount of whispers and gossip, and pandemonium erupted. And Matilda and Esmeralda had paid the price.

Elena couldn't imagine forfeiting her life and going into hiding. She couldn't imagine not being as she was. She might not understand why she was gifted with fire but she couldn't imagine not having the freedom to live her life and decide her own life's walk. If someone told her she'd have to give up her life here in Nola, her heart would break. This life she'd created with Gran and their store was filled with memories. And yes, Essie/Esmeralda had been a part of all of that, but as a cat, not as a female witch as she was born.

"I'm sorry I just saw everything from my side without giving you a chance. But now what? They think you're dead. Jealousy still runs rife in the covens. I already hear the whispers about me, about my fire," her hands seeking out and touching Essie's real ones. No longer black fur but the warmth of skin-to-skin. "You know everything there is to know about me, yet I know nothing except from what I've read in Gran's grimoire." She finally felt more at ease, Elena took a step in, her arms embracing her in a long hug, then stepping back.

"You don't look old enough to be my aunt, more my sister. " Elena said, taking in her long brown hair and hazel eyes, and she truly looked not that much older than Elena, turning to Killian- "What would your mother do if she finds out Esmeralda is still alive?" -then back to Essie- "Can you shift at will now back and forth? Tell me to stop, or the questions will keep coming."

***

His heart swelled with pride, watching Elena coming full circle with knowing precisely what happened and why not everything was as it seemed to be. Essie no longer had to hide who she was, and Red had finally had a piece of her Gran here with her through her sister's eyes, every question she had wanted answered too could now be answered by her aunt. Killian grinned wide because he knew he would do anything for Red.

Killian took a step closer to her, needing to be closer, letting her feel the warmth of his flames."I will handle my mother. We'll figure this all out. But I need you to understand something, Red. I've fallen for you. There's just you for me, forever. Nothing will get in my way when it comes to protecting you. I have an idea, but I need you and Esmeralda's help."

Esmeralda's gaze looked from Killian to Elena. "Elena, I can shift back and forth, but I'd like to stay in my human form as much as I can. I am done with hiding who I am. I may be an outcast because I hold a more feared power than others, but that doesn't give anyone the right to curse me to my own kind. I know the darkness scares you, Elena, but Killian is something amazing to behold. He is nothing like his mother. He leads with a true and kind heart. He loves his Coven and will always protect them. I have known him since he was a child. As a familiar with ties to the coven, I've been able to catch glimpses from the edge of the veil. I've watched him grow. His magick is mighty, and I see how your fire reacts to his. He is your twin flame, Elena. The person you are meant to spend your life with. Don't let your fear of his dark magick get in the way of something amazing."

Kil was blown away by the kind words Essie had spoken. It was his turn to blush and turn red like a ripe strawberry. It was nice to hear good things spoken about him. His mother was filled with such dark magic she let it completely take over, and now it felt like she had not a single ounce of light left. It was a sad thing to watch, but he'd find a way to help her see things differently.

Red laced her fingers with his, her gaze shifting from her aunt to Killian's. "I feel the same about you, Kil. This has all been so world wind, but I know I'm yours too. And you're mine." 

25

 emons and rosemary were the scents that greeted them as they all
walked into the house from the backwoods. It was strange how certain
moments were marked by emotion, song, or smell. That you could be
drawn back to a certain place in time, whether good or not, a marker
oftentimes unbeknownst to us, just filed away in a corner of our mind.
This was one of those moments.

The three of them stayed in the clearing for a short bit after confessing
their souls. It was a cleansing of sorts. The moon paying witness to the
words spoken, giving them all a chance to breathe and come to terms with
Essie's transformation back to Esmeralda.

Elena stayed within the strength of Killian's arms, knowing without a
doubt she was where she was meant to be. So much had changed in such

a short while and more would now that secrets were creeping out of the past.

But they would have to tread quietly and slowly. Killian's mother was a powerful witch with status to match. Covens all over the world were transitioning into the new era, yet there were some things that were still taboo.

Esmeralda was a siphon. That placed fear in many still today. She couldn't just simply step into the coven and announce she'd been a cat all these years in hiding because of her extraordinary abilities.

For now, she'd stay in the house with Elena, get her legs back under her, strengthen her skills, and allow Kil time to put together a plan moving forward. Esmeralda was reclaiming her life and she deserved everything and then some for imprisoning herself the way she had.

Turning toward them as the door closed she said, "How about if I make us some peppermint tea unless you want something stronger?" A nod from her aunt and she moved to the kettle, adding water and lighting the burner.

"I want to still call you Essie if that's alright. I have this strange urge to tell you everything, but in truth, you've been here for all of it. Maybe you could help me with Gran's grimoire. She was the worst at keeping notes. I swear some of it is written in a different language. It's a mess."

Grabbing the tin jar off the counter that Elena had filled with ginger snap cookies yesterday - "Sit down, let me get this all ready, and we can decide on a few things."

Taking a few steps toward Killian, her hand finding his chest, palm resting gently, she pushed up on her toes, her lips finding his, "I'm glad you're here."

***

Kil pulled Red into his arms and placed a tender kiss in the crook of her neck. This beautiful woman had won his heart three times over. He would do anything to make her happy. It also warmed his heart, knowing that she had a piece of her family back. Fate always had a funny way of turning and twisting its way down a path until it hit the perfect spot.

Elena needed her aunt in her life more so now than ever. She needed to know her true history and how to become an extraordinary witch whose powers were unmatched. Killian saw a glimpse into Red's future and found something he knew he wasn't meant to see. Red held another power of her own, and he realized why Gran didn't want to teach Elena about her history because she knew if she did that, it would bring the wrong attention to Red's front doorstep.

Now the question remains, does Essie know about Red's hidden power? Whatever it may be, Kil would do whatever it took to keep her safe. His worry was of his mother and the evil that was residing within her. He knew one person who could help, but it would be a difficult task. This would be a very touchy subject for Esmeralda, but he had to try his best to save his mother or possibly lose her forever. Something he didn't want ever to have to face because his father adored his mother, and he knew this would crush him.

His brother had a love-hate relationship with their mother, but deep down, he knew losing her would leave a gaping hole that could never be mended. Kil could hear the soft whispers of Essie pushing through, trying to soothe his nerves. His eyes closed while he held Red a little tighter to his chest. Essie's words came out as soft, soothing hugs.

<Killian, you my dear, have always been family. Don't fret about something you have no control over. You may have dark magic flowing through your veins, but your heart is pure of light. I will help you with your mother, but Elena will initially not understand. The only one that can truly draw the darkness out is the light of another. She doesn't know who she truly is, Killian. I am the siphon, but she is the moon. The one true light. She isn't your twin flame, Killian; she is much more than that. She is your soulflame. That only happens once in a lifetime, if it ever happens at all>

His chest rose and fell at the words that flowed through his mind. He remembered seeing the moon behind Elena in his dreams, and her eyes were as bright as the sun. Now, his vision made complete sense, but he only heard soulflame mentioned once when he was a boy. He overheard his father calling his mother that. Twin flames are a little more common, but soulflames were rare. Not only was he her darkness, but she was his light.

***

Elena held him a little tighter. She wasn't quite sure what was running through his thoughts, but his body language had changed in the last few minutes. So she clutched him a bit harder, the warmth from her inner flame hopefully flowing into him.

This was new ground for all of them now. From waking up this morning to going through the day, the three of them stood at a new precipice.

What worried Elena was herself, her own untried, very volatile power. Killian was powerful; she didn't know the extent of it but she could sense it. And Essie was older; she may not have been practicing her witchcraft for the last number of years but she had history and the knowledge which Elena did not have.

There was so much to think about, so much to do, a slight shiver racing its way over her skin because Elena Payne of the Coven of the Divine Spirit was a lightweight in the game that was starting to be played.

She made potions and sold candles & such. Gran was the power and wisdom within the store and their family. She wasn't sure how she could be helpful.

Stepping out of Kil's arms at the sound of the kettle, she said, "I'm not sure where we go from here? Are we going to be in danger" she said while pouring the hot water into the teapot and bringing it to the table and setting it on the cozy. Her gaze finds Essie's first, then turns to Kil. "How do you think the covens are going to take this once it starts?"

26

Killian loved Elena's scent. It lingered on him and in the air when she left his embrace. It was like warm cinnamon from a freshly baked apple pie that your grandmother baked. A smell that made your mouth water to take a taste. She was his little slice of heaven that he always seemed to crave. He grinned wide as he watched her float around the kitchen. Kil wasn't sure how he got so lucky to call her his, but he was grateful to have fate on his side.

"Red, they will have to know the truth. What happened to Essie, and why your Gran kept her secret? Things are not what they used to be, and just because each one of us holds different powers doesn't mean we are freaks of nature."

Essie nodded her head, agreeing with Killian. Essie knew the ways of the elders no longer existed for the most part and that his coven would follow whatever path he led. They wouldn't even question him because Killian always did what was best for the love of his people. After all, that's what a true leader does.

He looked over to Red, and he could tell she was worried, but he reassured her that whatever was to come, they would face it together. He would show her how powerful she truly was.

Essie took a cup of tea from Red and turned her attention back to Killian. "There is only one problem to all of this, and she is your mother, Killian. What if we can't drive out the darkness that has completely taken over? Are you willing to sacrifice her for the greater good?"

Killian let out a deep breath and ran his fingers through his hair. He loved his mother deeply, but he had seen what she was capable of and what evil had filled her heart. She was no longer the mother he once knew, but he did have a plan of his own brewing, and he could only hope that Essie and Red would be on board. It was crucial for his theory to work. He closed the distance between him and Red, gently running a finger across her beautiful freckled face.

"There is only one way to save my mother. Essie? What drowns out the darkness so the evil can't take hold?"

She shook her head like she knew the answer but didn't want to say it. Kil could feel Essie's power rise, knowing she wasn't happy with the question he bestowed upon her. Was it a fair question to ask? Maybe not, but he knew there was no other way. He waited for Essie to answer the question.

His witch was pure of light, and the moon flowed through her veins. She was the only one capable of destroying the darkness. Would this put a strain on his and Essie's friendship? He wasn't sure, but he couldn't see any other way.

Essie's voice rising, his name filling the air, "Killian Seamus Raven, I have known you since you were a boy, and I know how much love is in your heart, but you do realize what you are asking me to do? I've always promised to protect her with my life. And she's not ready for what you're thinking of. With that being said, the answer to your question is that light drives out darkness."

Red looked back and forth between Killian and Essie like she was missing what they were actually saying. "I need you to teach Elena every spell of the light and how to manipulate and control it. She's going to need to know everything for this to work."

***

Out of everything being spoken Elena's mind stopped on his middle name, which was so rare that she was sure she had read it recently in Gran's notes that were squeezed into her grimoire. She had loved her Gran, still loved her, but she had to be the most disorganized person she had ever met. She used to tell Elena there was an organization to her method of chaos. Still, to this day, she couldn't figure it out, and that's where she was hoping Essie could now help.

Staring back and forth between her aunt and Killian, Elena definitely felt like she was not a part of the conversation taking place right in front of her. She was definitely the third wheel on the bike that was being peddled.

Hearing again that Killian's mother was going to be a problem made Elena have doubts about how she and Kil were going to be able to move forward. She already had a certainty that his mother would not approve of her. She would find too many faults in comparison to herself. Elena would never measure up, but...she wasn't letting go of Kil. She'd find a way to make this work and wouldn't allow Killian to lose his mother.

She knew he led his coven, but a child's mother was always their mother. Memories, emotions, and family, all powerful motivators, and she didn't want whatever was slowly transpiring now between herself, Essie's evolution back into Esmeralda and Killian, and her finding each other to be a malevolent story. She wanted to bring love and strength to his world.

Killian's touch and question, her brows furrowed, her palm finding his heart, a place it rested often in their short time together. Her gaze shifted to see the worried look across Essie's face, feeling an awakening in the air that surrounded them.

Moving from Killian's arm toward her aunt, confusion racing through her at what the two of them were sharing, exclusion still marring the cobwebs of her mind as she tried to piece it together.

At Killian's direction to teach her every spell of the light and how to manipulate and control it, a spark ignited. Turning to Killian, she said, "You're going to use me against your mother?" Then, her gaze finds her aunt, "Are you both crazy?"

***

Kil knew how strong his little witch was and how powerful she was. All he had to do was teach her exactly how to use the light of the moon to drive out the darkness that lived in his mother's heart. Once this was accomplished, he knew his beautiful Red would be unstoppable. Her aunt Essie was an elder witch who could help Red master her powers. The two of them working together could give Elena the confidence she needed.

"Red, I know this sounds insane, but I promise it will work. You are more powerful than you know. I believe between Essie teaching you all the ancient spells she knows, plus how to tap into your light source, and me teaching you how to control your fire, you will be a force of nature to reckon with."

Essie grabbed Red's hand and smiled. "I absolutely agree with Killian. You harness your mother's light, Elena. Her nickname was the moon goddess. I wish you had got to know her because you are the spitting image of her. There is something that I have been keeping from you, and I hope you can understand why I did this. First and foremost, it was for your safety, and secondly, it was for her safety as well."

Kil raised a brow, not knowing what Essie meant by protecting her as well. Essie walked over to the window and opened it. She made a clicking noise with her mouth, and Red looked at me like she was just as confused as I was. In moments, a white owl landed on the window sill. Red gasped, moving toward Kil.

"Elena, I didn't think you were ready to hear this, but I believe you are. Your Gran is still here with you. Just remember, when a witch dies, she is reborn either to Mother Earth, or she becomes a protector in the form of a familiar."

Red turned to her aunt, her brows furrowed together. She had no idea what Essie was hinting at, but Killian grinned, knowing exactly what her aunt meant. This had to be the best surprise she could ever receive. He just hoped her heart would understand. Elena wanted nothing more than to be with her family, and now her dream was coming true.

"My sweet niece, I realize this will be a lot to handle, but there will be no secrets between our family anymore. So it's time for you to meet your new familiar. My sister and your Gran live within this beautiful owl."

***

She might need a calming spell at the end of the evening, maybe something even stronger. First, finding out that Essie had transformed back into her aunt Esmeralda, knowing that she'd been with her on every step of her life, including after Gran's death? But now another witchery bombshell that Gran was still with them, still a part of their lives?

Elena's existence, up to a year ago, had been pretty tame for the most part. The last twelve months had made up for that, and the last couple had taken her on an out-of-control carnival ride. How all of this had been going on around her and she hadn't known? She must honestly be a failure as a witch in standing, no third-eye awareness, nothing.

Killian's words just made her shake her head, that Essie agreed, made her wonder what they saw that she didn't in herself. Yes, she could call and hold her fire, but only to a point. If she was under duress, she didn't know if she could be relied on.

She heard the beat of wings first, then her gaze touched on the owl that landed in the opened window, so regal, she thought. The creature's eyes finding hers and holding hers, Essie's voice weaving a web around them, as her words sunk in.

"Gran?" A breathless whisper as her footfalls moved on their own, a little closer, unsure as her mind was in the 'I-can't-believe-this' mode.

Her gaze went between her aunt and the owl. How could this be? Yet as she stepped closer her hand lifted to softly run her fingertips across the downy softness of the owl's chest, its gaze holding hers.

"Essie, how long has she been in this form and how long have you known?" Her palm now fully resting against its chest, its heartbeat steady and strong, a splash of a tear falling onto her outstretched arm, just then realizing she was crying.

***

Kil watched Red as his heart swelled with so much love. He knew how much she missed her Gran, and now he was here to witness such a special moment with his beautiful witch. Her family was here all along and had never really left her. They kept quiet to keep her safe, which any family member would do. Tears began to sting his eyes as Essie came closer and gripped his arm.

She produced a barely-there whisper so he could only hear. "This is all because of you, Killian. Thank you for bringing our family together again."

Family was everything to him, and he knew the importance of it. No matter what happens, family sticks together and always has each other. This was why he was fighting so hard to get his mother back because she was his mother and his father's other half but she was letting the darkness win. He turned to Essie as his tears fell and whispered back.

"Red, you and Gran are my family now too. We'll figure this all out."

Essie reached out and wiped the tears from Killian's face. "We will find a way to get your mother back. I promise Killian."

Kil smiled, turned his attention back to his witch, and stepped to her side. Essie walked over to the owl and stroked her feathers. "I think it's time, sister. Your granddaughter needs to hear your voice and know why we kept this from her."

The white owl's head dipping slightly in a nod, the link through their bond connecting so all could hear her <I am so sorry, Elena. I wanted to tell you many times but couldn't risk taking that chance. I knew it would only put you in more danger. The day Killian walked into the store was a blessing because he is your soulflame, and I have known it since the day you were born, and so did your mother. She had the same power as Killian. Although she held the moon's light inside her, she had the power of sight. A raven would visit you when you were a baby and were crying. We tried to soothe you, but it was only him that could. You were drawn to him. To keep him safe, Essie would erase his memories of you so his mother would not find out, but somehow, he would still find his way to you.>

Kil's jaw went slack, and his raven wrestled inside his mind like he was trying his best to remember those memories but couldn't grasp them. "Why would Essie erase those memories?"

Essie stepped closer to Kil and grabbed his hand into hers. "Killian, think about it. We are not allowed to mate with a human. It is forbidden! My sister fell in love with a human, and your mother gave her an ultimatum to either leave the love of her life or to never return as a sister witch or have the backing of the clan. Your mother loved my sister and was heartbroken that she chose a human over their friendship. She couldn't get past it. It turned her into a bitter woman, which allowed the darkness to thrive. We felt it best that your connection to Elena be hidden, to keep you both safe until the time came that fate decided it was time. And if she was going to take too long we would have nudged it along. Killian, we both know how much your mother means to you, and we will help you get her back."

Killian was lost for words, which was the first for him. His heart felt like it would explode from all the love it held inside. He pulled Red, Essie, and Gran in his arms, hugging them to his chest. He whispered, "I am blessed to have you all in my life, and I am thankful that I get to call you family."

27

Killian smiled as he sat back in the chair and listened to Red ask every question she could muster to her aunt Essie and her Gran. Life seemed to be coming full circle for his little witch; it made his heart swell with pride. Red had very quickly become the center of his world. He couldn't properly describe it just that it was. He could feel it within every fiber of his body and he would make sure nothing would ever harm her, even if it were his mother. He would find a way to bring his family and hers together. Killian and Red would rule his coven together, side by side.

Essie told Elena she had to be open to her powers to be able to hear Gran speak through her familiar form. Killian had been teaching Red to tap into her powers by simply meditating, quieting the mind long enough to concentrate, drawing powers inwards, making it easier to control.

Every passing day, Red was growing stronger and becoming the witch she was meant to be. Strong, fierce, and soon, she would hone in the light from the moon, and when the opportunity arose, she would drive out the evil that lies within his mother's heart.

Kil's body went stiff as a vision invaded his mind's eye. He saw his beautiful witch standing in the middle of a field picking lavender and his raven flying around her in circles. Kil smiled because his familiar loved her as much as he did.

In an instant, everything shifted. Dark clouds drew in, the very air around his witch, thick and heavy with malevolence. His mother stood behind Elena, holding a blade in her hand. Killian transformed into his human form as the blade struck downward and pierced into his chest. He shifted in enough time to save his witch from his mother's rage but not himself. He could feel his blood bubble in the back of his throat, and the only word he could manage to get out was "Why?"

Essie ran to Killian's side, trying to pull him back to the earth's realm. He was stuck in a vision, his body thrashing like he was trying to fight against something. Blood spilled from his lips, and Elena was shocked to silence for a moment but then shouting his name. She turned to where her Gran sat perched nearby with pleading eyes. Her Gran flew closer and began to screech at Essie.

"Elena, my sweet niece. You are the only one who can help Killian. He is trapped in his vision. You are the light that he needs to drown out the darkness that has him hostage. Speak his name over and over again until he answers you. I will light some white candles. Once you see him, wrap your arms around him and praise the Mother Moon to guide you home."

***

Her mind was like a hamster cage spinning out of control. Once Elena actually came to terms with the realization that Gran was alive and here in the room with her, not in human form, but as an owl, the questions started one after the other. It took her a moment to understand that she'd have to stop talking and listen through their link.

Killian had been helping her master her powers. It was slower going than she thought it would be. When they said 'practicing magick' they meant it. Magick is a lifelong student, never-ending.

Whereas before, Essie had been her familiar, now Gran was in the form of her white owl. So similar science, but different. Once she settled her excitement and opened the channel within herself, she was able to hear and communicate with her Gran. It had been over a year since she'd heard the familiar tone and tears did well and blur her vision, but the good kind.

Her sight, back-and-forth on Kil as she and Gran and Essie caught up. It would still take a few more discussions to get herself to rights, but just knowing her family was back together and all because of Killian made her love for him deepen.

Then it all changed. Like there was too much love and happiness and a long-forgotten spell decided that this was the moment to reappear and up end her world.

Killian's body seized, and by the look on his face, Elena knew he had been thrown into a vision. She also knew to leave him alone when that happened and not interfere. Until the sight in-front of her turned into a horror movie.

Blood spilled from his mouth like a waterfall, his body wracked by seizures, Essie beside him, her magick touching like pinpricks along Elena's skin. Something was bad, very bad, her tears turning to ones of fear and a cry escaped her lips.

Turning to Gran for help, Essie's words halted all her emotions. How could she possibly end this? She'd never walked into another's dreams or visions. But the severity written on her aunt's face and Elena did as asked, repeating Killian's name over and over, only stopping to draw in more air, her eyes affixed to her love, hoping he heard her and turned toward the sound of her voice.

***

Killian could hear his name being called, but his body was shaking so violently that he wasn't sure who was calling to him. His blood flowed like a raging waterfall and pooled at his feet. His mother had stabbed him and pulled the blade out of his chest to watch his knees buckle beneath him.

He gazed up at her, but what he saw was barely recognizable. Dark ink-like swirls of magick whipped around her as she commanded the darkness to leave Killian and come to her. Although she was an elder witch, she couldn't break through the walls of his magick. He grasped what strength he could and whispered a spell of protection around his beautiful witch and engulfed a ring of fire around her. There was no way in hell he would let anyone harm the woman he loved, even if that included his mother. Killian would gladly give up his life for Elena if it meant she would forever be safe.

His mother knelt in front of him and stared into his face. A loud cackle roared from her thin lips. "My precious boy, do you think I would ever allow you to be with a witch of light? You are destined for great things, my son, and Elena isn't even close to being your equal. So tonight, you will be reborn and forget all about your little so-called witch, Red."

In Killian's head, Bram shrieked in protest. No way in hell was he going to let this happen. His mother did not realize how deeply he loved Elena. She was his soulflame, making her more powerful than his mother could have imagined. Killian closed his eyes and heard his Red calling out to him. He saw what looked like the full moon shining brightly behind her and through quivering lips he mouthed "I love you, Red, with all of my heart and soul." Those were the last words she'd hear him speak as his body went limp, falling to the ground and landing in a pool of blood.

***

It wasn't working. She was calling and calling, begging him to hear her, turn her way. Panic had set up house in her body. Flames danced around in protection of her, a gift from Killian, but he shouldn't be using his magick on her, she had her own.

Words echoing and dancing in her mind as her heart bled out that she couldn't reach him, "Essie it's not working, why isn't it working?"

"Elena believe in your strength child. Trust in your magick. It will protect you both, but you must believe." Essie's own anxiousness ratcheted hers up.

"What if I hurt him? What if..." Elena's thoughts halted as he collapsed to the ground, a gore film in the making.

Kil had said she was his light, but the anger and fear ruling her body right now felt dark and dangerous, more rage than anything holy.

"Elena call to him and shine your inner light" her Gran's words were harsh in her mind.

Calling to her flame, she let it build hot in her chest, then a chant to the moon goddess to lend her power and strength. Elena threw open the floodgates, a burst of light thrust from her open hands, not red or orange hues as usual, but pure and bright, circling Kil where he lay, then rushing skyward, grasping and banishing any evil intentions, the cycle recurring as Elena called his name.

Had he moved? Wondering if wishing made it so. Her gaze swept him from head to foot while her magick poured over him, the shimmer from Essie's candles lighting a pathway.

She blinked and blinked again. His hand had moved. "Gran he moved!"

Elena dropped to her knees, her fingers latching on to his hand, tugging, his name a constant fall from her lips.

***

Killian would have taken a thousand swords to his heart if it meant to keep his beautiful witch safe, but never would he thought it would be from the one person that he loved so dearly. His mother stood over his body with soulless eyes. Kil tried to use his magick to no avail. His hand reached up to grab his mother's shirt, but she backed away laughing.

"My son will not be with a light witch! You hold dark, powerful magic inside you, Killian. She will not know what to do with it. She doesn't have what it takes to be your mate. I will not say this again. Let her go, and we will never discuss this again."

Killian couldn't believe what his mother was saying. She had no idea what Elena was capable of or of the power she held inside her; it was nothing like he had ever felt before. There was no way in hell he was going to give her up. If his mother wanted a fight, then that's what she would get. A smile slowly crept along his face as he heard his witch calling his name. She was his beacon of light that led the way out of this fucking nightmare.

"Do you see that mother? You don't have a fucking clue how powerful she is. She holds the power of the moon inside her, and one more thing I forgot to mention; she is my soulflame. You know what that means, so let me be clear; if you harm one hair on her beautiful head. I will show you no mercy."

Kil didn't wait for an answer as the knife dissolved away. He practically ran towards the light, knowing what awaited him on the other side. His beautiful Red's smiling face that he couldn't wait to kiss and tell her how much he loved her.

***

A few days had passed and slowly her angst was wearing off, but Elena knew she would never ever forget the sight of Killian in the throes of his vision or forget how cruel a mother he had. She couldn't for one moment understand how a mother could inflict harm on their own child. That thought keeping her awake some nights.

That Killian had actually felt her magick and heard her calling to him during his attack, gave her the resolve to practice as much as she could. She'd been able to help him even though she hadn't been quite sure what she'd been doing. She'd just followed the feel of her magick and let it guide her.

Both Kil and her aunt were finding time to spend with her or she would find some moments every day to either strengthen the control of her flame or meditate and listen to her body and emotions. The more in tune she was, the stronger she'd become; at least, that's what they kept telling her.

Elena loved him with everything that she was. When people spoke of true love this was what it must feel like. She would do or give him anything he needed to ensure his safety and happiness. And that's when the idea had popped into her head.

Ribbon of harmony, braid of love, weave and bind, strengthen our hearts, to forever find peace.

Topsy-turvy, that's what she would call it. So much had happened once their magicks had crossed. Inevitable, fate, whatever word you'd choose. The past being righted by the present.

Elena knew that oftentimes you had to be stripped, to go to basics, to bare your soul to find your strength. And she and Kil had taken one pummel after another.

But they were healing, Essie and Gran were back and they had a path moving forward, but a little magick couldn't hurt.

She'd arranged the crystals and candles in a triangular pattern, lighting them, setting her intentions within moments of meditation. Cradling the crystals in her hand, the spell chanted over and over until the power of her words amplified within the room. Selecting three strands of ribbon, tying one end together, then braiding and visualizing, peace, balance, and love, then knotting the ends.

Making two, one for each of them, wanting him to know that she always thought of him and wanted them together always.

He'd barely taken two steps into her home, which was more their home now, even though they hadn't gotten that far physically yet. "I have a gift for you, for us." showing him the harmony ribbon, her fingers finding his front pocket and placing it inside, hers already safely in her pocket. Then her lips found his, her body warming as it always did when he was near.

*****

He could tell she was excited about something, but that wasn't new to him. Elena could make washing the dishes fun, or maybe it was just that he was that happy to be with her, no matter what they were doing.

Recognizing the ribbon for what it was, that she'd thought of him in such a way, when her lips touched his, he pulled her in flush to his front. His mouth took control, the flick of his tongue across her lips and she opened, and he dove in. His tongue stroked along hers, a growl curling up from his throat at her taste. His hands slid down her body and cupped her ass, shifting his hips for the perfect friction; he was rock hard just from kissing her.

*****

She was drowning; that was the only word for it. Her body weakened by his lips and then more by the press of his cock against her stomach. But then something else stirred her. She felt it in the center of her chest, a soft unfurling. A pulse, then a flicker, then a glowing warmth.

Killian was calling to her magick. She didn't know how he was doing it, but she could feel it between her breasts, reaching out, looking for his, twining when they touched, then blooming and bursting.

Never had she felt anything like what was happening to her now. She gripped him tighter as their magick danced, rubbing against him, not wanting this to end. This was potent and drugging, and she never wanted it to stop.

28

Killian felt a slight pang of shame when he confessed his undying love to Red. He knew their circumstances were a little unorthodox and he'd kind of just blurted it out in front of Essie and Gran. He wasn't ashamed of his feelings. His love for Elena was pure of heart and he'd tell anyone proudly that he was hers and vice versa he knew for Elena. She loved him right back.

Still, as someone who had lived for close to a hundred years, he should have been more prepared since he knew where this had been heading. He knew before he'd met her. He'd already been spellbound by his beautiful redhead.

He had a romantic heart, and Kil was always extremely organized. But this whirlwind of events, once the goddess had begun, it had run at full speed.

He had a little bit of OCD when it came to things, especially putting them back where they belonged. However, his witch had him running around like a love-sick puppy. In all his years, no woman had ever held his heart, but the day Elena came into his life, she grabbed it with both hands and had no intention of giving it back.

Tonight, Killian was determined to make up for the lack of romance in the past. Earlier in the day, he had met with an old friend Morgana. She was an artist when it came to fabricating pieces of jewelry. Kil wanted Elena's ring to be special and unique. Just like his beautiful fiance. It was the first time he acknowledged it to himself, he loved how it sounded, fiance soon to be wife. If he had his way this was going to be the shortest engagement on record.

Killian hurried back home and gathered everything he needed with Essie's help. They had arranged everything outdoors in the forest behind the house, which was one of Red's favorite spots. Essie told him that Elena was going to love everything he had done for her. It was really simple; a blanket in the center of the clearing, candles of various sizes, lit and arranged near where he was planning to kneel, and him. He thought it looked beautiful and he knew how Elena loved the simpler little things.

"Killian, it's perfect. She's going to love it. I'm so proud of you and so happy to call you family."

Killian kissed her cheek, "Thank you Essie for everything." The moment rushing over him that his witch would be home soon. "Now to get myself ready."

He hurried to the house, taking a quick shower, and donning a suit; he wanted to look his very best for his little witch. Why he was nervous he wasn't sure but his hand shook slightly as he left a note for his Red on the bed along with a gift he'd bought for her, laying it out on the duvet.

[Meet me in the forest. I have something special for you.]

Everything was in place. His beloved was a simple woman who didn't like extravagant celebrations, which was one reason amongst so many why he loved her so much.

***

Today was her late day at Beliefs and it had been a long one but a good one. The hustle and bustle of the store always a few steps ahead of her, so that late morning had turned into afternoon, which had turned into dinner time. And not far from her thoughts, all day was Killian.

They'd fallen into a sort of routine. During the day they did their lives, her at the store and him at his coven. Sometimes they'd squeeze in a lunch but mostly evenings and some nights they'd spend together. They hadn't gone all the way yet but they couldn't keep each other's hands off the other either. It was just a matter of time. He was giving her the time she needed.

Pulling into her drive, Kil's car was already parked, she made her way in, the house quiet.

"Killian you upstairs babe?" Her footfalls taking her up to her bedroom, the scent of his shower present in the air, her eyes falling to the note on the bed [Meet me in the forest. I have something special for you.] her insides warming at thoughts of her warlock.

Wasting no time, Elena stripped down, pinning her hair up, jumping into the shower, erasing the busy of the day, then dawning on fresh underwear, then the slip of a dress he'd bought for her over that, she rushed down the stairs, stopping long enough to slide her feet into sandals, throwing open the backdoor and heading off down the path to the clearing.

How many times in her life had she taken these steps, run down this path, she couldn't count. But this time, she was running to her future.

And then she saw him and he saw her. The spark that always ignited at his nearness firing in her chest. He looked incredible in his suit, not understanding why so formal until he dropped to one knee, the setting of candles and the patchwork blanket that her Mama had made but was normally draped over the porch swing registering. Her breath rushing out in a gasp, his name whispered as his words filled the night.

"I wanted to do this the right way. I've told you before that you're mine, that I'm not letting you go. I knew before I met you that you were the one. Will you marry me, Elena Payne?" Her eyes dropped to the ring he held. Her vision clouded and she fell to her knees before him.

"My freckles, my fire, my heart, all of me, is yours. I give you my mornings, my nights and everything between. Yes, Killian Raven. I'll marry you."

He placed the ring on her finger, pulling her in his arms, his power a swirl of magick around them, lifting them off the ground, toes no longer touching, spinning them in a circle, "She said yes!" This woman made him the happiest man alive. "I vow to love you with everything I am for this life and into the next. We will face whatever life throws at us, together. You're my everything."

Wondering who he was telling, looking around to see if the woods hid prying eyes. Her gaze fell back to the depths of his, her world spinning, but she only had eyes for him. "I love you." Their feet back solid on the ground and their lips finding each other again.

Then apparently the woods did have ears, as shrieking from up above cast their eyes skyward to see Gran doing dips and dives in the sky, her gradual descent to the clearing and a nearby branch where she settled herself. Then, the yelling that came down the path that Elena had just used to get here herself. Essie ran faster than her feet allowed and Elena hoped she didn't fall face first.

"Congratulations you two," Her words were breathless as she flung herself into them. Hugs all around with squawking from overhead. Then Gran's voice connected with each of them - [I knew this day would come. I've known forever. I just didn't know when it would be. My children, you are our future. Be happy and love to the fullest.]

"I'll do my best, Matilda, for Elena and the coven." Killian's voice was emotional as his gaze shifted from where she perched in the tree back to Elena's.

"And I'll do the same for you." Elena's voice falling into the same emotional vortex as his.

"We need wine. And I have some ready because I knew there was only one outcome." Essie retrieving a basket that was hidden behind one of the large trees in the clearing. "Then we'll leave you two alone."

Flutes of aged crystal were filled for the three of them. Gran, on soft feathers, brought herself down closer "To the both of you" Essie joined one of Killian and Elena's hands together, placing hers on top. "From this day forward, you will never walk alone. This is the beginning of your always. To a forever of dark binding to light. To finding peace and love within the shelter of each other's arms. A covenant binding two souls. May you always find what you need in the other."

Glasses were raised and tears did fall, witnessed by Mother Earth and the Goddess up above.

29

She sent the text just after lunchtime. The morning had been beyond busy and even lunch was eaten on her feet. Was it the change of the coming season that had everyone looking for renewal and introspection? She and Sophie were mixing spells and potions one after the other, orders coming in by phone and online. To be fair, she may have fudged up a couple and had to start again because her mind and body were both distracted by one thing, Killian.

She didn't know if it was the full moon intensifying the cravings she had for her warlock, but she had dreamt hot, dirty things about him and her. She'd come to work with her nipples hard and her panties wet. She was going to text him that, but she wasn't that outgoing with her sensuality yet.

When they were alone, it was one thing, but what if someone saw the text. Just a thought and her blush rose up her neck and over her cheeks, her eyes lifting to catch the blue ones of Sophie, a questioning look on her face, and that blush turned full scarlet because she'd been caught, that all-knowing grin touching her friend's lips.

"You wanna share what caused that blush because I'm all ears." Sophie's brows doing that suggestive 'give-me-all-the-details' look.

"No, but I can show you the ring again." Her happiness overflowing and if there was a cloud nine, she was definitely walking on it today.

Sophie's smile was genuine. "He did so great. That ring is perfectly you."

And she was right. Killian had told her a friend had made it per his thoughts. The ring was simple. Not gold or silver but a liquid dark fire that seemed to have a life of its own. Killian had said the magick of the ages infused the ring. Elena loved it and that he'd created it for her touched her deeply.

They'd stayed in the clearing until close to midnight. The glow of the candles slowly diminishing one by one. She'd barely noticed, being wrapped up in her warlock's embrace, the heat of his kiss keeping her warm, small talk about this and that. But mostly just connecting with each other and the elements around them. Then, a slow walk back into the house where they'd crawled into bed and fell asleep nestled together.

Everything for her and Kil had been a tempest since they'd met. His position in his coven had to come first, and she understood that. She had her own obligations which were nothing like his, but this need had overpowered her today, to touch and hold him, so overwhelming, she knew it was time.

She wasn't experienced. What she knew she read in books or maybe overheard from some of the other witches her age in the coven. Elena wasn't very forward, so what she was planning was out of the box for her, but she knew she'd have to be the one to make the move.

Killian had told her there was no rush; when she was ready. But now it was like she couldn't get there fast enough. So, leaving Sophie to close up for the night, Elena headed home.

She had thought of a romantic dinner and candles, but she wouldn't be able to eat. Her need was too great. She just wanted to touch, kiss, and love on him, her fiancé. And oh my gosh that sounded so incredible to say that.

It had taken her longer to say that word, love, even to herself. But he was her light, her flame, and she needed him to know how much he meant to her. He'd been so patient with her, never pushing her farther than she wanted to go. But she was ready now. She wanted everything with him.

So she changed into something she had bought on a whim. Something that resembled the color of her hair and left nothing to the imagination. She lit jasmine and lavender throughout the house, the scent always stirring her.

Her bedroom took up half the second floor with two beautiful balcony doors that she opened, tiny garden lights strung overhead, giving off a low glimmer as the sun slowly set behind the giant trees that sprawled the woodlands behind her place.

On the bedside tables, a few tea lights glowed, her bed turned down and ready. The hunger became consuming and she hoped she could be everything he wanted and needed because he was already all that to her.

When had he struck a match and held it to her heart, enticing her flames to come out and play, she didn't know. His eyes full of desire, his soul full of fire, the burn euphoric. He was pieces of poetry and lyrics sung on a night deep in lust. He wasn't butterflies, he was wildfires. And her choice was to burn with him. She just needed him to show up.

***

Kil just finished meeting with the sister witches reassuring each of them that his mother would not interfere with the new order of his coven. No one would ever be considered an abomination; that was all in the past. He wanted them to know they would always be safe, reinforcing the wardings he had implemented over the last few weeks in case his mother wanted to test the waters.

And now his thoughts were just on Elena and her earlier text. He loved that she thought of him as much as he thought of her. Their connection was something beyond anything he had ever imagined.

Transforming into his raven, he flew to the place he called home. Kil had practically moved in with his beautiful witch, both just wanting to be with the other. His love for her was soul-deep, and he couldn't wait to spend the rest of his life with her.

Her bedroom window was halfway open, and his raven squawked; he could see the room was illuminated with candles, and his witch was sprawled on the bed in lingerie that matched her hair. Fuck she was the sexiest woman he had ever laid his eyes on. What a lucky man he was to call her his.

He flew through the window, returning to his human form. He stood before Elena completely naked, and his witch's heated stare traveled down his chest to his waist and stopped on his now throbbing cock. He ached to be inside of her, but he never pushed himself on her. He waited patiently until she was ready to make love with him.

They'd had nights of touching but tonight, seeing her waiting for him, tonight would be so much more. Tonight would be their first time together, and he would make sure it would be unforgettable.

He could taste her arousal in the night's air, a growl erupting from his chest. The flicker of the flames touched the fairness of her freckled skin. He never knew how dull his life had been without those sunkissed dots.

Her eyes held his as he took the few steps, his fingertips lightly running along the inside of her thigh, "I've never seen anything as beautiful. I love you so much Elena. I hope you're ready to be ruined." Because he wasn't going to leave any part of her unmarked.

He not so gently grabbed her thighs and pulled her to the edge of the bed. Her gasp jacked him up further, the wet spot on her lacy undies giving his cock a jerk.

"I'm going to try to be..." His words lost on him because he'd never lied to her. "Fuck. I'm wound so tight. You tell me if you need me to slow or stop.

I will. But right now, my mouth needs to be somewhere. First here," Bending to take her lips in a scorching kiss, his tongue delving deeply, hers meeting his. Shifting back on his heels to gaze into the auburn depths of hers, seeing her need blaze up at him, "And now here."

His head dipping, a slow drag of his tongue from her belly button to the top of her panties, his blue hues capturing hers where she watched his descent, then moving lower, his tongue a soft touch of the soaked fabric between her legs.

Holy hell, he wasn't going to be able to go slow. Not after that faint taste sliding through his mouth and down his throat. She was the sweetest ambrosia and he wanted to drown in her.

His fingers slowly found the edge of her panties and pulled them downward. Her little gasps made his cock jerk in anticipation. Kil wanted to be buried balls deep inside her, but he needed to feast on her peach first.

He pushed her legs back, her delicate flower dripping her want down onto the sheet. His tongue traced along her petals, making her moan out his name. Her hips arched at each swipe. His thumb found her sweet spot, rubbing her clit as he lapped up her sweet nectar. His Red tasted like wildfire and he knew he'd never get enough of her.

"That's my good girl. Look how wet you're getting for me. Tell me, are you ready for me to fuck you until you're a puddle beneath me?"

He liked to be vocal. He wanted her to know without a shadow of a doubt what she did to him and what he wanted to do to her.

***

She heard the beat of wings, her head turning to the open doors. Ebony appendages larger than any she'd ever seen, their flutter soon shifting to the man she knew. It was so surreal to see that transformation before her eyes. He was magnificent in any shape. But right now before her, the flicker of candlelight's touching on every defined muscle including the one between his legs, her gaze lifted to see the same need staring back at her.

It was like a shroud was placed over them and at his first touch, her body had softened, and where she was wet before with just thoughts of him, she was now soaked.

"Don't be gentle. I want everything you want babe."

His touch and pull told her she was with another Kil tonight. Their nights of touching and stroking were all preamble to this; tonight was something different. He was just so much more, his lightness had disappeared, his touch firmer, his own scent muskier.

At the bend of his head and the pull of her panties, her mouth dropped open because she knew where he was heading. She'd dreamed about this and he wasted no time. Her legs pushed back, her pussy open and ready, and at the first swipe of his tongue, his name fell from her lips, the fire in her chest surging, the room taking on a heated charge.

Then his thumb found her clit and her hips begged for more, both of her hands skimming across her stomach and moving upward, finding her nipples and squeezing tightly, knowing she wasn't going to last, not with him and not like this.

His voice dragged her gaze to his, his lips wet from her, his words barely spoken, a whisper of a "Yes" falling from her lips, when another touch to her clit and she screamed, her legs locking around his head, her orgasm ripping through her.

***

Her legs were a vice; her screams the most precious gift. His tongue lapped up every single drop spilling from her cunt, a delicious honey he was going to crave daily. He was addicted with one taste. He could feast on her forever, her legs slowly unlocking, his name on repeat from her beautiful mouth.

Killian wanted more, and the need to be inside her was a primal drive. He didn't want to rush her or to seem greedy, but he dreamed about how she would feel on his cock.

Kil wasn't a man to boast about his size, but Elena was small, and he didn't want to cause her any pain. But he couldn't wait.

Leaning forward, grabbing the base of his cock in his hand, he slowly swiped the head through her folds. Up and down, passing over her clit, then pushing slightly inward, coating himself in her honey.

His gaze lifting from where he held himself, up to her beautiful face - "Do you feel me baby?" he said while holding her gaze, he pressed a little deeper, her hips lifting, pushing him in further. "Fuck Elena, you're so hot and tight. Like being wrapped in a hot flame."

Holding himself there, he leaned forward a little more, his teeth teasing a nipple through her bra. Her strangled cry and another arch of her hips and he sunk deeper.

He wasn't going to survive. Everything inside him wanted to slam home. Rip her innocence and claim what would only ever be his.

"Killian, I need more please. Move. Do something." her hands lifted, her nails found his back.

And he pushed past her barrier until all of his thickness was buried inside her tightness. Then he pulled back and drove in again, over and over. His mouth lifted from her breast to find her lips, her walls clamping down on him, milking him for all he was worth. He moaned her name and kissed her hard, taking her every breath. Her hips became frantic against him, meeting his every thrust.

Then she shifted his world by rolling him onto his back, straddling his waist, and rotating her hips in a motion that must be illegal. His grunt and groan filled the air, the pleasure unlike anything he'd ever experienced.

Her head tipped on her shoulders, the fire of her hair falling down her back and touching the tips of his thighs. The visual would stay with him forever, his balls tightening to near painful. He knew at any moment he would lose the battle he desperately was trying to hold back. He wanted them to lose control of euphoria together.

***

Through the cloud of eroticism that hung over them, she slowly drifted back to the now. Killian had licked her through her climax, let her have every moment of pleasure and basked in it. His face now just above hers as he slowly fed his cock into her tight embrace.

The pressure was such a good bad, spreading her wide, a burn at the tear, but the pleasure creeping through her took the edge off the deeper he entered her until he buried himself to the hilt. Her hips lifted and met each one of his thrusts, her fire a slow and growing roar within her; she was burning up. She didn't know if he could feel it, but it was like crashing waves, building and building.

The bite at her nipple pulled something out of her, and she grabbed Kil pulling him closer, then turned them, so she was looking down on him, the flare in his gaze causing the true redhead to emerge.

Her hips lifted, then slid back down his length, hitting her in that spot that spiraled her flame higher. Her head tipped back and she rode him, her hands greedy on his chest, her own fingertips, finding his nipples, and giving a hard squeeze.

The first ripple caught her off guard, the second following quickly, and then combustion. Her pussy clamping down on him and heat scorched her through her clit up into her chest, her nails an attack against his skin, and she lost the ability to breathe, just riding out the orgasm, waiting for the afterglow.

***

His name left her sweet lips and he felt her orgasm drench his cock as he pumped his seed deep within her womb. Their bodies were coated in sweat as they rode the wave of ecstasy together. Red collapsed on his chest, his arms wrapped around her while they tried to catch their breath.

He slowly rolled them on their side, his cock still deep inside her as they drifted off to sleep. He couldn't have asked for something more perfect than this night they shared. Red was made for him and her body was utter perfection. His witch had him completely under her spell and that's where he would forever stay.

30

Killian gathered the sister witches, excitement a heady mixture in his veins, but he just couldn't wait. Revealing he'd proposed to Elena, she'd said yes and that she'd be joining their coven, their happiness so genuine for him.

Eager to share his thrilling news, he was bursting with anticipation to disclose it to his younger brother, Keegan, and his dearest confidante, Iris. Following the meeting, he revved up his engine and raced over to Keegan's home, where he spilled the beans with a contagious enthusiasm that lit up the room. Their joy was palpable, filling the air with infectious excitement. With his inner circle now in the loop, the next milestone awaiting him was to reveal the news to his parents,

Killian knew Elena would have to discuss her engagement with her own coven, the Divine Spirit. He knew she really didn't feel at home with them, but he would be there to offer his support when and if she needed it. His own Raven coven was a much more powerful coven with ties all around the world. He was proud of how his coven had grown. How diverse the witches' powers were, offering those a real home, building trust and security for everyone under his care.

Thirteen was a number he didn't adhere to. All were welcome. He was bringing in a new era of witching.

Killian was having a private introduction to his family a bit later in the day, one he knew Elena was a bit nervous about, considering how unsettled things were with his mother. But again, he'd be there, supporting her, standing beside her.

And that's where he found himself a short while later, standing, his gaze on her in a stunning emerald green dress, nervously fidgeting with her hair. She was about to meet her fiance's family for the first time, and the thought made her anxious. Killian was confident that his father would be charmed by her immediately. How could he not be? Elena was perfect in every way.

His only worry was his mother, but Killian had a plan in place. His hope was that his little witch would be the light he needed to cast away his mother's darkness.

Essie had also agreed to come along despite her reluctance to shift back into her cat form. However, if it meant keeping her niece safe, she was willing to make that sacrifice. Essie was apprehensive about Killian's mother finding out she was still alive, but for now, Killian had the upper hand, and Essie was determined to keep it that way.

Killian embraced Elena and planted a gentle kiss on her forehead. "You look absolutely stunning, Red," he said reassuringly. "Don't worry, I promise nothing unfortunate will occur tonight. Essie and I have already cast protection spells, and Keegan has done the same. And now, let me show you a neat little trick."

As Essie clutched to Kil's pant leg in her cat form, he started chanting an ancient spell she knew very well. This was one of her favorite spells, especially when escaping from one realm to another. Suddenly, the door flew open, and Elena gasped in surprise. Kil took her hand in his and led her through the door.

"Welcome to Raven Estates, my love."

***

She knew she'd have to meet his family eventually, eventually being the key word. Killian's surprise of their engagement, especially since they hadn't known each other that long, had barely dimmed when he dropped the big one on her. "I gathered the coven and told them we're engaged." All the breath in her lungs expelled at that one sentence. Elena hadn't expected things to move so quickly. In all honesty, she hadn't really thought that far ahead, she was still basking in the glow of their night in the woods, and how magical he had made such a special moment.

Killian knew she wasn't into the over-the-top extravaganza stuff, she was simple and down to earth. And maybe naïve. She'd avoided a lot of interaction and socializing with her own coven because she always felt like she didn't measure up.

When Gran was alive, it was different; everyone held great respect for her. But since her death, it had all changed. Gran was back with them now in the form of her owl familiar but that was a secret at this time until they all decided how to move forward.

Elena had stood within her small walk-in closet, her selection of dresses she was sure not on the grand scale that Killian's coven would be used to. She just knew she couldn't meet them being something she wasn't. If their union was going to pose a problem, she wanted to know right off. So she selected the green gown that had been a gift from her Gran at her graduation.

Elena remembered saying that how could a redhead wear green. And Gran had given her a mischievous smile and said; a redhead can wear anything she wants.

Did the jitters rise and play a bit of havoc? Yeah, they did, but Kil was there to reassure her and be by her side. That Essie had agreed to shift back to feline form and support them both added a bit more flutters. Her aunt's life had forever been altered due to coven jealousies. So Elena had performed a protection spell before getting dressed, because any little bit helped. Those four words -so mote it be- still resounding in her head.

At Killian's touch and kiss her hands lifted, touching him and grounding herself, the movement of Essie at his feet, adding a layer of completeness.

Then his magical trick had a gasp fall from her as a door opened in their living room, his powers always leaving her in awe and questioning why he would choose her.

Their fingers entwined, she took the steps by his side that led them to his coven and her new future. Her earlier gasp was nothing compared to the one that left her lips at the first sight of Raven Estates. Her head turned to see Killian's gaze already on her.

"Killian, who are you?"

***

Killian grinned wide from the question Red asked of him. Who was he? A powerful Warlock whose magick was still evolving. Something he had worked hard for. He didn't see the world through hooded eyes. Killian believed in trust and loyalty and, most notably, protecting the ones he loved.

Tonight was about introducing his beautiful fiance to his family. He wanted them to love her as much as he did. How could they not? She was kind, caring, and loving. Red fought for what she wanted and loved her family immensely. She had the same values in life as he did. Another reason why he loved her so much.

As they crossed the threshold of Raven Manor, Killian tenderly clasped Red's hand, leading her into the familiar embrace of the home where he and his brother had forged countless memories. Despite its decor of rich dark reds, mysterious blacks, and subtle shades of gray, the manor exuded a warmth and welcoming aura that enveloped them both. Killian had always found solace in its unique charm, and he hoped that the cozy ambiance would soothe Red's frayed nerves, casting a comforting spell over her as they ventured further into the enigmatic depths of the manor.

As they ventured further in, Keegan and Iris emerged as the first to greet them, playfully engaging in their usual brotherly banter. Keegan couldn't resist teasing his brother, delivering a friendly punch to his arm, while Kil retaliated by ruffling Keegan's perfectly groomed hair, disrupting his meticulous morning routine that often involved admiring his reflection in the mirror.

Meanwhile, Iris enveloped Elena in a heartfelt hug, her warm words dripping with genuine joy and affection. "It's wonderful to see you again, Elena. Congratulations on the engagement! I couldn't be happier for both of you. Kil truly deserves all the happiness in the world. You've chosen a remarkable man." The genuine warmth in Iris's words resonated throughout the room, solidifying the bond between the newly engaged couple and their cherished friends and family.

Elena thanked them both as Kil whispered against her ear. "The answer to your question earlier. Who am I? The answer is simple. I am yours."

***

Her heart felt like it had grown too large for the confines of her chest. Stepping through the magical doorway, Kil had created and into Raven Manor was possibly the most overwhelming, awe-struck moment of her life. It was kind of an Alice in Wonderland meets Cinderella.

Elena had never been to anything like this before. Her eyes widened in wonderment, trying to absorb everything she saw. She and Kil were from two very different worlds, and it was definitely brought to her attention as she stood there beside him. The overall grandeur of the place was on an entirely higher level than her coven.

A bit of self-doubt taking a slow creep into her thoughts until Killian's voice broke them apart "I'm yours" her gaze lifting to his, the love she had for him, answered in his own gaze.

"You are that, but you are also so much more. So how about you show me where you grew up."

At first glance, it had taken her breath away, but now that she'd settled herself and her hand had gripped Kil's a bit tighter, to realized he had matched her effort. He wasn't letting go. He somehow knew without words that she needed his touch.

She hoped freckles weren't all his family saw today. She knew she was more than decorated by them. She'd grown up being teased about them by girls and boys, both in school and the coven. She'd grown into them though, they suited her. Gran had always said she walked around with constellations upon her skin.

Her Gran had been her best friend. Had helped her get through the loss of her mother, taught her the craft in her unorthodox way, and never pushed her one way, or the other about their own coven.

And now she knew why. Her Gran had known her element was fire, even when she herself hadn't. Gran had an idea of where that power could lead her, she had let it and Elena evolve in its own time.

Elena had her family in her aunt and Gran, like Killian had his. The question now was, how would they blend and would his mother allow it. She needed to be the woman he deserved. He said he was her fiancé, but he really was so much more than that. He was a leader, a ruler, and when they married, she would rise as well.

Was she out of her element? Definitely, but she was fire and a redhead, and if her aunt was right, part of the moon.

In a moment filled with warmth and gratitude, Elena embraced Iris tenderly, finding solace in the presence of familiar faces that eased her nerves. "Thank you, Iris. I feel truly fortunate to have found Kilian. He is an exceptional man, and I vow to always cherish him, bringing happiness to his life every day. I promise to love him for the rest of my days," Elena expressed earnestly, her words carrying a heartfelt commitment that resonated throughout the room, enveloping them all in a sense of shared joy and anticipation for the future.

<h1 style="text-align:center">31</h1>

Killian held no doubt that his brother and wife would quickly come to adore his enchanting little witch. How could they resist? Elena exuded a rare blend of kindness, love, and care that rendered her nothing short of perfect in his eyes. The warmth that surged through his heart as he witnessed Keegan and Iris warmly embracing Elena filled him with profound gratitude. Their instant acceptance of Elena sparked a flicker of hope within him, a hope that she would forge a deep and lasting friendship with them, weaving a tapestry of shared laughter, love, and support that would enrich all their lives in the days to come.

Keegan leaned in towards his brother, his voice barely above a whisper. "I know Dad is thrilled about meeting Elena, but when it comes to Mom, we both recognize she's not the same person we grew up with. If she stirs up any trouble, Dad said he's ready to ask her to leave." The unspoken understanding between the brothers hung in the air, a silent acknowledgment of the complexities within their family dynamics and a shared commitment to protect the newfound happiness that Elena had brought into their lives.

Iris patted Killian on the back. "Let's get ready to rumble!" she laughed. Killian and Keegan joined in with her laughter. Iris knew how to cut to the chase and make humor out of anything.

Elena blushed as they walked towards the dining room table. Killian's father pulled out a chair for Elena to sit beside him. She looked at Kil with pleading eyes. He smiled and took a seat on the left side of her. Killian's father sat on her right side. His father was such a wonderful man that he hoped Elena would love him as much as he did.

"It's nice to meet you, Elena. My son has told me such wonderful things about you. It makes my heart happy that he has found his other half."

Kil gently squeezed Elena's inner thigh. He couldn't be happier with how things were going so far. He didn't have any doubts about his family not loving his witch as he did. His brother and father were always supportive when it came to him. The only unease he had was his mother.

He was about to ask his father where his mother was when she walked into the dining room with a man and a woman flanking her side. Killian could feel his fire ignite as his anger rose to the surface. The man he knew all too well, and he couldn't believe his mother would bring Damien, the god of monsters, to his family dinner. Who the fuck was the woman, and why was she here?

"Mother, what the fuck is he doing here, and who the hell is she?"

***

Elena wanted to think of another word besides overwhelmed, but she couldn't grasp another at this time. Between the manor and its grandeur, she was definitely that word. But on the good side, her nerves had finally settled down enough that she wasn't shaking, especially since Killian had stayed by her side.

Everything here was on the grandiose side of life. Elena had not been raised with all this. Her gaze shifted to Killian while the three of them spoke, and the true bond they all shared was so tangible, her heart loving him even more in that moment for giving her this extended family.

His head turned as if he knew she was staring, that instant excitement she always felt leaping to life. He gently squeezed her fingers and she followed him and the others, as they headed toward a large dinner table set with more plates and cutlery than Elena had ever seen. And to add to that, Killian's father, their likeness giving it away, his gentle timber easing her a bit more as she sat down between father and son.

And Killian stayed with her the whole time. If this event wasn't so important, she'd ask to be excused and drag him behind the nearest door and have her wicked way with him. But that would have to wait.

So in tune with his emotions, she knew the instant the room changed. Looking up to see what had to be his mother making her entrance, accompanied by two others and her nerves rose at the imposing group they made.

It was Killian's anger that surprised her though. It was instant, and she could sense the shift in him, her hand falling onto his leg under the table, giving him a gentle touch. Her gaze lifted to the others at the table, and then back to his mother. It seemed everyone was waiting for an answer to Killian's questions.

***

"Damien, please for me. Would you go see what's going on? She asked for you specifically."

Damien slammed the phone down, nearly shattering it into pieces. He didn't like meddling in anyone's business, especially family business, but his mother had a way of wrangling him in. She laid the guilt trip on so damn thick it was almost impossible to breathe.

Black magic was temperamental all on its own, but adding greed seems to feed the darkness even more. It often consumes the host entirely and destroys the person they once were. The only source to beat such powerful magic is a pure light source. One that is born of it.

Damien knew his aunt had been dancing with the devil lately, as per all the gossip that made its way to him, but she didn't realize that there is always a price to pay, which often ends with death.

He arrived at his aunt's home, not really knowing what it was she wanted of him. He wasn't necessarily welcome here for the most part. Knocking on the main door, his aunt greeted him personally, so that should have tipped him off. His aunt didn't answer the door. Top that off with a smile that would put fear into a hyena. What the hell was she up to? She tugged on his arm, pulling him into the house, explaining that she needed him to see if Elena, Killian's new plaything, was born of pure light, and if she was, whether or not he would help kill her.

Damien was a complete asshole; you could ask anyone and they'd tell you that, but this? What the hell was going on with his aunt. He needed to see firsthand what was going on in his cousin's coven for himself and his own mother. He agreed that he would see if Elena was of light or if she wasn't; all the time wondering what the hell was going on here.

Following his aunt into an adjoining room, he came face to face with Killian. He and Kil never got along; tonight would be no different.

"Come on, Killian. Is that how you talk to your favorite cousin?"

***

She had not, not, adding in a big huff, wanted to be here. But the problem was the sketchy group of people she ran with. It was like dominoes. You owed one, and then the one became two, and so on, until the column with the owing was longer than the column that owed you.

So the phone call earlier in the day, that asked for a meet turned into more of a hijacking. But when Donovan Caine said 'come' you came.

For the most part, he'd always been decent to her, fair if that word even existed in his vocabulary. Sadie thought it was maybe that she might slightly, on a very low scale, frighten him.

She knew he was a bad guy. Correction, everyone did if you lived on the West Coast of the States. He was THE drug lord if you were into that which she wasn't, but he had helped her one random morning and she had taken the bait.

The unexpected part was her talent. She'd saved his life indirectly after touching a bag he gave to her to deliver for him. The trace of ugliness had sent her into a mild seizure right there in front of him. Sadie didn't know how to explain that to him, just that she sometimes had visions.

"You can tell the future, ma petite?" Her gut had done a dive because she couldn't control it and she didn't want others to know.

"No, it's very random and not always right."

But in this case, it had been, and she'd been pulled in a little deeper, given more money, a better place to live, all for her loyalty to him. If he found out that she just gave him little bits to stay in his good graces, enough that he wouldn't suspect, her life might end.

"I need a favor from you. You'll be well rewarded. I have a friend who wishes you to touch a book she has. I would consider it a trust of faith if you'd go, Sadie. Antoine can drive you."

And he wasn't asking.

And here she was at Raven Manor, where she didn't want to be, surrounded by people that weren't fully human, if that little show she'd witnessed a few minutes ago by the woman Rissa, she was sent to see was anything to go by.

And then she said to follow her, so what choice did she have. Unsure who the large male was that joined them, but Sadie wanted to be anywhere but here, especially as one doorway opened, leading them into a much larger venue where others seemed to be waiting.

She needed to leave, like right now. Her eyes scanning for an exit, when one of the men at the table stood, anger clearly visible as he asked his mother what the hell she was up to which included her and the other tall one next to her. This was bad, she felt it. Why did this always happen to her?

32

$\mathfrak{K}$eegan couldn't believe how low his mother had stooped to bring Damien to a family dinner, especially to celebrate his brother's engagement. His mother knew Damien and Kil never got along, so why on earth would she decide to invite him tonight of all nights? What the hell was her agenda, and who the hell was little Miss Blondie? She wasn't even family.

"Mother, what in the world is going on here? Why would you invite Damien here tonight, knowing that it is a night of celebration for Kil? How could you do that to him?"

He watched his mother pin Elena with her eyes and tap her black nails against the table. Keegan shook his head, he knew Kil was getting ready to lose his shit. He could feel his power surging in the room making the hairs on the back of his neck stand straight up. Damien crossed his arms, waiting for his aunt to answer the question.

***

Rissa narrowed her eyes at Killian. Did he think he could bring his witch into their coven and she would not be suspicious of who Elena was or what she truly wanted with her son? One, she didn't play games. Two, she knew Elena's grandmother very well, hell they were best friends and what did she do? She fucking betrayed her and the sister witches. Why? Because she fell in love with a pathetic human. That alone was treason!

Damien was essential to this little gathering; his powers were like no other, plus he had the ability to know when someone wasn't telling the truth. So little Miss Goodie Two Shoes couldn't get away with her silver tongue like her grandmother had. Rissa didn't care if her son was angry with her, his protection was paramount.

"Killian, do you think for one minute that what I am doing isn't for your protection? You are my son and the elder Warlock of our Coven. I will not let a pretty face walk in here and try to take that away from you. I know the bloodline that she comes from. Her grandmother was my best friend, and she committed treason against her own coven! Damien is here for one reason: to ensure your witch speaks the truth." Then her gaze shifted to her left "and Sadie is a little extra insurance."

***

Kaden couldn't believe the words that came out of his wife's mouth. He noticed a change in her, but this was beyond anything he ever witnessed when it came to her. The woman before him was cold like ice, and her words dripped with disdain.

Rissa and Kaden had met at the tender age of sixteen, and it was love at first sight. Five years later, they got married and spent every day together. A year later, Killian was born. Kaden couldn't have asked for a better mother for his son. His wife was always happy, and she spent all her time with their son. Two years later, Keegan was born. Their life couldn't be any better. To see her now made his heart sad. He didn't understand why she had become so harsh and paranoid.

He slammed his fist hard against the dining room table. His magick wrapped around his wife, pulling the air from her lungs. It broke his heart to do this, but he had no choice but to remind her of her place. Kaden didn't blame Elena if she wanted to run and never come back. He was so embarrassed by his wife's behavior that he wanted to disappear in the shadows.

"Rissa, I will not tolerate your behavior any longer. I have no idea what has gotten into you, but you will stop this nonsense right fucking now. You will remember your place, Rissa! Tonight is about our son's happiness, not about your agenda. Elena has nothing to do with her grandmother's actions, and she will not be judged for them. So what? She fell in love with a human. The heart wants what the heart wants. You are the only one that had an issue with it. No one else did. You are the one who drove your best friend away, and I will not allow you to do that to our son. Damien, I am sorry she brought you into this; I need you to leave. Sadie, it would be best if you went as well. Whatever she has asked of you, please don't do it. Again, I am sorry she dragged you two into our family affairs."

If she could have casually backstepped quietly out of the room, she would have. But there was nowhere to go amidst this family feud. When she did get out of there, she was going to ask Donovan not to peddle her out again. Thinking that Sadie knew it was stupid of her to request that from him, but this wasn't the first time she'd been put in an unstable position.

And being privy to all these details wasn't good either. Knowing too much got you in trouble or in someone's debt or their bad books, she was sure she could think of more.

Looking about, Sadie caught the stare of the other brother on her. His look 100% unwelcoming, and if he would have offered to escort her out, she would gladly have accepted but no it didn't happen.

What did happen was more dirty laundry being thrown about and from what she could tell the family gathering was going to take a nosedive.

At the mention of Damien, Sadie realized they were talking about the big moose that had walked out with her and Rissa, the mom and troublemaker of the group.

So just great for everyone to see her in the same boat. And that it was an important day for her other son, who was the head of the coven. Was it possible the floor would just open and swallow her?

The loud bang that rends the air brought her head back round to the father of the group, her name being spoken. This was getting more tense as the minutes passed by.

The pleading in his voice towards her and Damien not to be involved in whatever his wife had planned hit her in the heart, and she spoke before she realized she had.

"I was asked to find out whether Elena's intentions were honorable"- her gaze finding the angry ones of the redhead. "I didn't realize what was happening until a few minutes ago. I shouldn't be here. This has nothing to do with me and I'm fine to go just point me in the right direction."

***

There was a rabbit hole somewhere or an ulterior dimension of some kind, Elena was sure of it. How this had changed in such a short span of time, she didn't know. She knew Killian's mother had issues, but never had she expected this outright attack or the underhanded methods that she had obviously sunk to.

Her Gran had raised her to be humble and kind; she truly didn't have a malevolent bone in her body. But maybe she had just grown one because as Killian's mother spoke about her and her Gran, she could feel an unfamiliar rage slowly stoking within her. And it was white hot.

How could someone that had raised such a wonderful son as Kil and obviously Keegan be this horrible a person. She hadn't even given Elena a chance. She'd condemned her without so much as a 'how do you do'.

Elena knew most of what had transpired with the sister witches from Kil and Essie. Oh my gosh Essie! She had come with them, looking left and right but not seeing her.

The bang spun her around to see Killian's father, overwhelmed in his own disbelief. His words trying to reach the woman he married. His pain evident that she had ruined what should be the happiest of moments for their son.

Elena had almost forgotten about the other two, she was so focused on feeling Killian next to her and watching his mother. She didn't fully know if Damien or this Sadie girl knew what was expected of them, but they were standing on the wrong side of the table. They were standing with Rissa.

Like that day in the forest, Elena hadn't realized how her element had built. It had gone from small embers to an inferno, setting everything around her ablaze.

Voices around her slowly faded away, the comforting warmth of her heat, soothing. Her only thought how could Rissa do this to them.

***

All jokes aside, Damien didn't realize how deep his aunt had slipped into the darkness. Indeed, his family practiced dark magic, including him, but his dedication was more to his uncle Kaden; he was of blood. Damien knew how much his uncle loved Rissa, so he would also protect her.

Damien could see the hurt in his uncle's eyes; hell, he could hear it in his voice. How could she do this to him and her son? Even he could see that Elena was true to her word and loved Killian.

Killian and he always had a little rivalry between them, but he did want his cousin happy. Damien was a softy, but outside his family and friends, he didn't want anyone to know that. He would talk with Sadie, who looked like she was looking for a place to escape and explain what was going on. He didn't want her to think wrong of the rest of his family.

He turned to face his aunt, "What you have done today is inexcusable. I might be an asshole, but Killian is your son. You are sworn to protect him and love him as his mother. Not to humiliate him in front of his future wife. I should strip you of your powers right now, but I will leave that up to your husband."

***

How could she be so cold towards Killian? He is her son. Essie wanted to come out of her hiding place and bitch slap her. Did Rissa not see that Elena truly loved him and they were soulflames. Kil had the kindest soul and was a fantastic elder Warlock. Why wasn't Rissa proud of her son?

It saddened Essie, and there was a time when she remembered how sweet and loving Rissa was. She didn't have a mean bone in her body, and her love for her husband was undeniable. Rissa would light up like a candle every time Kaden would walk into a room. Their love for each other was envious of others.

When she gave birth to Killian, she was a doting mother. She took him everywhere with her, and she would gush over milestones he made. Then, when Keegan came along, she was the same as him. She did not falter her love for her boys.

Whatever happened to her to cause her to act this way, they all had to find a way to get her back for Kil and Keegan's sake.

Essie felt Elena's flame take flight, her anger very apparent. She would protect Killian even if it meant from his mother.

Manifesting from her cat form to her human self, she stayed hidden, at least for now. Why add more drama to the shit pile. Essie released her powers and siphoned her niece's fire before they could emerge and damage could be done. Essie knew Elena would not want to cause any harm to Killian's home or damage the family dynamics anymore.

***

Kil's jaw almost hit the floor when his cousin, Damien, took his side regarding his mother's outrageous behavior. Kil hated to admit it, but maybe Damien wasn't so bad after all and stripping his mother from her powers until they could get to the root of the problem was the best resolution.

Somehow, he would make this up to his beautiful witch. He had hoped that his mother would be at least decent and be happy for him. Never would he have thought she would have ambushed her like that. Elena gave her no reason to make her believe she was anything but what she said she was. Just because things went wrong with Elena's Gran, she didn't have to blame Red.

Kil kissed Elena and turned his attention back to his mother - "I have no idea what has gotten into you Mother, but I will no longer tolerate it. You took what was supposed to be one of the happiest nights of my life and completely destroyed it. I was hoping you would put whatever vendetta you had with Elena's family aside and get to know her. You would see for yourself how extraordinary she is. She is nothing but kind and loving. Elena doesn't have a mean bone in her body. So I have no other choice but to bind you! You will be completely stripped of your dominant powers. I bind you to me!"

Killian waved his arms, drawing the air in the room towards him. His mother fell to her knees, screaming out his name. Pieces of her raven-colored hair attached itself to Killian's flesh. He chanted a binding spell over and over again. "Your eyes I will see through, your ears I will listen from. I bind your soul to mine. There will be nowhere to hide, no place that will be unseen. Your powers are mine to will."

Rissa looked up at Killian, "You can't do this to me. I am your mother. I will make you all pay for this betrayal."

Kil's heart sank; he didn't want to do this, but she left him no choice. She was a threat to herself and her family. "The woman I see before me isn't my mother. My mother is loving and caring; she would have never done what you did to me tonight. I don't know who or what has convinced you to allow the darkness to take hold, but I will vow that whoever it may be will be punishable by death."

33

They had stepped back through the doorway Killian had created with his powers, leaving his coven and family behind...for now, those last two words weighed heavy on her. Hurt, anger, grief all just clouding her head.

She had woken up so happy this morning, nervous but otherwise happy. She should, by all rights, be celebrating her engagement to Killian with his family.

But in a few moments of time, everything had disappeared as her element started to bleed out around her, drowning out her hurt, replacing it with power. Until Essie had siphoned it away, saving her from herself and setting the room ablaze, leaving her standing raw again and exposed.

What if she wasn't the girl for Kil? What if she didn't have the backbone he needed to be his wife.

He had stepped forward, not his father, but himself to bind his mother's powers, to stop the tirade and the ugliness she was throwing over them and the coven.

What kind of mother did that to their child? Elena could never imagine treating another person like Rissa had just done to her own family. She had no idea how this would now unfold. How could their lives be what they wanted if his own mother despised her?

Not even looking at Kil, her gaze set on the floor of the living room, "Killian, I'm sorry. Maybe we should wait until you can get this all sorted out. Obviously, there's more going on with your mother and I don't want to be in the way." Her darkened gaze lifted to his, "I love you with everything that I am, but I can't come between you and her or your coven. You need to figure this out first...don't you? Your father looked so defeated and Keegan so lost. Maybe you all should repair this before we move forward with the wedding"- her hands clasped in front of her, fussing with the band of her ring.

Then not being able to withstand the need to touch him, she took a few steps to bring herself up to him, her palms resting against his chest, "Are you OK? I'm so sorry if my presence made this erupt like it did. I want to help, but I have no idea what to do." The sound of her aunt behind them reminded her they weren't alone. Tilting her head, her forehead resting against his chest, the beat of his heart so strong. Letting out a deep sigh; not really sure where to go from here.

***

His heart sank for his father, knowing how much he loved his mother. How could she sink so low and be so cruel to ruin what was supposed to be one of the happiest nights of his life? He wanted to wrap Red in his arms and just disappear.

Somehow or other, he would make this up to his witch. He should have known better than to have planned something special with his family, knowing his mother would fuck it up, but deep down; he had hoped his happiness would take the front-row seat to his mother's selfishness.

Killian was almost lost for words when Red said they should wait to get married. It felt like all the air in his lungs was sucked out from his chest. The last thing he ever wanted his witch to feel was blame for his mother's actions. There was no way in hell he would wait to marry her.

He cradled Red in his arms, hugging her to his chest. Killian could keep her safe in his arms forever. She was everything he ever hoped for. His fingers threaded through her red locks. His eyes looked over to Essie, and his shoulders slumped. He hated that she had to witness his mother's behavior as well.

"Red, I waited what felt like centuries for you to come into my life. Every night, I closed my eyes and dreamt of the beautiful woman with the crimson color hair. You stole my heart a long time ago, and I refuse to let anyone stop us from getting married. My mother can't hurt us. Her powers are bound to me. If you want, we can elope, but I will not wait to marry you."

***

Her heart saddened as she watched from her spot off to the side. A long time ago, her and her sister, and Rissa, were thick as thieves. They did everything together and were each other's best secret keepers. The three of them vowed to always stay close.

Essie had stared at the shell of the woman that was so dear to her. She couldn't believe the words that came out of her mouth or how she could humiliate her son on one of the happiest nights of his life. Killian not only found the woman he was supposed to spend the rest of his life with, but she was also his soulflame. Something so rare, and her son was lucky enough to find his.

The audacity of her inviting someone who wasn't even family to use her as a pawn in whatever game she was playing. That poor girl.

Rissa knew Killian and Damien never really got along, and to throw him in her son's face was appalling. Essie didn't even know if there was anything left of her friend to save.

Essie could hear the hurt in her niece's voice when she told Killian they should wait to get married. It infuriated her because she knew how much they both loved each other. They were a perfect match for one another. Essie couldn't ask for a better man for her niece. He was kind, loving, respectful and led his coven with a caring heart. There was no way she would let Rissa ruin this for them.

"My dear niece, do not let Killian's mother stop you from marrying him. That is exactly what she wants to happen. You two deserve nothing but happiness, and I couldn't ask for a better man for you, Elena. Anyone with eyes can see how much he loves you. So please be strong for him and don't back down. Show Rissa she doesn't mess with a Payne because she will most definitely get burned."

***

Back at Raven Manor...

A mother will stop at nothing to protect her son, even if it's from himself. When Rissa discovered her son was in love with a Payne, she jumped into action. There was no way in hell she would risk Elena leaving her son as her so-called best friend had done to her. Elena's grandmother and aunt made a vow to Rissa but didn't honor it. Elena came from a family of liars and she was not the right choice for her son. As soon as things had gotten complicated, her friends had left her behind.

She never got to explain what happened, and it wasn't Rissa who ordered Matilda to leave her human mate; it was her father and his hate for any species outside their coven. Her father was despicable and extremely controlling, not to mention how jealous he was of not being the elder Warlock of their coven.

Rissa had married into one of the most powerful covens, and her father plotted to take over her husband's coven one day.

Rissa was keeping a horrific secret from her husband and her sons to keep them safe from her demented father. He told her if she didn't do what she asked her to do, he would kill her husband and children.

Draven, her father, had the ability of possession. He would take over his daughter's body when he wanted to find out information, no matter what it was. Matilda being in love with a human was the perfect opportunity to drive a stake in the sister witches and cause dissension. Rissa told them they were abominations when it was him all along.

Tonight was supposed to be nothing but happiness, but yet again, Rissa's father was jealous of her son being the elder of the Raven Coven. Draven told his daughter he would make them all pay for not making him the elder. That he deserved it, not Killian. Rissa stood before her family, screaming at her father to get out of her body and leave her family alone.

Draven laughed as he humiliated his daughter. They had no idea he was in control, not her.

Rissa broke apart as she heard the anger from her son's mouth. Her heart was breaking, and she never thought she would see one of her best friends again, and yet there stood Essie off to the side, hidden from most but not from her. She could see the disappointment in her eyes and inwardly begged her father to stop.

Elena had every right to hate her, with what happened tonight. Rissa hoped she would get the chance to show her the real her. Then her husband spoke, and her heart bled even more. She loved her husband and sons more than anything. How could her father do this to her?

When everyone had left, the real plotting began. Rissa dropped to the floor as her father's possession left her body. She wept like a baby and begged her father to leave her family alone. He laughed in her face and told her that she better not breathe a word. The real fun begins on Killian's wedding day.

"You remember what I said, Rissa. Do what I say, or they will all die."

34

To the Goddess up above, surround my family with your love, protect them each and every day, keeping them in your sight and in your light. Hold them safe and protect them from what they fear. As I will it, so mote it be.

The saying was true. Sometimes you had to go full-on witch, flip the switch and let the cauldron bubble and boil. Elena had to remind herself that she was the main ingredient to her magic. It started and ended with her and some days, she just had to weave some witchery.

'Be strong' - her aunt's words to her. 'I will not wait to marry you' - Killian's words to her. She was so lucky to have them both in her life. She had felt empty when they had returned from Kil's coven, but within his arms and the touch of both their love, Elena had squared her shoulders and realized how fortunate she was. This was just a stumble and yes, a big one, but they'd already had their share and they'd righted themselves and moved on.

After a short bit of time, they'd each gone their own way, Essie to find Gran and fill her in, Killian to speak to Keegan, and Elena to find a few quiet moments and think.

She needed something positive to come from today. She needed to feel like she was in control when it felt like everything was casting whirlwinds around her. She needed to know her family was safe and protected. Killian, Essie and Gran, all three, were about to enter the past to strengthen the future, a little extra sorcery couldn't hurt. At least, that's the way she thought.

Standing before her altar, her candles, bowl and crystals the extension of herself, she thought of her family, knowing she would do anything she could to keep them safe.

She watched her finger slowly move the ingredients she had chosen in the bowl, her voice steady and strong as each was added to the mix.

"Tiger's eye bring me courage. Sage give me wisdom. Cinnamon help my spirit grow. Bergamot bring me clarity of mind. Pine strengthen my resolve."

Elena held her hands over the bowl, visualizing energy coming up from the earth into the bowl, through her hands and into her core, imagining the bowl flowed with a golden light until it did. Until the spell was created for her to overcome fear and embrace risk.

Removing the tiger's eye, she attached it to her bracelet, worn as a charm as she went about her day. Clasping the bowl within her palms, her footfalls took her out the backdoor and down the few steps to sprinkle the rest throughout a piece of her garden because a storm was slowly brewing over her and Killian. Her powers and skill were going to be tested and she just hoped and prayed she didn't come up short.

The coolness of the evening, a nice touch after the warmth of the day. The sound of the woods was so different as night approached. It was strange how that happened, but it was the truth. Those animals that slept by the day, now awake and the others finding a resting spot until morning. Even the breeze took on a different feel as the sun dipped and the moon took its turn.

Her feet on an automaton, being pulled a little deeper, passed the gardens into the thickness of the trees. The bright fire from the setting sun spilled through branches and lit her way until the further she ventured, even those tendrils couldn't reach. And she stopped and listened.

The earth spoke if you opened yourself up to her; Gran had taught her that early in her life. She closed her eyes drawing in the fresh air, feeling a subtle warm pulse in her chest in response. Her magick saying hello at the small taste of life she drew in. Her lids lifting, her tawny hues drawn to the moon that hung silver and swollen in the sky, Killian's words rising in her thoughts.

Could she be what he said?

Anything was possible in the world of magick; she just needed to get past her own uncertainties.

"I am no one. Why would you give this power to me?" her words spoke out as if she would get answers from the giant glowing orb. Her thoughts again went to Killian because he was her flashlight. She was so truly blessed with him. And if he believed it, so could she. She just needed to give herself a daily pep talk, remind herself that she was so much stronger than she knew. And she'd get there; to the there that was meant for her. She was a Payne. She needed to remember that.

***

There were so many emotions running through Killian: anger, sadness, disappointment, disgust and, most of all, shame. Killian never would have thought his mother would have ever sunk so low to humiliate him in front of his future wife. Once a loving mother who would do anything for her children, now was nothing but a soulless, heartless woman with an agenda.

Kil would bury the pain deep from his mother's betrayal; he knew she wouldn't be able to harm his soon-to-be wife or him. Now, he could concentrate on the most crucial thing in his life. He was marrying the woman of his dreams and spending the rest of his life with her. He would give her the life she deserved. No one would stand in the way of that; he would ensure it.

He'd known deep within himself that this had to happen and happen quickly regardless of the hour. He'd sent out a demand for his members to gather in the ritual hall.

Killian stood before his Coven with his brother and father flanking each side of him. That they'd kept his mother out of this was no oversight. Killian allowed his magick to flow freely and weave around each coven member, a ritual of weaving magick to strengthen the bond of accepting Elena's light magick.

Killian held a few strands of Elena's red hair in his hand as the magick of his coven slowly threaded her light magick into every one of the members, making an oath to their elder to protect Elena and accept her as an equal, to see her not only as his wife but as an elder witch of the Raven Coven.

Keegan and Kaden clapped their hands together in nothing but pure admiration for Killian. They couldn't be prouder of him and what he has accomplished as their elder warlock. He led with a kind and loving heart. He would sacrifice himself before letting any witch or warlock get harmed. Kaden clutched Killian's shoulder, smiling wide.

"Son, I am so proud of you. No matter what life has thrown at you. You didn't let it break or destroy the person that you are. So many warlocks let the power of the title destroy who they once were. They use their magick to harm others, which only shows their weaknesses. I know your mother hurt you yesterday and for that, I am sorry. We will find a way to help her, but first, my son, I will watch you marry your Elena."

Killian pulled his father and brother in his arms, hugging them tightly. He tried his best to fight back the hurt bubbling to the surface, but at that very moment, he let the tears fall. Whoever said a man is weak by showing his hurt is a coward. He didn't cry often, but what his mother did felt like a punch to his heart. Killian needed to release this emotion so he could move past it. He slowly released his father and brother from his embrace and faced his coven.

"I want to thank every one of you for everything you do for me as your elder and for our Coven, nothing goes unnoticed. Elena will lead by my side, not only as my wife but as my equal in every way possible. I am not above her. We lead together. Her heart is so pure of light and love.

Tomorrow, she will thread her light magick and weave it with the dark magick of every member of our coven, making all of us family. A new journey awaits us."

A few hours later, Killian opened a doorway to Elena's so he could wrap his arms around his beautiful witch. He needed to smell her cinnamon scent and hear her little giggle that always made her nose wrinkle, showing off her cute freckles.

She sat in her favorite chair with her legs pulled up, a blanket around her, and a book resting on her lap. Her hair was pulled in a messy bun, and she wore his old Metallica shirt. Killian couldn't help but stare at her. She was so gorgeous, and he counted his lucky stars that she was his.

Elena was so engrossed in her reading when Killian appeared she gave a bit of a jerk. She jumped up, giving him a swat. He laughed and scooped in her arms, plopping down in the chair. He planted kisses all over her face, bringing that giggle out. Killian told her all about the weaving of magick, and tomorrow, she would meet with their coven and join herself to each of them.

***

Elena had the house to herself, everyone was somewhere else, she liked the quiet. That's one thing about her home, she truly felt settled and herself here. Even more so now that her family had come back together. If only her mother could have returned too. It wasn't meant to be that way obviously, not in the cards. She was blessed, though, to have those she did, and she'd take a moment every day to remind herself of that.

Killian said he had coven business to attend to. So once he left, Elena had made a cup of chamomile tea and changed into some comfy clothes, which included going to Killian's side of the closet and finding a worn soft T-shirt. Then, putting up her hair and finding her favorite chair.

She'd decided to get back to a book she had started reading weeks ago. It was a good one too but with everything happening, relaxing time had been far and in between.

So absorbed, she hadn't heard or felt Kil. She startled and jumped up, then finding herself in his lap, her freckled face getting some serious lovins from his lips.

Leaning back to stare at him, she said, "You're lucky I didn't send fireballs your way," her laugh slowly faded as he told her where he'd been and what would be happening tomorrow.

"Killian, your entire coven will be there?" her amber gaze locked with his, "I don't know what's expected of me. This is all becoming so real now. It's not just you and me anymore, is it?"

"No and yes. We'll always have our own place or a retreat we can go to be alone Red. I will always show you and tell you how I feel about you. My coven, our coven, is going to be your new haven, a circle of trust where you will strengthen your powers and forge deep and meaningful friendships. That's my hope anyway."

And she wasn't even gentle at all when she threaded her fingers through his hair and brought his lips to hers. He made her feel so cherished and loved, her moan slipping passed her lips into his mouth because her warlock could kiss. Mumbling against his lips- "You should take me upstairs so you can play connect the dots with your tongue."

Those words barely spoken and he was up and out of that chair, with her in his arms, taking the stairs two at a time, and she just held on until she was dumped in a heap onto the bed. Killian's shirt was pulled over his head, pants undone before she could blink, his hands rubbing together, "Where should I start?" but he didn't wait for an answer, just jumped onto the bed and pulled her underneath him.

The next day ....

Killian had opened the doorway into his coven like the day of their engagement, Essie following along. To say Elena hadn't slept the night before was an understatement. At one point, Killian had just dragged her against him, locking her in tightly, words murmured at her ear, and that's all she remembered.

Taking a sideways glance at her sexy man, she said, "You put a spell on me, didn't you?" Then she turned her gaze back to the members that were awaiting their arrival.

She was nervous and hoped she was dressed alright because she had no idea what went with a weaving ceremony. Her floral dress and light sweater seemed maybe underrated, but Killian made introductions and she tried to follow along as best she could.

"Elena, don't fear you'll harm anyone. Everyone here is here for you, for us. They have vast experience in our craft. I'll be right here beside you and Essie on your other side." Her nod to him as she took in all their faces, and she decided to say something before they started.

"I'm sure Killian has told you or you've heard my element is fire. I have some control over it, but I have a long way to go. I guess that's why they call it practicing magick." A few smiles from the faces looking at her calmed her nerves. "I just wanted to say thank you. I love Killian with everything that I am." Her eyes lifted to him, "Ok, I'm ready."

Calling to her flame, letting it build slowly, her hands raised, palms skyward, a slow ember igniting, then like Killian had shown her, she gave it a slight push, strands extending, a bright trail slowly weaving around each member standing in attendance until the circle completed itself back to where she stood. A smile lit her face as she felt the intertwining of their magick to hers. She didn't know when the tears started to fall, but they had. But she didn't care. All she felt was love and acceptance in this moment.

***

Killian watched his coven stand before his fiancée, their magick weaving with hers. It was something to behold. Elena was in complete control of her magick, and the smile on her beautiful freckled face was radiant. Her flames swirled around her like an intricate dance, her confidence making her glow.

There was no doubt that his witch would soar like a bird with wings. How could Killian's coven not fall in love with her? She was kind-hearted, loving, and fierce. His coven would thrive with her as a leader. The way she moved drew everyone's attention. The other witches whispered about her, their voices filled with awe and envy. Elena had a way of connecting with the element of fire like no other witch that he'd seen before her.

Her laughter echoed through the sacred room, weaving spells of protection and healing. Killian watched from the shadows, his heart swelling with pride. He knew that Elena's leadership would bring prosperity to their coven. She would guide them toward unity, strength, and compassion, the very essence of magick itself.

Killian didn't think his heart could hold all the love he had for her. He couldn't wait for her to have his last name and to proudly call her his wife. They were only a week away from their wedding.

Killian's emotions were a tempest, swirling like a storm-tossed sea. The weight of his affection threatened to burst through his ribcage, a temerarious tide that threatened to consume him whole. His love for her was no mere whisper, it roared, fierce and unyielding.

He imagined their future together, the shared laughter, the quiet moments, the stolen kisses under moonlit skies. The thought of her bearing his name, woven into the very fabric of her identity, filled him with a heady mix of joy and vulnerability. It was as if he held a fragile glass bauble in his hands, one wrong move, and it would shatter into a thousand shards.

Killian's nights were spent weaving dreams of their life together: cozy mornings sipping coffee by the window, evenings tangled in shared secrets and whispered promises. He envisioned her laughter echoing through their home, her touch leaving trails of warmth on his skin. The thought of her as his wife, a partner in adventure, a confidante in sorrow was intoxicating.

35

Rissa's fury burned hotter with each passing moment. The betrayal and malice of her father pierced her heart deeply. How could he harbor such animosity towards her sons and husband simply because he was not selected as the elder of their coven? She knew her father had always been self-serving, but the extent of his cruelty towards his own blood left her reeling.

Meanwhile, Draven, a man shrouded in ambition and cloaked in secrecy, observed Rissa's sons with a covetous hunger that bordered on obsession. The boys possessed extraordinary powers that defied the laws of nature. Yet, it was not just their abilities that captivated him; it was the enigmatic nature of their gifts that drew him in like a moth to flame.

In Killian, Draven saw eyes that held the wisdom of ages. He pondered what hidden truths lay within them. Could they unlock ancient knowledge or shape reality itself? Killian's potential was a riddle waiting to be solved, a puzzle that enticed Draven's curiosity.

Keegan, on the other hand, presented a unique allure. A rare being capable of manipulating time itself, a true temporal voyager. Draven envisioned himself as the puppeteer of Keegan's strings, orchestrating events from the shadows to serve his insatiable desires.

Driven by thirst for power, Draven believed that the boys' gifts were rightfully his, a culmination of generations of sacrifice and ambition. He was consumed by the desire to possess their powers, convinced that they belonged to him by birthright. He vowed to stop at nothing to claim what he perceived as his due.

Rissa remained resolute in her determination to safeguard her family at all costs, even if it meant being vilified in the eyes of others. The mere thought of a world without her sons and husband was a chilling void she refused to entertain. She would go to any lengths necessary to shield her loved ones from the malevolent grasp of her father, no matter what shadows lurked on the horizon.

The ominous specter of her father's scheme hung over Rissa like a dark cloud, casting a pall over everything she held sacred. His chilling words, delivered with cold precision, warned her of dire consequences should she dare to defy him. Yet, Rissa knew she could not stand idly by; her family's safety was paramount.

Beneath the pale glow of the moon, she steeled herself for the confrontation that would lay bare the truth, shattering the fragile facade of secrecy and deception that had shielded them thus far. The burden of her father's malevolence had become unbearable, urging her to act despite the risks.

In the hushed stillness of the room, she stood face to face with him, the air heavy with tension. His gaze bore into hers with a malevolent intensity, a twisted blend of fury and disappointment. "You will not betray me," his voice dripped with menace.

Summoning her courage, Rissa drew a deep breath, her heart drumming a frantic rhythm in her chest. "I will do whatever is necessary," she spoke softly but firmly, her voice unwavering, "even if it means sacrificing myself."

With trembling hands, she unraveled the sinister plot that threatened to unravel their lives, laying bare the treachery that lurked in the shadows. In that moment, she willingly embraced the role of the antagonist, knowing that by exposing her father's malevolence, she was taking the first step towards safeguarding her family, even if it meant shouldering the weight of their condemnation.

As the damning truth spilled from Rissa's lips, a palpable tension filled the room, crackling in the air like electricity. Her father's expression contorted with a mixture of disbelief and rage, his features contorting into a mask of hate. The revelation hung heavy between them, casting a long shadow over their once-tangled familial ties.

In the silence that followed, Rissa braced herself for the storm that was sure to follow. Her father's eyes narrowed, a storm brewing within their depths. For a fleeting moment, she glimpsed a flicker of something akin to regret, a shard of humanity buried deep within the darkness that consumed him.

"You dare defy me?" Her father's voice echoed with a chilling finality, the words laced with a venomous edge. The weight of his wrath bore down upon her, threatening to crush her resolve like fragile glass.

But Rissa stood her ground, her conviction unwavering. "I will not allow you to harm them," she declared, her voice steady despite the tumult raging within her. With each word spoken, she fortified her defenses, drawing strength from the fierce love that bound her to her family.

As the confrontation reached its crescendo, a sense of liberation washed over Rissa, a feeling of freedom born from the courage to confront the darkness that had haunted her for so long. In that moment of truth, she embraced her role as protector, determined to shield her loved ones from the cruel designs of her own flesh and blood.

With a heart heavy with dread and determination, Rissa raced down the dimly lit hallway, her footsteps echoing like thunder in the stillness of the night. Each stride brought her closer to her husband's study, where she sought solace and strength in his unwavering love and support. The thought of his embrace, of his comforting words promising protection for their sons, fueled her resolve.

As she approached the study door, her hand outstretched to grasp the doorknob, a sudden chill seized her. A cold shiver ran down her spine as if an invisible hand had gripped her soul. Draven's insidious presence slithered into her mind like a serpent, weaving its dark tendrils around her thoughts, paralyzing her with fear and doubt.

In that moment, Rissa felt herself slipping under her father's sinister influence, a marionette dancing to his twisted tune. The weight of his manipulation pressed down upon her like a suffocating cloak, threatening to extinguish the flicker of defiance burning within her.

Yet, amidst the suffocating darkness, a spark ignited within Rissa, a flame of defiance that refused to be snuffed out. She vowed to break free from her father's hold.

In that pivotal moment, as the battle between light and darkness raged within her, Rissa stood at the precipice of a harrowing choice, a choice that would determine not only her own fate but the fate of her loved ones. With a resolute heart and unwavering courage, she steeled herself for the confrontation that lay ahead, ready to face her father's tyranny head-on and reclaim her autonomy, no matter the cost.

36

$he glanced once more at her desk, weighted down with a pile of old spells and notations she'd found rummaging through some chests. The cellar under the house was a collection depot for everything that had been moved after her Mama had passed. Elena had figured that these had made it down there by mistake, probably mixed up with other things.

Not that Gran was the most organized person when she was alive and on two legs, but anything pertaining to any magick history was usually in their own library or housed in the coven.

Remembering the pain when her mother had crossed over, she herself had been so young, just five. But it was watching Gran go through her grief that forever ingrained the emotion within Elena.

Children didn't pass before parents; Gran had said that over and over again.

She supposed that out of sight made living easier, moving her Mama's things where they couldn't be seen, except when Gran looked up and saw eyes so familiar, mine, staring back at her. Elena knew it had been a bit of a struggle, a grandmere raising a granddaughter. She also knew somewhere in there, a shift had happened, a bond so tight-knit that nothing could pull it apart.

Her original familiar, her cat, was now her walking, talking Aunt Essie again, shedding her cat form to stand by and help them in their fight against Kil's mother. And her current familiar was now her Gran in owl form. Confusing? Slightly. Elena understood why they did what they had, keeping secrets hidden. It had taken some inner soul searching, but she had got there.

She loved them both and was so thankful she had them in her life again. Now, if only they could get through to Killian's mother. Elena would never forget the look on Rissa's face the day they'd been at the coven. Killian had tried to convince her that all would be well, that they would get to the bottom of what had his mother changing so drastically. She truly hoped so because she wanted Kil and his family to have their mother and wife back.

Her thoughts turning as well as her nerves, Elena stood, grabbing her sweater, she needed some air, her steps falling into their pattern, out the back door, through the gardens and down the well-worn path

***

"Gran, I love him so much. How is this going to work if his mother hates me?" Elena said while sitting on the fallen trunk of a tree in the backwoods.

Her place, her spot, her haven where she came when she needed space, quiet when she needed to center.

And Gran had felt her through their connection, that her granddaughter had needed her, appearing like an avenging angel, wings an ethereal white, the rhythmic beating a comfort to Elena's ears as her gaze lifted skyward to see her familiar circling downward, talons reaching and extending to the jagged stump next to her. Settling, her appendages drawn in, the soft down of her chest ruffled as her head turned, and the dark soulful eyes of her Gran found hers.

Elena's hand lifted, her fingertips gently running through the softness of her feathers so grateful her Gran was back, no matter her form.

"Gran, I want to help Killian, but I don't know how? I feel helpless. I've spelled and I've cleansed. I don't know that much about his coven yet. I know every coven has its own niche and I know I'll get there. I can tell he's worried and upset and I want to take it away from him. You should have seen his mother. She was so hateful." Her words drifted off, her head dropped, a deep sigh fell through her parting lips. The clacking of the owl's beak, brought her head back up, their link opening for Elena to hear her Gran-

[My beautiful flame, everything will work itself out. You are not alone anymore. Killian knows his family and your aunt and I know the history that he doesn't. We will prevail. I feel it.]

Elena held Gran's gaze, her eyes' reflective pools reminding her of the fullness of the moon. The steady thump thump of her heart felt where her hand still rested within her plumage. A nod from Elena, feeling the love through their link.

The sound of crunching debris had her head turning to see her Aunt Essie, worry on her face, coming toward her from the same path she had just come earlier.

[I reached out to her Elena, when I felt how upset you were. We're both here for you. We won't leave you].

Pushing herself up, Essie's arms already open, Elena stepped into the hug, wrapping her own arms around her and hugging tightly.

"Thank you for coming. I don't know where this came from. One minute, I was fine and then the next, I just couldn't breathe and needed to be out here." She eased back to see into her aunt's dark brown eyes. It still freaked her out a bit that her aunt still looked so young, but that was magick for you.

"Elena, I've always been here for you, even when I was in cat form. Was it right what we did not to tell you? We thought it was…" Her aunt looked over to where Gran perched and listened. "And even though the dynamics have changed, we're still together. It was meant to be this way. I truly believe that. We are all where we are meant to be at this moment in time. And my beautiful niece, we are going to be right beside you on your wedding day."

At those last few words, Gran's thoughts came through - [Your aunt and I can not wait to see you become Killian's wife. Your mother would have loved him, loved seeing the love you have for him.]

Elena pulled Essie over to where her Gran still sat on the stump, gently putting her arm around her, then watching Essie do the same. Anyone watching would have thought them all shades of peculiar, but Elena couldn't be happier. Her family was working their way back to the whole.

Giving them both an extra squeeze, the idea taking light, as the sun started to make its nightly descent, she blurted it out, a smile touching her lips, her heart feeling full and the anxiety that had her come here tonight disappearing, "You both are going to be my bridesmaids right?"

37

Good witch? Bad witch?- those two words flipping through her head during the day.

She'd woke up feeling off. Ever since their engagement party, that hadn't actually been one, she was restless and a bit out of sorts. It wasn't interfering with her day, but it was a constant little niggle in the back of her mind.

Elena thought of herself as a good person. She had a deep love of nature, and she tried to see magick in all places throughout her day. Goodness ran through her veins alongside her fire. But that day at Kil's coven with his mother saying such hurtful things, her fire had taken over, slowly getting out of control, she'd almost fallen over into the bad category.

Almost, but that was then and today was now. And today was the day she was going dress shopping for her wedding. No matter how many times she said that it still felt all kinds of magical.

She was meeting Essie and Keegan's wife, Iris, at an eclectic thrift store known for its unique style. Elena didn't want new, she was fairly simple. All she needed was a quiet spot in the woods, and their vows. But she also understood the need for close family and a few friends to be a part of their special day. It was going to be very intimate, which was perfect.

Minutes later, she was behind the wheel of Gran's old Volvo, heading toward Jackson Square. There were a few secondhand stores that she had found, hidden gems if you took your time and searched through the racks. Elena wasn't quite certain what she was looking for, but she was sure when she saw it, she would know.

She left with plenty of time to spare, so when the Estate Sale sign had appeared at the bend of the all-familiar road, she found a spot under some overhanging trees and parked, grabbing her bag and allowing herself fifteen minutes to have a quick look around.

The Pearson home had been passed down from generation to generation. Elena had only been inside a couple times when she was very young and that was with her Gran. The family had a very peculiar background, she rarely saw any of them in all the time she lived in the area. To be honest, she thought the house sat empty most of the time.

There were others milling around, and even though she was curious to go inside the three story, she didn't have time. She'd just take a quick look around outside at the tables.

Trinkets and kitchen items lined both sides of the walk, but it was the toe of her sandal hitting a box that sat pushed under one of the sale tables that caught her attention. 'Books' labeled across the top, bending and pushing back the flaps to reveal some paperbacks and hardcovers.

Elena was always looking for something to read outback in the porch swing. So kneeling down, she sorted through selecting a few romance novels, her eyes falling on a book, leather-bound and dirty. Her curiosity piqued as she opened it thinking at first glance, it might be a diary, but no, it wasn't.

Turning the pages carefully, the words were slightly faded, but it was unmistakable. It was a book of shadows. How could this have possibly ended up in a box at a yard sale, her insides doing a little jig dance. Turning her head and looking over to the front of the house, her gaze drawn to the top floor window, an odd sensation making her straighten and gather all the books she'd chosen, then turning to find the agent that was handling the sales.

"Did you find something my dear?"

"I did. I'm going to take all these books!" but she decided to pry a bit, "I didn't realize the Pearsons were moving?"

"There's been a death. I don't know all the details." With that, she told Elena the amount due, she paid, without another word being said.

Her phone chimed so she took a quick look - [Elena see you shortly. I'm on my way.]

Oh crap, she stayed longer than she expected, and her aunt was on her way to their meeting spot.

Walking back to her car, stowing the bag in the back and within twenty minutes, she was parking again, sending a quick text to Essie- [I'm here] then speed walking around the corner to see Essie and Iris talking in front of Treasure Trove their first stop.

"Hi. Sorry I'm a bit late," she said while hugging them both and not mentioning why she was.

"So let's see what we find here," Iris's excitement was contagious.

"Your Mama isn't here, but your Gran and I are. So this is our gift to you. No matter the price, so no arguments," her aunt Essie laid that out before they stepped foot in the door. Her eyes misted up and she knew not to argue because stubborn ran in her family.

Her arm was linked by Iris, "And I'm buying the accessories and I don't want to hear a thing about that either. We're all sisters now and I'm so happy for you and Killian. Him and his brother are some of the best men I know. So let's do this," she said while tugging her along, the chime above the door heralding their entrance.

***

"That's the one!" Iris's voice reached her as she walked out of the changing room.

"She's right Elena," her aunt's look almost brought tears to her eyes again.

Elena hadn't looked at the mirror inside the changing room as the attendant had buttoned up all the small little clips at the back. Thoughts of her Mama, a soft caress on her memories, the moment completely overwhelming her.

"I'm done miss." The girl's voice brought her back to the moment. Then she stepped out where the others waited, turning to the bank of mirrors in the sitting area, her breath caught in her throat, the sounds of the store behind her drifting away. "Yes. This is the one."

38

Elena? Do you need to rush off straight away? I know you probably have a hundred things to do, but I was wondering if we could talk?"

Sophie couldn't put this off any longer. It had been bothering her for a long time, especially after really getting to know Elena and spending their days together. She was truly a sister to her and not just because of the coven. Sophie felt like they'd become quite close in the year she'd been working here. They were close in age and they liked the same things. Elena made Beliefs feel like a home to her and that said a lot because Sophie had an ugly past and to have something that made her feel the way Elena and the store made her feel meant a lot.

"Of course I have time. And you're right. I do have stuff to do, but not that much. This is a simple wedding. Well, it started out that way, but everyone wants to add their own this or that but still low-key compared to some. Let me flip the sign and we can have some iced tea and talk."

Sophie didn't know if she could do this now that it was here. Watching Elena walk to the front door and turn the lock, flip the sign and start taking off her apron and she knew there was a chance that Elena could fire her and tell her to basically get the hell out of her life.

Why had she ever said yes to Mira and the others? She wouldn't want it done to herself and that was always the way to know if you were doing something wrong.

Elena's arm found its way around her shoulders, steering her towards the nook and giving her a nudge to sit. "I'll grab the jug and some glasses. You sit. You look sort of off. You ok Soph?"

No. No she wasn't. Out of sight, out of mind worked for only so long. Sometimes weeks would go by and no one asked her a thing about Elena and the store. Her guard would drop and she'd feel so normal and happy. And then, out of the blue, one of the elders would ask if she'd seen anything untowards, anything they should know. They'd never really said anything precise, just for her to watch the comings and goings; watch who visited the store. And Sophie never went to them first. She waited for them to approach her. And even then, she tried to circumvent their questions.

"Ok so what's up?" Elena's cheerfulness made her feel worse because ...timing. Elena was getting married soon, like in less than thirty-six hours and here Sophie was going to hurt her.

A glass was pushed in front of her and she looked up into Elena's deep brown eyes and it was like a dam burst. Sophie couldn't stop the tears. "Elena, I'm so sorry. I should have come to you right away. But I was scared and I didn't know you that well so I thought there must be a reason why they'd ask me to spy on you. But then I got to know you and I knew they were wrong. But then I didn't want to disappoint you, so I said nothing and now I screwed it all up!" Her voice rose as she went on, her crying making parts of what she said distorted.

Elena reached across the table grabbing one of Sophie's hands and squeezing tightly, her other hand grabbing a napkin from the holder and setting it in front of her. "I don't have a clue what you're talking about? What spy and who? And Soph, take a breath because you look awful."

Sophie squeezed her friend's hand back, then let go to wipe her face and take a breath and have a sip of her tea; the first purging of her thoughts calming her slightly.

"Ok Sophie, start again and in a language I can understand this time."

Giving Elena a nod, Sophie started, "A few months after I started here, Mira called me into her office after a coven meeting and asked me to keep an eye on the store and you," her gaze was looking down on the table, her fingers fidgeting with the napkin. "I asked her why and she said it wasn't my place to ask. If I wanted to continue to be a part of the Divine Spirit, I would do as I was told. I didn't want to, but I had no one and nowhere else to go. So I did."

Sophie's eyes drifted up to see the hurt and confusion on her friend's face. "I didn't really tell them much. Nothing important anyway. Elena, I care about you so much and when months went by and I realized you were such a wonderful person, I went to Mira and told her I didn't want to do it anymore. She basically just told me that I had no choice. If I didn't, she'd tarnish my name so no coven would want me." Tears started welling again. "I'm so tired of being alone. I know it's no excuse Elena, but I needed to tell you. I can't live with this any longer. I'm going to leave the coven and I fully understand if you tell me to fuck off. I know you rarely say that word, but you can use it. I expect you to. You can't hate me more than I hate myself right now or how I've been hating myself for months."

To say Elena was shell-shocked was accurate. There was no way that sweet Sophie would do such a thing. But she didn't put it passed Mira or the other two elders, Abigail and Ursula, to conspire against her. And what and why would they want to know about the store and her? Nothing went on here. She was pretty boring really.

The store had old-time regulars and some odd characters, who Elena never pried as too what they were. Sometimes, they offered their supernatural information up, but even then, Elena never shared it, not even with Sophie. She respected everyone's privacy to be unique.

"So what did you share with them, Sophie? And why didn't you come to me sooner? This has been ongoing for what? Like nine months? I trusted you with everything. You should have just opened up to me. I would have helped."

Sophie knew this was going to be hard and awful. But seeing Elena's face and hearing it in her voice made it so much worse.

"Honestly, Elena, nothing important. And that's why they started holding meetings here in the nook, to see for themselves. I gave them nothing important. I never even mentioned Killian. I just didn't know how to get out from under it. I'm so, so sorry. I'll leave if that's what you want. I'll be leaving Nola too. They'll make my life hell if I stay. I should have had more backbone, but I didn't."

Elena stared at her friend trying to wrap her head around what had been going on underneath her nose. And it's weird how she kinda had an inkling the last time the coven was here for their meeting. All those sideways glances she felt as she was going about her day, helping customers and preparing potions.

Elena understood what it felt like to be alone and not have someone to turn to. The last year of her life before Killian had walked into it had been hard. She knew people did things out of fear and out of love, the lines blurring at times. And then sometimes you got deeper and deeper and it seemed impossible to find your way out.

Forgiveness was something she believed in. She'd just lived through it with her Gran and Essie. Sophie had been here with her since before her Gran's death, working and keeping the store open when Elena had taken time away. They'd had girl's nights and lunch parties and laughed at each other's mess-ups while spelling. She'd always been a friend and she knew how the coven could be; that's why she'd been reluctant to give them her full acceptance. Her gut had been right.

"Sophie. I'm not going to lie. I'm hurt. I'm disappointed. But I understand how things like this can happen. I know you've had a hard life. You've never told me and I've never asked, but our experiences can screw us up at times. You've become family to me and I'm choosing to believe that you gave them nothing of importance. But going forward, you don't lie to me no matter what it is. And you and I both will be going to see Mira together to let her know we won't be a part of the Divine anymore. Are you ok with that?"

Sophie just stared at Elena. Could she have heard right? She was giving her another chance?

"Elena, are you sure? If you have any doubts I'll understand. And I swear I'll never lie again. I love being here with you. You've given me a home and life and I'll never be able to repay you for that. Why don't you hate me?" Sophie had to ask that. She'd jeopardized everything and it would take her a long time to get over what she'd done.

"Sophie." Elena's had outstretched towards hers and Sophie placed hers into it and held it tightly. "We all make mistakes. I have too. I know what it feels like to be in your place; it was a little different, but I still remember how I felt. Let's put it in the past. And start fresh right now. You wanna do that?"

And the tears started again, Sophie pushing herself out of the nook and coming around to Elena, Elena already halfway up and she wrapped her in a hug and that's how Killian found them.

***

He wasn't sure what he'd walked in on but the charge in the air was telling him something really heavy had gone down in here and very recently.

He'd parked in the back alongside Elena's car, a chuckle in his chest at the old vehicle she drove. He'd suggested getting her something new and her reply still made him grin from ear to ear. "You're the four-wheel addict. I'm fine driving Gran's old car. It's got a certain flare."

And he couldn't argue with her when she looked at him with that look that she had. But he wasn't giving up. She needed something bigger, safer and faster. In the meantime, he'd keep spelling the old car because it made him feel better.

The look on Sophie's face, said she'd been crying. The look on Red's face said something completely different.

"Tell me before I jump to conclusions. The energy in here is setting off my alarms." His gaze went from one to the other.

Elena was about to speak, but Sophie unfolded herself and stepped forward, "Elena let me. It's all my faul!t" Her gaze going from Elena to Killian. "I did something very wrong. The coven asked me to keep tabs on Elena and the store. I've explained it all to Elena. I never gave them anything private or important. They said if I didn't I'd be kicked out. It was wrong I know that." Her voice going quiet and she just remained there.

Elena moved into Killian's side, her arm going around him. She could tell by his expression he was keeping his temper in check and knew she needed to keep his emotions in check. He wanted her safe and she loved him for it.

"Killian. Sophie and I have talked it out. I know how they can be; that's why I've tried to keep my distance. Maybe this is partially my fault. If I'd just been straightforward with them, maybe they wouldn't have asked her. I want her to stay with me here. She's my family. And what have you said before? Family sticks together." Her face tilted up to his, seeing the moment he realized she'd turned his words back on him.

"Is that what I said?" His arm pulled her in tighter, his gaze dropping to her lips and then just as quickly turning to Sophie.

"My first priority will always be Elena and her happiness and safety. If she's forgiven you, then I'll stand by her decision. But Sophie if anything more comes of this? You come to us. I'm not the enemy you want. I'll have your back, but I expect you to have ours. And I'll be paying a visit to the coven."

At that, Elena stepped out from his embrace "Killian, Sophie and I were going to go together and let them know that it's over and we both won't be a part of the Divine."

"Elena, my love. This is something for me to do. I want to. No elder should threaten a member of their coven or risk expulsion. You know how I rule. I'm not standing by when others could be affected as well. The Raven coven is very powerful and I'm just going to let them know that. So you two stay and do whatever it is you were doing. And I'll be back."

"You're going now? Like right now?" Elena was shocked. The smile that lit up his face was so damn adorable to her.

 "Why not? Catch them on the defensive. I'll call when I'm done. See what you witches are up to." He gave Elena a wink, then pulled her in for a kiss, "Be good while I'm gone. But once I'm back, you can be bad." The blue of his eyes finding Sophie overtop of Elena's red curls. "I'll square this away. Is there anything at the coven you need returned to you?"

Sophie couldn't believe Killian was going to stand in for them, for her. Months of anxiety seemed to just flow out of her body. She was going to cry again, so instead, she dug her nails into her palms to recenter. "No, there's nothing I need. And thank you for understanding and believing me. Both of you. I hope I can regain what I've lost in your eyes."

"If Elena's good, then I'm good. Ok, I'm off." Giving Elena's butt a quick smack. "That's just so you don't forget me."

Elena watched him go, still staring at the door even after it shut. Sophie's voice bringing her around, "You're really lucky Elena. He's a wonderful guy. And just thank you again for understanding. Is there anything I can do? Do you want to do more orders or restocking while we wait for him?"

"I know I'm lucky and I remind myself of that every day. And I have a better idea. You're gonna love it."

***

Killian could tell he'd taken Mira completely off guard; which was the point. When Elena had first mentioned the Divine to him, he'd done a bit of digging. They were an old coven but small, with member decline over the years. It was obvious to him that leadership was the issue.

"I'll keep this brief. I had an interesting conversation earlier with Sophie and Elena. It appears she's been doing some spying on your behalf." He raised his hand when she was about to speak. "Let me finish. I believe her. You've heard of the Raven coven. You know what we stand for. You know my family tree. As of today, both Sophie and Elena no longer have ties to your coven. As Elena is soon to be my wife." He paused there, letting that be the surprise he knew it was. "My coven is now hers, and Sophie if she chooses. I have ears everywhere. Do your coven a privilege; be the leader they need before you find yourself extinct."

And with that, he turned and left, knowing he'd made his point.

***

"Elena, I love this idea and thank you again. I'm going to sleep well tonight."

Sophie had gathered what they'd need for the spell. Elena's idea was perfect. After the bumpy road, they'd just had, a spell of compassion and friendship would bring them back to center.

Two pink candles, two rose crystals and some rose essential oil.

They both sat across from each other on chairs they'd pulled over from the workstation. Elena poured the rose oil into a diffuser, giving it a few minutes to infuse their space. Then both lit a candle placing it against their hearts, both grasping a crystal in the other hand, setting their intentions and opening themselves up.

Both take indrawn breaths of the sweet fragrance, then exhale anything unwanted or negative, imagining the love light from their hearts spreading from the candle to the crystal, forming a bubble of love and compassion.

Elena, feeling lighter and more at peace, offered up her chant - "kindness and compassion find the one I seek, and find her a path to a better peace. This is my will. So mote it be." Her gaze held Sophie's, a soft smile touching her lips.

"Forgiveness heals me, love fills my soul. I move forward with true intentions. This is my will. So mote it be." – Sophie's words and smile reflected back at Elena.

And that's how Killian found them, the space around both of them filled with positive energy and warmth. Witchcraft erased what had transpired earlier and left healing in its place.

She stood in her bedroom looking at her wedding dress hanging from her closet door. This all felt so surreal. She was getting married to Killian tomorrow.

"Tomorrow" that one word spoken out loud in her room, the rise of butterflies across her tummy.

All of the yesterdays had gathered speed and rushed forward to create the tomorrow that would change her life. And that it was all happening here, where she grew up, made it so much more special.

Elena had always thought of her home, along with the few acres of land that spread out behind the house, as an enchanted sort of realm. She knew they were truly blessed with the forest that surrounded them. They just had to walk out their back door, down the path, and find one of the several clearings and let the magick consume them.

Shadows and starlight, sunlight and moonbeams, nature's power and beauty, blessing the rituals performed here over the years. There was only one thing missing, her Mama. But she had her locket and Elena would be wearing it as her footsteps followed the path to her new life.

"Penny for your thoughts?" Her aunt's voice caught her in a daydream, Elena found her standing in the doorway to her room.

A soft smile played on her lips, "Tomorrow's the day. I can't believe it's come so quickly. I'm a bit nervous. I'm not gonna lie about that."

"That's one of the reasons I'm here, Elena. With everything that's gone on lately with the covens and Killian's mother, I'd let this take a backseat, but an urgency woke me from my afternoon nap and I don't want to wait or postpone it."

Elena had a bit of an inner laugh when her aunt brought up her nap. She wasn't sure, but maybe her aunt was still partly a cat because she napped a lot.

Essie spoke as she walked towards her, "I promised Killian and it was also a long-ago promise to your mother. You and I have been practicing with your control and you've gotten so much stronger with the harnessing of your flame." Essie took her hand and clasped it gently "There's a full moon tonight, and I'd like us to go to the clearing and pull on the power of the moon."

Elena, looked down at their joined hands, "It can't wait until the next one? I have so much I want to do tonight."

"Would you do this for me Elena? I feel very strongly that it needs to be tonight. I'll leave you alone now to do what you need, but if you could meet me later?" her grip squeezing lightly. The tawny brown eyes of Elena's searching the hazel ones of her aunt and she could tell this meant a lot to her.

"Give me a couple hours and I'll meet you out back."

The smile on Essie's face was instant as she drew her into a big hug, "Thank you my dear."

***

And it was more like two hours and fifteen minutes, looking at her phone, the 10:52 p.m. lighting up her screen.

Elena had a few things she wanted ready and prepared for tomorrow. First on her list was her dress, shoes and jewelry, having gone over all the small buttons on her secondhand find just to make sure she hadn't missed anything the first time. Now, it hung over the top of her standing mirror, her locket and earrings laid out on top of her armoire.

Then she'd sat herself down and wrote her vows. They hadn't discussed in depth the entire ceremony, they both wanted it to be spontaneous, no real agenda and she loved that Killian was so open to that.

Iris had taken the decorating and the after-wedding plans completely out of Elena's hands. She'd told her a few times she'd loved to help, wanted to, but Iris had very plainly just told her to zip it.

Elena liked her. She was feisty and because it was a small wedding, she'd given in. So other than herself, she didn't have that much to worry about.

But what she did do was take a few moments to re-read three letters that she'd written over the last week. One for her aunt Essie, one for her Gran and one for her Mama. The last one she was going to deliver in the morning before the rest of her day started.

Taking herself downstairs, she filled a few glasses of tap water and set them out on the windowsill to absorb the lunar rays, so when the house woke in the morning, they'd all have a charged drink full of energy. The same went for her crystals. There was nothing that could amplify the power of crystals like the light of a full moon.

Sliding her feet into her sandals, she pushed open the back screen door and ran down the path that she had run down hundreds of times, probably thousands, the moon keeping vigil overhead.

Essie stood beside a circle created from the rocks that speckled the ground around the clearing. Her long blood-red robe dusting the ground, "Elena I need you down to your birthday suit and then to lay within the circle and I'll close it."

"You want me naked? You never said that earlier." Not that she hadn't done that before, but it had been with others, and there was kind of a security in that.

"Trust me. I'm going to be right here with you."

The cool air caressed her skin as first her pants hit the ground, then her shirt, and then the lace of her bra and panties. Her footsteps silent as she made her way through the opening left for her, Essie closing it behind her.

"Lay down in the center, you can see where I smoothed the spot for you. All you need to do is be open and accepting to the sacredness of the light. I'll begin."

Elena settled herself, her gaze immediately lifting and taking in the brilliance of the mother moon. Ever since she was a young girl, she could recall the comfort she felt while gazing upward.

Her aunt's voice softly weaving through the air around her, connecting the rhythms of life and earth – "mother moon, full and round, from sky to ground, we call upon your sacred gifts, to fill us with your light, and make us glow within."

Essie's voice spilled the chant over and over, its strength and assurance coming from all around her, Elena's eyes never leaving the moon above her. Opening herself to the deepest intentions and aspirations, a renewal and restoration of her inner self. To become the light in her world, to heal and be of pure heart.

She didn't know how much time had passed. She had fallen into a state of trance, just her, the universe and the moon. Her body absorbing the energy granted to her by Luna.

"Elena? Elena?" Essie's voice brought her back around, her head turned to see her aunt watching her from the side of the circle. "It's late my dear. And you have a big day tomorrow."

A soft smile, tugging at her lips, her mind and body so full of peace, she hated to move, but as she quickly realized the later it got, the cooler it got.

Standing, her aunt opening the circle, she quickly dressed, going to her aunt and sliding into her outstretched arms, "Thank you Essie for everything."

Her aunt's hand stroked along her back, "Your mother would have been so proud to see you tonight. To see you accepting your light."

"I wish she could be here with us," Elena stepped back, knowing, of course, she couldn't but it was a wish that filled her heart.

"I know. We all do."

As they walked back towards the house unbeknownst to Elena, a white owl watched from its perch, deep in thought. Her Gran had stood guard over both, just in case, sending out a link to her sister as they disappeared behind the thickness of trees - [Essie thank you. I hope this was enough.]

40

Killian was filled with excitement and disbelief that this was the day he had dreamed of for years. Today was the day he would finally marry the love of his life. As he woke up, he couldn't wait to see her in her wedding dress, walking down the aisle towards him. With anticipation and joy, he reached out for his phone to text Elena.

[Good morning, my beautiful bride-to-be. Can you believe the day we've been waiting for is finally here? I feel so lucky to be marrying my dream girl today. I can't wait to see you in your stunning dress. I'll be waiting for you at the altar, eagerly anticipating the moment when I can call you my wife. I love you more than anything, Red.]

Essie wanted to bring a little tradition when it came to her niece and Killian's wedding. She'd asked Killian to stay the night with his brother.

Essie wanted Elena to have the house to herself and for her to be relaxed in the morning for her wedding.

Kil was content with the idea of spending time with his brother as he didn't mind staying with him. Moreover, Elena's aunt was always hospitable to him, making him feel welcome in their home and staying with his brother would give Essie some much needed quality time with Elena.

Kil pushed back the covers, stretched his limbs, and headed to the kitchen to make himself a cup of coffee. The aroma of freshly brewed coffee filled the air as he walked in. His brother, Keegan, was sitting at the kitchen table, his face lit up with a grin as he looked up at Kil.

"Are you nervous, brother?"

It was evident that Killian was not nervous but rather excited. He had eagerly awaited this moment, which felt like an eternity. This was the beginning of something extraordinary. He was thrilled to have her as his partner to lead their coven as elders and possibly reconcile with members of her coven as well; that was on a wait-and-see basis.

Killian sipped his coffee and placed the cup back on the table. "No, I'm not nervous," he thought to himself. "I couldn't be happier than I am now. Have you seen how beautiful Elena is? I'm more anxious than anything, worried she might change her mind. So let's get going."

Keegan's laughter filled the room- "Don't you worry, my dear brother. It's plain as day how much she adores you." He patted Kil on the back. "Let's get you dressed, shall we? Iris is eager for us to leave a bit early so you can witness the magic she's created with the decor for your special day."

An hour later with the sun shining on their beautiful day, Killian, Keegan, and Iris arrived at Elena's home. The three of them were all dressed and ready for the wedding ceremony that was about to happen in a very short time.

They had strict instructions to stay away from the house, so there was no chance of them seeing each other. Even though for a small moment Killian wanted to give himself over to Bram and do a fly by the window because that's how excited he was. But he'd promised and he always tried to live by his word.

The woods behind the house were the perfect location for their wedding. It was a spot that Elena always found solace in and felt close to her family. As they descended the path, the birds sang their sweet melodies, and the leaves rustled in the gentle breeze. The atmosphere was serene and peaceful.

Iris enthusiastically pulled at Killian's arm, pointing out all the intricate details she had added to the decorations. As Killian's best friend and sister-in-law, Iris was known to be the finest designer/organizer in town. She was highly dedicated to her job and derived immense pleasure from seeing the happy couple brimming with excitement. Her work brought her tremendous joy.

Iris smiled as she watched Killian's face light up. "So, Warlock, I assume you're happy with everything I've done here?" she asked.

Killian wrapped an arm around her, grinning. "It looks amazing, Iris. Elena is going to love it. Thank you so much for this."

Iris poked him in the side. "That's what best friends are for. By the way, you clean up nicely, Warlock. Your guests are going to be arriving shortly; let's get you married, shall we?"

Killian had worked a bit of his magick behind the scenes. He'd gone back to have a talk with Mira and a few of the members at the Divine Spirit, extending an invite to their wedding. They knew Elena's future was as part of the Raven coven, but Killian wanted them to know his door was open to them if they decided to have a discussion with merging into his clan. But also to know without a doubt that she had a very powerful husband and coven behind her. He wouldn't tolerate any disrespect when it came to his Red. So, to see a few of their faces arriving gave him comfort in knowing they'd hopefully be able to work together.

He knew this would be a surprise for Elena, but on talking to Sophie she had told him that a few of the younger witches were looking for something more in a coven; he could give them that. But that would be later. Right now, he had something else to do.

He couldn't help but feel a little anxious that his parents hadn't arrived yet. As the entire coven sat eagerly waiting for the bride to come down the path, Killian took his place beside his brother, his eyes a constant back and forth to the trail where his witch would make her entrance.

***

"Mama, I wish you could be here today. I wish you'd have been here everyday leading up to today and I wish you could be here for all my tomorrows. I'm in love with the most amazing man. I know I've told you this before but so much has happened since my last visit. Mama, you'd love him so much. Gran and Essie might be a little over the moon about him too. You're the only piece missing. But I'll have you with me today. Just like I have you with me every day and I'll bring Killian with me the next time I come. He's asked to meet you, so expect a plus one next time. I should have brought him by already and that's my fault. I love you Mama. I got to go get married now."

Tucking the letter she'd written for her against her stone, taking a moment, and just sitting in silence, remembering the smaller version of herself and her Mama running hand in hand through the woods where she now sat. All her memories wrapped up within the treed acres of their little forest and the house just up the path and under the roof of Beliefs.

Memories, the foundation of her life and today she was creating new ones to add to the picture book in her mind.

.....and her warlock was waiting.

Pushing herself upright, the sun letting her know the morning was getting on, one last look - Selene Payne, *mother and daughter, always loved-* inscribed on her headstone.

"See you soon Mama."

***

Arriving back at the house from her visit with her Mama, she grabbed a jar of moon water to sip while she was getting ready. Her phone chimed and with a swipe, a smile covered her face; a text from Killian. Her gaze ran over it, rereading the last lit bit - [I'll be waiting for you at the altar eagerly anticipating the moment when I can call you my wife. I love you more than anything Red] Sending back a bunch of heart emojis and an- [I love you right back] she was literally over the moon today. Her eyes completely blurred with tears, the good ones. She was so happy. The kind of happiness that gave you wings and made you feel like you could do anything and everything.

Killian was the warm pulse in her chest. From that first day, her magick had recognized his and reached out, never letting go since. And every day thereafter, he'd left a touch, a small imprint of his love on her, turning her pages gently and enriching them with words. He was pieces of poetry and lyrics sung on nights deep in lust. It had started out as butterflies and quickly built to wildfires. He was her eternal flame and she needed to stop daydreaming and get her butt in gear so she wouldn't be late to her own wedding.

Rushing into the bathroom, leaving a trail of clothes in her wake she washed and took a loofah to her freckled skin, thoughts already going to their wedding night and spending it wrapped in Killian's arms with him buried deep between her thighs. Her warlock knew how to love, he was a raging storm, and she never walked away unscathed, but in the best of ways. She wore his imprints as she went about her day. The soft smile on her lips as thoughts of him made her freckles seem all the more noticeable, her blush a faint caressing. She was sure those close to her knew the look already but she didn't care. She was head over heels in love with Killian.

"Elena, we need to put some fire under you, or Killian's going to be stomping up here wondering where you are shortly," her aunt Essie's voice came from the other side of the door.

"Give me ten minutes. The dress and everything else is all ready," she knew her aunt was joking. She had plenty of time yet, but grabbing the nearest towel to dry off, so glad she had woken up a bit early and washed and twisted her hair in fabric bands, so all she had to do was untangle them and add her hair clips.

Her tangerine citrus body lotion filled the air as she started with her legs and moved upwards. Letting that soak in for a minute, she brushed her teeth again, then applied a light bronzer to her cheeks, then dusted her eyelids with her favorite topaz pumpkin shade, finishing up with mascara to her lashes.

Elena was pretty simple, rarely wearing makeup, but today called for a little bit of fancy. Carefully slipping into her undergarments, she splurged on these, remembering the afternoon she spent at the lingerie store, hoping to bring that look to Killian's face when she stepped out of her dress and stood there in these for him. Her gaze lifted to the mirror to take herself in.

"Elena, it's been 15 minutes," her aunt's voice bringing a smile to her lips.

Opening the door, slightly embarrassed, but the look on Essie's face was somewhere between love and tears. "Don't you cry. I just put on some makeup and you know I rarely do that."

"I know, it's just all hit home seeing you now, realizing how much you've gone through, to see you so in love" - her hands finding mine as she spoke.

"He's such a good man Elena, and to see your lives joining makes me believe in miracles."

Elena pulled her in for a hug, her own tears threatening, stepping back, "I need help with the buttons on the back of the dress and then I have a favor to ask," hoping her aunt would understand, "I want to walk to the clearing on my own. I love you so much and Gran," Elena stopped just realizing she hadn't seen her familiar as of yet. "Where's Gran?" Her voice showed slight panic and Essie started stroking her arm. "She'll be here. She had one important thing to do. Don't worry she'd never miss this."

***

"Oh Elena you're breathtaking," her aunt's voice behind her as they both stared into her floor-to-ceiling mirror.

Her dress was perfect, simple and elegant, matched with her Mama's earrings and locket, her slip-on sandals with their amethyst beading playing peekaboo as the bottom of her gown swayed.

The sound of wings drawing their attention to the garden doors of the balcony, Gran's white owl form settling on the wrought iron railing that surrounded the deck, their link opening immediately - [my beautiful granddaughter look at you] - Elena gave her aunt a kiss on the cheek, then made her way to her Gran, her hand lifting to rest against her down feathers above her heart - [your Mama is here with you as I am. Just because you can't see us doesn't make it any less so. You'll be glad to know I just did a flyby and your young man is waiting for you. Go Elena. Go walk into the arms of your forever.]

"Oh Gran, not you too. I already told Essie I have makeup on." A soft laugh filled with love going out to her family. "I am. I'm going now. I'll see you both out there. I just need one minute alone."

Her Gran's soulful eyes gave her one last look before she ascended to the clear skies overhead. Elena turning to see her aunt pause at the doorway of the room. "We'll see you down there." She turned to go.

She nodded because it all came down to this.

Giving herself a last look in the mirror, lifting her locket and giving it a kiss, her murmured words soft, "Love you Mama." she picked up the two letters for her Gran and Essie, dropping those off in Essie's room before she made her way down the stairs, passing all the photographs of her life. Stopping at the fridge where she lifted the tiny bouquet of sunflowers she made the day before and with the sun giving her own blessing, Elena made her way down the trail of dreams.

Even this far from the clearing, she could see Iris's touch on their special day. A trail of flowers and Elena couldn't imagine where she found the variations. Colored hydrangeas symbolized luck and good fortune, white cornflowers for blessings and love, and because she knew they were her favorite, sunflowers for happiness.

Her sister-in-law was a true gift and had a beautiful heart. Not only was Elena marrying the love of her life, but she was gaining a family too.

The soft sound of the music eased through her at the first bend of the path, her hands clutching on the stem of her bouquet. The sound of wings above her head, and she tipped her head back to see her Gran flying above her, and a tear did slip onto her cheek.

Her Gran had always been there for every step of her life. Elena's heart couldn't be more full than it was today.

***

Killian shifted his weight anxiously, stealing glances down the wooded path. Any moment now, his parents would arrive - he hoped. He wanted them here. He just hoped his mother could find it in her to see how happy he was. But he also wanted his father to bear witness to the miracle he'd accomplished, bringing the two covens together for this union. He wasn't sure yet what the future held for both, but it was a start.

Keegan gave his brother's shoulder a playful shove, jolting Killian's focus back to the present. "Don't worry about Mom and Dad," he said with a reassuring grin. "Today is about you and your happiness with Elena."

Elder Allister, like an uncle to the brothers, stood beneath the handcrafted altar adorned with sunflowers and hydrangeas lovingly woven by Iris herself as a tribute to the blushing bride. Allister and their father, Kaden, had been inseparable friends since his youth, making him the perfect choice to officiate.

A swirling plume of black mist announced Kaden's arrival. He materialized behind his sons with a mischievous chuckle, relishing their look of surprise. Killian immediately pulled his father into an embrace. "Cutting it a bit close, don't you think, old man?"

Kaden laughed heartily, returning the hug. "And miss witnessing my son's happiest day? Never." His expression softened as he cupped Killian's face. "Your mother sends her regrets. An unavoidable matter demands her attention. But you mustn't let that dampen your spirit today. This celebration is about you and your Elena alone."

Killian nodded, his father's words reassuring his heart. For this was his and Elena's day, the rest of the world could melt away.

Essie descended the forest path first, a snowy owl sweeping around her and then heading skyward, then another swoop over the clearing, blessing the scene. Killian's chest flooded with love for Essie and Gran, who had championed his love for Elena from the start.

The opening strains of "A Thousand Years" filtered through the trees, signaling the bride's arrival. Killian's breath hitched as Elena appeared, awash in ethereal beauty that stole the world away. Her vintage lace gown sculpted her perfect form while her wild red curls danced like flames caressed by the breeze. In that moment, she was the only magic that mattered.

***

The tiny lights nestled within the trees that lined each side of her walk caught her attention. Flowers of every kind filled nooks and crannies, and there, on the last turn, was Killian.

It hit her at that moment how truthful he'd been from the start. He'd told her that she was his and he wasn't going anywhere. She'd fallen to his magick on that first day. Her gaze so transfixed on him and how handsome he looked that it took a few more forward steps to realize that their quiet, small wedding had grown.

Their covens were here. Both of them. That a few had come from the Divine had Elena questioning how that had come about. Sophie's smile and wave brought a smile to her lips. Her gaze touched each member before returning to Killian, then to his brother and Iris, to Allistair and Kaden, his father, then to Essie and finally her Gran.

Where was his Mother? Her eyes did a quick sweep, her footsteps taking her to Kil who stood waiting, his eyes on her.

Suddenly, slightly shy as she stood before him, Elena tugged on one sunflower she'd left loose amongst the others, giving it to Killian. "I love you with everything that I am. I just wanted to say that before we started." Then, leaning in towards him, so only he could hear, "Where is your mother? Is everything ok?"

41

Killian was ready to simply just sweep her off of her feet right there and then after hearing those words of love from her, and the sunflower, which he popped into his chest pocket. She was the most precious thing in his life.

Leaning in so he could whisper into her ear he said, "I love you Red. And everything is alright. Let's get married."

Elena's hands trembled, passing off her bouquet to her aunt, then taking his, tears shimmering in her eyes. This moment would be forever etched into their memories. They turned towards Allister, who would officiate the ceremony.

Allister beamed at the couple. "What a profound joy to bear witness to the union of two exceptional individuals. Killian, as your uncle, I've watched you blossom into a remarkable man. Not only a powerful elder warlock but a leader guided by compassion rather than selfishness. You have opened the discussion between two covens present here today. And now, to see you joined with your true love, Elena..."He paused, eyes crinkling with emotion. "You both deserve every bit of happiness. Killian, I believe you've prepared your own vows?"

Killian gazed into Elena's soulful eyes. "I vow to fight for you, pursue you, and love you wholeheartedly and unconditionally for the rest of my days. I promise to dream with you, laugh with you, celebrate with you. To comfort you through life's trials and walk beside you whatever the future may bring." His voice thickened. "You make me feel whole, complete, alive. You are my breath, my heartbeat and my soulflame."

Allister turned to Elena with a tender smile. "And now, your vows to Killian."

The moment was so much more than she'd imagined, trying to absorb every little thing. Their woodland wedding, their circle of loved ones, filled her heart to bursting; she truly hoped she remembered every moment of today. How the magic of their love seemed to flow and wrap around the two of them and spread to include all their guests. She could see in Killian's expression, so unguarded, what she knew without a shadow of a doubt, he loved her. Elena Payne, with the flaming hair and the overabundance of freckles, would make connecting the dots impossible. He painted colors in her heart and filled it with treasures she'd never known.

The deep azure of his gaze found hers, Allister's deep timber hovering at the edges as she lost herself in her lover's eyes. The vows he spoke, she felt through his gaze, the warmth of his touch, and each word that he'd written, then brought to life for her here today.

She was so ready already for the kissing, and 'I Do' part. A soft smile touched her lips at her thoughts. Her warlock had totally bewitched her, she was a lucky girl.

"I choose you. I choose you for everything. For all the steps we have yet to take, for all the moments we have to come. This redhead promises to love you with all that she has. I promise to love your family as my own. I promise…"

A darkness disrupted their moment, Gran's shrill screech renting the air as Killian's mother appeared, pain and grief written all over her face.

*****

Rissa gazed at herself in the mirror, wiping away the tears that streamed down her cheeks. Today was one of the happiest days of her life. Her son was getting married, and she was determined to ensure no one, especially her father, ruined it. She felt her magick surging within her, like a protective veil, ready to strike out against anyone who threatened her family.

She decided to wait until the ceremony was over to inform Killian and Keegan, and her husband about everything. She planned to ask for their forgiveness and understanding of the situation she had been dealing with. She had to protect them all from her sadistic father and his malicious plans. She wanted to free herself from his torment and make sure he was exiled for eternity.

Rissa's heart skipped a beat when her husband walked into the bathroom wearing a perfectly tailored suit. He had to be the most handsome man her eyes had ever seen. His hair was peppered with silver strands that complemented his beautiful face. It had been what felt like a lifetime since they married, and to this day, he still took her breath away.

After all, she had put him through for the past ten years, he never left her. For so long, she wanted to run into his arms and confess every single detail of what her father made her do. Rissa hated herself for being so cold and unloving to the most important man of her life. She could only hope he would forgive her.

Kaden kissed Rissa on the forehead; she practically melted beneath his soft lips. Rissa's arms went around him, pulling him close, breathing in his masculine scent, letting it wash over her, calming her nerves. More than anything, she wanted to break down and tell him every last detail, but it would have to wait.

He cupped her face, and tears threatened to fall once more. Kaden had to see how broken she was and how much she had missed him. "Rissa, you are so beautiful. You always have been."

Butterflies erupted in her belly; her legs were shaking, and at any moment, they would fail to hold her up. "I love you, Kaden, with everything that I am. Tell our son that I will be there for his wedding, but first, I have something I must do."

She sensed his disappointment, but this urgent matter brought no delay. Before he could interject, her name fell from his lips, and in a swift motion, she vanished, employing her magick to materialize inside her father's residence. Moving through the familiar hallway adorned with her mother's portraits, she paused and ran a hand over her mother's image.

Rissa gazed affectionately at the photos, at the one who always captivated her with warmth and kindness. She couldn't fathom how her mother had ever ended up with a man who was so distant, self-centered, and manipulative. A soft sigh escaped her lips as she observed her mother's striking beauty. Her long, jet-black hair cascaded down her back, perfectly framing her face. Her eyes, the color of a clear blue sky, sparkled with joy and contentment.

"Mother, give me the strength to protect my family. I don't understand why he hates me so much. Maybe it's because I resemble you, and it's a constant reminder of losing you. Regardless, it all ends tonight. This will be the last time I ever speak to him again."

Rissa opened the doors to her father's study, and his prudent face greeted her. "What are you doing here, Rissa? I gave you a direct order, and your defiance will not end well."

A tumult of emotions surged within Rissa as she held her ground. "I refuse to be a mere puppet any longer, father. My sons and husband need me. I never want them to doubt my love for them. They are my world, and I am determined to shield them from your selfish behavior. Resembling my mother is not a fault of mine, nor should it be a burden for you. I will not bear the weight of your blame for her passing any longer. Take this moment to mend the fractures within our family before you lose me, and all that remains to warm you at night is your avarice. I have a son's wedding to attend, where I will lay bare the truth. This stops today."

Without waiting for her father's response, Rissa's heart raced as she hurriedly left the room, her footsteps echoing down the hallway like a drumbeat, marking the urgency of her message. With each stride, a mix of determination and uncertainty tugged at her emotions, a tightrope walk between hope and fear. She prayed that her words, delivered with a raw honesty born of necessity, would penetrate the armor of his pride and touch the depths of his soul. As she ventured forth into the unknown, she carried with her the fragile yet resilient hope that her father would open his eyes to the pain he had caused and, in doing so, find the courage to mend the hurt he had caused.

A short while later......

Rissa brimmed with excitement as she hurried through the dense woods towards her son's wedding. The cool breeze whipped around her face, her heart beating rapidly with anticipation. She knew this day held immense significance for her son and was determined to cherish every moment of the ceremony. As the wedding venue came into view, a wave of emotion washed over her. Tears of joy welled in her eyes at the sight of her son, handsomely dressed, and Elena was the most beautiful bride she had ever seen.

Maybe her father did listen and wasn't going to cause any more hurt to her family. Perhaps he would finally be the father she always hoped for, and finally, she could put all this behind her and be the mother and wife that her sons and husband remembered. A chill crept up her spine, and her eyes darted everywhere. No, this couldn't be happening; a glimmer of hope snatched from her instantly.

She rushed towards her sons and husband, stumbling and collapsing to the ground. Kaden hurried to his wife, extending his hand for her to grasp. However, Rissa did not take it. With pleading eyes, she gazed up at him. Sobs tore from her throat as she uttered, "Kaden, he showed me horrifying visions of you and our sons, lifeless and mutilated. I couldn't bear the thought of losing you all. There was blood everywhere, and he threatened that those visions would become reality if I didn't comply with his demands. I did what I had to to protect you. Please, find it in your heart to forgive me. My love for you and our sons knows no bounds."

Kaden pulled his wife in his arms. "Who showed you these visions?"

A piercing scream shattered the night air, signaling Elena's capture by Rissa's father. His face twisted into a malevolent grin, exuding a chilling aura. "Rissa, your defiance was bound to lead to this. Your son took what is rightfully mine, and now I'll take what matters most to him. Don't waste your efforts searching. You'll never find us. Killian bid farewell to your wife. If you remember, I told you once you hold a title that was never rightfully yours."

In an instant, Rissa's father vanished into the shadows with Elena in his grasp. Killian's anguished roar reverberated through the forest, unleashing a torrent of magick that sent everyone sprawling to the ground. His gaze locked onto his mother, his eyes ablaze with searing fury, threatening to consume everything in its path. Rissa felt her son's agony rip through her, shattering her heart in silent agony.

"Killian, we will find her," Rissa vowed, her voice a whisper of determination amidst the chaos.

***

The sound of hurried footsteps came from the entrance of the clearing, Elena's vows drifting off and stopping as she turned to see Rissa late, but yet she had arrived. Elena would take that as a win, at least for today.

What mother would want to miss her child's wedding, squeezing Killian's hands, knowing that even though he was upset with her, she was his mother, his family, and now their circle of family and friends was complete, here to share the day.

The shrill screech of her Gran rose above the soft lyrics playing in the background, clouds drifting in where moments before a blue sky crowned their day. A whisper of unease lightly called to her from everywhere, starting as a tip-toe but slowly rising as a crescendo.

Rissa's stumble and fall added to the change in the air. Her purging of a secret she'd been carrying for far too long, then lifted into her husband's arms, and that was when Elena felt the bony grasp of inky darkness set cold hands on her and douse her flame.

On a magical level, she already knew, but her eyes had yet to leave where Rissa and Kaden embraced and spoke. Who would do such a thing to another, she thought.

And then, like her thoughts had been read, a voice of pure malice spoke from behind her, her gaze shifting from those of Killian's mother and father to her love, to her one true love. Her scream inflicting all sorts of emotions to cross his face at once.

He wanted to take her from Killian, but she wouldn't allow it.

Calling to her flame, a slight spark, then nothing. Trying again as he spoke, his words putting sheer terror into her body and soul, "You'll never find us Killian."

Elena tried to move but couldn't. It was like she was bound tightly in restraints. Her eyes latched to Killian's, the sound of his name spilling from her lips, but then a distorted haze draped over her, and a vortex spiraled around her, hands gripping her, tightening to almost pain, and then again nothing; she'd slipped under his thrall.

42

Cobwebs feathered themselves as she crawled, one movement at a time. Awareness and strands pulling on her to wake up. Slowly, the darkened edges broke away, her lashes slowly allowing fragments of her surroundings in.

At first glance, the bedroom appeared Victorian, dated but elegant. One door, two windows. The bed she lay on was soft and comforting. In any other circumstance, she could see this room being a haven, a cocoon to find solace.

Thoughts of Killian and their wedding slamming back into her, Elena sat upright, shaking her arms and legs: she could move.

Desperation taking place now that she was fully back in herself. She called to her fire, placing her clasped hands against her chest, adding a silent prayer for it to hear her. But still nothing. She felt where the glow should be, but it was like it was behind a locked door.

One tear fell, then another; this couldn't be happening. Her life had come together again. Had this been what the nightmares were about? Premonitions of what was to come?

She had to find a way out. She had to get back to Killian and her family.

Her feet touched the floor, taking her to the door, her hand reaching for the knob, but her hand was met by a surge of energy causing a painful ripple and she pulled her hand back.

Wardings. She turn and ran to each window to be met by the same barrier, a film of sorts layered over the pane so she couldn't see out.

She had no idea where she was. Was she still in Nola? Then a small hope flickered, opening a link - [Gran can you hear me? Gran?] but just static. [Essie? Can you hear me?]

And nothing. Elena thought a familiar's bond was for their life, no matter where they were.

A chill formed where her flame used to live. She was alone, a prisoner because of jealousy. Her heart broke for Killian. The last look on her beloved's face would haunt every waking moment and thereafter.

She gave herself over to the tears, letting them stream down her face. She knew that purging set things to rights. She had learned that. The sobs carrying her hopes onto the dress she picked for her special day, the one that had brought her to the altar, where her warlock stood waiting.

At the image of him in her head, the tears slowly lessened. A deep breath, remembering the power and strength that Killian lived by.

She was his. He loved her. She could do this. She could figure out a way to escape. She came from a long line of capable witches.

"I'm going to find a way back to you Killian. I swear on our love."

End of Book 1.

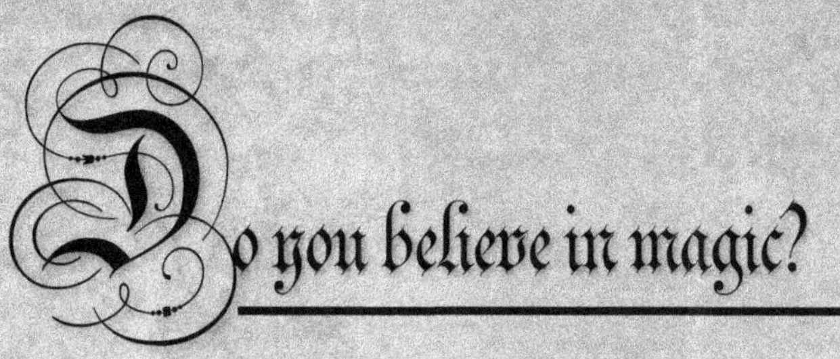

Killian's Enemy Binding Spell

Chant these words

I cast this spell into the night,

to bind my enemies and limit their fight.

By earth, by wind, by water, by fire.

I wish to stop their evil desire.

The evil words and actions they spread.

Shall only cause them to feel great dread.

To lead this fight against their deeds.

As I will. So mote it be.

Killian's Enemy Binding Spell

Chant these words

Elena's Love Spell

Carve a heart onto a candle. Light the candle, feel its warmth.

Whispers….

As I watch the flame dance.

I draw to me hopes of romance.

As it warms my face, I'll warm others' hearts.

Who gaze upon the feathers of cupid's dart.

Blow the candle out

Sophie's Truth Spell

With the power of the Universe coursing through my veins,
I lift the veil from my eyes.

Show me what he/she hides. Let his/her truth be told.
Let he/she lies to me be shown.

I lift the veil from my eyes.
There is no secret he/she can hide

Essie's Spell

Black Cat Curse

Twist the bones and bend the back,
Trim him/her of flesh and fat
Give him/her fur, black as black

Gran's Grounding Spell

On the earth is where I stand,
Digging my roots in the land,
Fill me with the energy so bright,
And fill me with your strength and might,
So mote it be.

Rissa's Strength Spell

Strength of day
Strength of night
Give me strength
Beyond my sight.

Rissa's Strength Spell

Killian paced the dimly lit chamber, desperation gnawing at his insides as he sought out spells to locate Elena. The air was thick with the scent of burning herbs, and each incantation he whispered felt like a lifeline slipping through his fingers.

"Where are you, Elena?" he muttered, his voice barely above a whisper.

He traced the symbols on the ancient parchment, hoping for a glimmer of guidance, but each spell he spoke hung heavy in the silence, yielding no trace of her presence.

Frustration mounted as he grasped at the remnants of his fading hope. "Reveal yourself to me, spirit of the lost!" he chanted, his voice rising in intensity. But the shadows around him remained stubbornly still, offering no answers.

Just as despair threatened to swallow him whole, a blinding pain shot through his temples, forcing him to his knees. The weight of his uncertainty crashed down, and he gasped, struggling to breathe.